Hurt Me

C.G. BLAINE

To the year two thousand and twenty
Fuck you, bro

Part
One

Eden

Everyone has their breaking point. The one thing that can catapult them from a completely rational human being to whatever the hell I am right now. A spiteful ex, a woman scorned, someone who's about to commit fraud. *Light* fraud. Daddy was a lawyer back in the day, and I'm sure he'd want that distinction made right from the start.

I found my breaking point after a drunken journey that started and ended in my bathroom. The twelve hours between are rewinding in my head like jumpy and grainy black-and-white security footage while I'm curbside in front of the airport. Only the classiest moments stand out. And, holy hell, are those in Technicolor.

I fidget, waiting for the driver to gather my bags from the trunk and doing everything I can to avoid my tinted reflection in the window. The oversize sunglasses are necessary since I'm on the verge of a devastating hangover. But when combined with the large-brimmed hat, I look guilty. And I haven't even set foot in the airport yet. I haven't flown on the plane ticket or checked in under a reservation I should have canceled months ago.

But I'm about to do both, and I'll have the time of my life.

Even if it kills me.

In my defense, when I was getting ready to go out last night, I expected to spend today doing anything *but* what I'm doing. I envisioned sleeping late and then shopping. Maybe grabbing lunch with a friend, if any dragged themselves out of bed early enough.

I hadn't even thought about the trip in weeks. The romantic escape I'd planned every perfect minute of, only for my boyfriend to have the audacity to ask me to cancel.

Seconds after dumping me.

I was still shaking my head, shell-shocked from having two years ripped from under me when Ashton curled his fingers under my chin and tipped my face up.

"Will you be a sweetie and cancel the Bahamas for me? You've always been better at that stuff."

Then he tapped me on the nose and left me standing in his living room.

Well, I wasn't a sweetie. I wanted him to pay for plane tickets that went unused and be charged by the hotel even though no one showed. Not that he'd notice either way. In the entire time I'd known him, he'd never once glanced at a bank statement.

Regardless, wasted tickets and an unclaimed getaway—that was the plan. Only now, I'm checking luggage and hauling my carry-on through the terminal. Still bordering on tipsy, if I'm being honest.

Once I pass security, I slip my phone out of the side pocket of my bag, only to shove it right back in. If I call before I land, Eli will find a way to stop the plane. My big brother hasn't laid off the overprotective routine in twenty-one years. I wouldn't put it past him to make a suspicious call or tell security that a mentally unstable woman was loose in their terminal. He and his latest girlfriend were still asleep when the town car picked me up. I wouldn't have made it out of our apartment otherwise.

I collapse in an empty row of seats outside the gate, bypassing the first-class lounge out of principle. They don't recycle the hundreds of plastic water bottles they dole out daily, and I refuse to help them suffocate our planet. Plus, I prefer the people on this side of the doors.

They trickle in, filling the waiting area around me. Stressed-out mothers herd children, who are plugged into devices, while the fathers participate in various capacities. All the voices and movement distract from the steady pulse of my recently reawakened heartache. For a short time anyway.

I really thought my heart had healed. That the scar tissue Ashton had left behind would act as a barrier against future breaks. Then my friends, who predate our cotillion days, buzzed my damn phone off the bathroom counter last night and proved me oh-so very wrong.

I fish out my phone again and scroll up through the group chat, past the *So sorry, hon*s and *Complete prick. You're better off*s until I reach the first of many *OMFG*s. All caps and the *fuck* are reserved for true emergencies. Not unfortunate haircuts or gossip from the previous night's party. Real. Shit.

The words didn't make sense the first time I read them. Ashton, proposed, engaged. I dropped my mascara wand and backed to my claw-foot tub. My stomach sank at the same speed as I did, lowering onto the ledge while the screenshots flooded in. All I could do was stare at the screen, each message numbing me more.

I'd picked the ring last year. A pear-shaped diamond with a double pavé band that gave me actual chills the first time I saw it. I'd told him I wanted white rose petals and a rooftop dinner and him on both knees instead of just one. He did everything down to the tiniest detail. All of it. For someone else. And in under two months.

I was still sitting there when the cavalry rode in shortly after. My friends were dressed to kill and determined to help me forget that I'd just been filleted, my bones still on the tile. We spent the night bouncing between clubs, sweaty men, and open drink tabs. I usually shepherd them around and hold back hair, but I danced until I couldn't breathe and drained every drink they slid my way.

At no point did it enter my sloshed brain that today was the day Ashton and I would have left on our trip. Until around four a.m. when one of my friends shouted a reminder in the back of an Uber. The music in the SUV was so loud, she had to scream it a second time.

"You should go," she yelled, to which my wasted ass replied, *"Hell yeah, I should!"*

I remember the exchange clearly because I then proceeded to puke into my handbag.

Classy.

Everything blurs again after that, but I woke up in my tub. I was clutching an empty bottle of vodka with my bags packed and waiting by the door. I also found a note on the mirror, telling me to grow a pair and act like the badass bitch I am. It said Ashton *owed* me this trip, and I needed to screw every guy on the island while I was there. It was signed *Drunk (AND SO FUCKING RIGHT) Eden* with black smudges all over the page.

I rolled my eyes, unimpressed with myself. But then I noticed the mascara wand in the sink, where it'd landed after falling from my hand. Black streaked down the white porcelain from its slide to the bottom of the basin. I looked into the mirror, no longer blocked by the paper. My hair was a knotted mess, my makeup smeared, and I had similar black streaks down my cheeks. I remembered writing the note then. The tears he never deserved had been streaming down my puffy and red face, no matter how fast I had tried to swipe them away. Then I'd crawled into the tub with my security vodka.

Everyone has a breaking point. That douche canoe brought me to mine.

After another chest-compressing glance around the bathroom, I washed my face, perfected a look to shimmer under the Caribbean sun, and was out the door in under twenty minutes. Woman. Fucking. Scorned.

As the terminal further crowds, I throw my phone to the floor, not coming close to hitting my bag. Sighing, I bend forward and grab it off the carpet. Before I put it away, I mute my messages, sign off social media, and otherwise drop myself off the grid for the next five days.

A worn green duffel bag lands in the row facing mine. The owner drops into the seat beside it a second later, attention fixed on his phone. He extends long legs in front of him, holding his head up with an index finger pressed to his temple. I've just settled back when he looks up. Tan skin sets off steel-blue eyes, the contrast disarming, even from ten feet away. I offer a small smile before his gaze lowers. It sweeps all the way down to the red-bottom heels on my feet and back up, his voice bored when he says, "Not my type, princess."

Thank God his eyes are already back on his phone because my mouth actually falls open. Neck tats, a lip ring, grungy jeans, and a generic black tee that stretches over even more ink on his biceps. He's not *my* type.

By the time he checks to see what damage he caused my ego, I've recovered enough to force out a cold laugh.

"Don't flatter yourself."

He lowers his phone when I match his stare from across the aisle, unwilling to give him a win by looking away first. But even though my outside locks down the bitch act, his disinterest struck dead center in that ache in my chest, and it wrenches tighter.

They announce first-class boarding mid-staredown. As much as I want to continue a scowl battle with a complete stranger, I break my eyes away. I grab my bag and earn a smirk.

"Figures," he mumbles, shaking his head.

I shoot him one last glare on my way past before flipping the expression to friendly for the woman at the gate. While she checks my boarding pass, a little boy darts by us. His dad swoops him up, throwing him over a shoulder, and the candy wrapper in his hand flutters to the floor. Father and son keep going, so I pick it up and toss it in the wastebasket behind the attendant.

"Thank you," she says, sounding surprised. She smiles, handing back my ticket. "Enjoy your flight, Miss Monroe."

I nod and head down the tunnel, already focused on what will happen when the plane lands. Getting on a flight, using a ticket with my name on it, was the easy part. Checking into a resort under a reservation held with someone else's credit card … now, that will take some serious finesse.

Beck

The fucking Bahamas.

White beaches, hot as shit, and crawling with PDA-obsessed couples and dude-bros in board shorts. When my cousin said she had a place for me to lie low for a few days, I expected another zip, different prefix. The flight here alone would have wiped me out if not for an airline employee who owed me a favor. But so long as everything works out and the only money I spend on this little island getaway is on cab fare and cheap food, I won't bitch about the color of the sand or umbrella drinks.

Much.

I stuff my passport to the bottom of my duffel bag once I clear customs. Ma insisted we have them for when she saved up for a "real" vacation. Six years later and I'm using it for the first time. Shit. Until wheels up, I'd only flown once—a pilot trying to bang my aunt took a bunch of neighborhood kids up in a four-seater when I was twelve.

With no checked bags, I head straight out the door, squinting at the sun despite my shades. I spot the princess from earlier, not that she's easy to miss. She's dragging her suitcases and juggling another bag, her blonde hair falling over her face. She stalls out next to a cab idling at the curb to check her phone. I swoop in before a family of four can make their move.

She offers a halfhearted, "Hey!" when I step in front of her and crawl in the back seat, but someone was going to steal her cab. I won't apologize for getting there first.

"The Grove," I tell the driver.

He pulls away, leaving her wandering back toward the airport on her phone. While we fly past other cars on the highway, I unzip my bag. He glances in the rearview mirror as I strip off my shirt, but after that, he keeps his eyes straight ahead and out of the back seat. I grab the white button-down, carefully folded on top of the rest of my clothes to avoid wrinkles.

"You been before?" he asks, his accent heavy.

"Nah, first time." I readjust the collar, leaving the top two buttons open. "I'm not really the resort type."

He nods, going quiet again, and I unbutton my jeans, arching up to push them down. The light-wash, rolled-up bottom pair I put on look as wrong as the shirt, but they're both necessary if I'm going to pull this off. Once I switch my boots for sandals, I lean between the seats and jerk the rearview mirror to see myself. I run my hands over my head, flattening my hair until I can't stand the sight of myself anymore. There's sellout, and then there's the dude staring back at me.

We turn into the resort just as I finish my transformation. The driver parks beside a massive fountain, spitting water. Large bronze arches overlap the entryway on the other side of us. He twists around in his seat and gives me a once-over.

"How do I look?" I ask, smoothing down my hair one more time.

He hesitates, lifting a brow. "Do I lose my tip if I say ya look like a rich prick?"

I chuckle, slapping cash into his palm. "Rich *douche* was the goal, but I'll take it."

When I reach for the door handle, he says, "Wait." He pops open the glove box and digs around. "If you're going for douche…"

A leather cuff lands in my lap. I snort, fastening it on my wrist. "Thanks, man," I say, climbing out.

I throw my bag over my shoulder and stop on the sidewalk. My eyes follow one of the arches, up and over the entrance. On the other side of the glass doors, white marble covers the floor, and chandeliers drop from the ceiling.

Fuck, this could go all kinds of wrong.

"Hey, Tourist."

I spin around, and the cab driver grins, ducking to see me through his passenger window. He hooks his head for me to come back. I dip down beside the car door, still fastening the cuff on my wrist.

"Whatever your scheme is, designer might be more convincing." He passes me a pair of sunglasses along with a scrap of paper.

Bringing the square frames through the window, I check the side. *Gucci.* I slide them on and let my cheap pair from the gas station land on his passenger seat. "You're like a poor-man's fairy godmother."

He snorts and nods to the paper in my hand. "Hit me up when you get sick of rich pricks and want a warm beer."

I glance at the torn oil-change receipt. The name and number scribbled down are barely legible with all the ink smudges. "You got it, Winston."

He reaches out, slapping my palm twice before sliding his hand back. As he shifts into drive, he shakes his head. "Fucking tourists."

The car speeds off, nearly taking out a polo-clad employee on his way toward me, almost at a run.

"Sir," he says, reaching for my bag, "let me get that for you."

Becker Donovan would tell him to fuck off, but since that's not who I am right now, I let him drag it off my shoulder. He holds the lobby door for me before taking the lead. The marble stretches to the opposite side where the entire back wall opens to the beach. Not many people are buzzing around the lobby. A kid on a leather sofa plays a loud-ass game, and a group of ladies in flowy dresses walk through, almost spilling their drinks when they cackle.

I'm trying to decide whether a lack of guests works in my favor when the dude makes a sharp left.

"This way, sir."

Around the corner, we step into a little alcove. He sets my bag down in front of the white desk stretched from one wall to the other and slaps a bell on the counter. He turns to me with dollar signs in his eyes. I flip through the bills from my pocket, pausing on a ten. His eyebrows draw in, and *fucking damn it*. I'm supposed to throw money at people like it's candy at a parade. I fork over a twenty and murder him with a stare until he scampers away.

I slap the bell again. I doubt the guy I am right now likes to wait for anything. It takes a bit, but the door behind the desk jerks open. And then out comes the best thing that could happen to me. A sexy brunette in a skirt, which I can't imagine meets the employee dress code of a place like this. Even if it does, the neckline of her dress shirt can't, plunging halfway down her chest. But while her outfit is appreciated, my ticket to a free vacation is the fact that this girl gives no shits about her job.

"Welcome to The Grove." She stays monotone, annoyed at being bothered. She stops in front of me, popping her gum while tapping at a keyboard. "Can I help you?"

"I'm sure you can."

I lean on the counter, and when she looks up, I slide off my shades. Her eyes complete a scan—the hair, the clothes, the cocky-as-fuck smile.

That's right, baby. Fall for the rich-asshole vibes.

She tips her head to the side and pulls back her shoulders, so her tits push out. "Checking in?" she asks.

Before I answer, I pluck a sucker out of the cup of candy next to the computer on the desk. "The reservation is under my sister's name." I remove the wrapper and pop the sucker in my mouth, chewing on the stick, and as she looks down at the computer, I ask, "What's your name, gorgeous?"

She bites her lip and tugs at the name tag pinned to her shirt.

"Macy," I say. "What are you doing working the desk at a place like this?"

"A friend and I moved down here from Miami last year." She looks up and shrugs. "It sounded fun to live somewhere you'd always feel like you were on vacation."

I fight back a laugh at her twisted logic. "That's the dream, right?"

"Is your name on the reservation too?"

"It's not," I say, sounding uninterested. "Will that be a problem?"

She hesitates, her eyes darting between me and the screen. "Well, technically, I need a photo ID and the card on file…"

"Look"—I throw the sucker straight into the trash can against the wall behind her—"my sister begged me to come along at the last minute. All I want to do is get in the room, shower, and hit the bar." I reach out and twist her name tag. She watches my fingers graze the exposed skin next to it, then her eyes lift to mine. "Come on, Macy," I say, my voice low. "You asked if you could help me. So, help me. Check me in."

After glancing around, she bites her lip again—only this time, it's because she's thinking. "Do you at least have your ID?"

"No. I left it in my other bag with our driver." I bring my hand back and pull out my phone like I'm bored of her.

A few seconds pass before Macy finally takes a deep breath. "What's the name?"

Fuck. Yes.

Gina's latest meal ticket really did me a solid, running his mouth about his sister's abandoned trip.

"Macy, I'm buying you a drink after your shift." The smile is genuine now, and I slip on my shades. "My sister's name is Eden Monroe."

Eden

The airport sidewalk empties and refills from another flight while I coax my mother off the phone. She rarely checks in anymore. Her time is better spent helping husband number four schmooze clients for his luxury-car dealership in California. No hard feelings. She's working toward a nice alimony payment, I'm sure.

Growing up, Eli and I knew the score. Our parents' "love" never extended beyond Darla's interest in Daddy's money and his desire for a boy with strong bone structure and a doe-eyed baby girl. We were even written into their prenup—Elijah Dean and Eden Rose, no more than two years apart.

I would get in a cab—another one since the jerk from the gate stole my first one—but if I give directions to the driver, my mother will ask where I am and why. Adding to the pile of humiliation I've laid claim to recently, I haven't told her about Ashton. As in she thinks he missed our Christmas Skype session because of a family trip to Europe.

I know.

I know.

Healed hearts don't cling to the person who wounded them.

Only one cab waits by the curb when I finish. The driver props a knee on the dash, tapping away on his black sunglasses with a finger. Rather than try to fill the silence, like I usually would, I loll my head back on the seat. I listen to the rush of wind through the open windows, blowing my hair about, and relax with the sun on my face. The entire morning feels distant—the heaviness hours away, then days and months and finally years.

"You awake, mama?"

"Yeah," I say, but I don't lift my head or open my eyes.

I can feel the cab turning into the resort. The tires switch from highway to the stone of the driveway I saw in the photos online. I'd dashed to the living room and bounced on the sofa cushions next to Ashton, wiggling the screen in front of him.

The clock starts to fast-forward until the present hangs over me again.

We roll to a stop.

"You look like I killed you."

I peek open an eye, and the driver has twisted around, his black brows pushed together.

He holds up his hands, shaking his palms at the roof. "She lives."

Almost smiling, I raise my head and hand him cash for the fare and a tip. When he grins back, I reach for the door handle.

"Take care."

He responds with a nod. "You too, She Lives."

As I climb out, I notice the license displayed on the dash. Daddy's middle name is Winston, and I glance at him one more time through the rearview mirror, liking him more than I already did.

A guy in a navy polo rushes over for my bag before both my feet touch the concrete. "Welcome to The Grove, miss." He drops his grin long enough to throw a quick glare at Winston while shutting the door.

Winston laughs, sliding the sunglasses down his nose. "Relax, kid. I wasn't anywhere close to hittin' ya last time."

The employee gathers my luggage from the back, and the second the trunk slams, Winston tears off. Tire squeals bounce around the arches overhead, and the guy's jaw tenses as the car speeds back toward the highway.

I think he mumbles, "Asshole," before he goes back to smiling. He gestures for me to follow him. I hesitate, giving myself a chance to back out, but then I jut out my chin and march through the doors into the lobby.

I've watched my mother flit from one bag of money to another long enough to understand how, when worn right, confidence can seamlessly mask a person's truth. I spent the flight rehearsing every possible scenario from here on out. I have an answer for everything. Nothing can throw me.

A woman stands behind the front desk, picking at her nails. So much for my hopes of a college-aged guy, so I could giggle and hair-flip my way through this exchange. She sees us coming and rolls her eyes. At me, at the kid holding my bags, at the world.

If I were less versed in the language, I might miss the way she sizes me up. In all honesty, I did the same thing the second I saw her. Straight, dark hair and a style that probably earns irritated glances from women and overly appreciative ones from men.

Ordinarily, I'd smile and say hi, but I need to be someone you don't fuck with right now. Plus, she's already dropped her gaze to a computer in front of her.

"Eden Monroe," I say dismissively.

She looks up from the screen. "Monroe?"

I nod, my nerves not a fan of how she says my name. Like it's familiar to her tongue.

Before she asks, I hand over my ID, the reservation confirmation, and the receipt the resort sent. With the package I chose, they charged Ashton's credit card the full amount at booking. Thanks to their cancellation policy, he lost any chance at a refund forty-eight hours ago, but she'll still more than likely want to see the card, which I don't have.

But I have something else.

I drum my nails on the counter and wait until she lays my ID and papers back down before I sigh. "Now, if there's nothing else, I'll take my key."

Then I push five hundred in cash across the desk.

She zeroes in on the money, then looks at me, and I raise a brow, daring her to challenge me. Macy—according to her name tag—considers me. Her eyes narrow, and I think she's about to call me on my shit when she drags the cash off the counter.

"It's 112." She forces her lips up at the corners and juts a keycard in my direction. "Enjoy your stay, Miss Monroe."

Holy shit. I can't believe that worked.

The tension holding my insides hostage vanishes as I gather my things. "Thank you, Macy."

She drops her nice act and rolls her eyes again. As she disappears through a door, I turn to the kid with my bags.

"Room 112 is this way, Miss Monroe."

"Eden," I say, falling into step beside him. "What's your name?"

Balancing my bags, he reaches for the front of his shirt where his name tag should be and winces when he doesn't find it. "Devon."

We walk back outside through a large opening opposite the main entryway. People mill about, laughing and lounging by a pool. I feel relatively myself for the first time all day and slow as we pass an outdoor bar.

"Can you drop my things in the room?" I ask.

Devon nods, and after I give him a tip, he disappears down a path that leads to the beachfront rooms. I head over to order a shot of tequila. I don't even sit down, tipping back the glass and biting my lime. My eyes water, and I shake my head, considering my vacation officially underway.

By the time I make it to my room, I've checked out the beach and completed my ritual at two other bars. Being three shots deep, I let the heavy door slam shut behind me. Someone set the thermostat to Antarctica, and I shiver, going to shut off the air. I slip off my heels and close my eyes, falling backward onto the bed beside my bags. I take a couple of deep breaths before I notice the masculine scent surrounding me—spice and citrus and … motor oil?

When I turn my head, my cheek rubs against a rough material, but it's definitely the source. I sit up fast and stare down at the bed. My matching Fendi suitcases sit next to a canvas bag. Worn and green.

What the fuck?

My head jerks up when the bathroom door opens. Steam pours out, and I scramble to my feet as the man from the airport casually strolls out. He drags a towel through his dark hair, another wrapping his waist.

He comes to a dead stop, recognition flashing over him when our gazes meet. He looks equally surprised to see me, one brow drawing in while the other lifts. We stay locked with each other, neither of us moving. And in my case, not breathing or thinking past an endless cycle of, *OhmyGodOhmyGodOhmyGod,* as scenes from those crime shows about women vanishing on vacations flash through my head. I can't even open my mouth to try and talk myself out of whatever situation I just stumbled into.

A long few seconds later, his eyes dart from me to the bed to the door. They return to me, setting off a starting pistol in my brain. Air sucks into my lungs, and I mad dash for the door. I pull it open, but a large hand lands next to my head and shoves it shut again.

"Wait," he says in my ear.

I spin to face him, and his arm stays outstretched beside me, his chilling eyes on me. My chest rises in short spurts, but my voice is still MIA while he stares me down.

After a beat, he lowers his hand. "Eden—"

The second his raspy voice says my name, I squeak.

And then I punch him in the face.

I go all out, too, using the form an MMA fighter who worked at our house taught me in case my prom date pushed too far. Which he did. Only that asshole's head snapped back. Unlike now, when my fist connects with the airport guy's jaw.

"What the *fuck?*" he shouts.

Not the smartest idea to attack the ripped, tattooed dude in my room, though it does get him to take a surprised step backward. I break for the glass doors on the other side of the room.

"Son of a—"

I'm rounding the end of the bed when he sprints over the mattress and beats me there. I skid to a stop so I won't run into him, my hand throbbing from colliding with the rock that is his jaw.

He grabs his towel with one hand, holding out the other. "I'm Gina's cousin."

"What?" The word is air with a hint of whimper, but it's progress.

I take a slow step backward to gain space, and he takes one forward.

"Gina," he repeats.

I shake my head, not sure how his family tree matters right now. He appears as thrown off with my response as I am by everything about him, and he gives a harsh look, rubbing his jaw.

"She's screwing your brother?"

It clicks then, and I narrow my eyes at him. My disgust toward my brother's current flavor overrides all else, and I spit out the name, "Regina?"

The guy lowers his hand, readjusting his stance in case I run again. "Yes," he says slowly. "She told me no one would be here. That I could crash for the week without issue."

I have no reason to believe him. Except I have every reason. Eli's constant rotation of women is something I've dealt with since moving in with him two years ago. He uses them; they use him. The whole thing is very reminiscent of our parents. But Regina Cruz has been pissing me off since she practically moved in on day one. She invites people over, leaves her rolling papers everywhere, and even had the balls to use my shampoo once. I've been begging Eli to get rid of her, but he keeps her around. I have no idea why; she's terrible. Scratch that. I know exactly why. It just still can't possibly be worth it.

Without taking my eyes off him, I sidestep to the bed. I dig in the pocket of my bag for my phone and only glance down long enough to find Eli's number.

"Who are you calling?" He comes toward me but stops when I hold up a hand.

"My brother."

He nods, relaxing. "Have him tell Gina *fuck you very much* from me."

Gladly.

It takes several rings before Eli groans into the phone. Here, I've fled the country and committed fraud and bribery, and he's still facedown in his mattress. Typical.

"What's up, Edes?" he asks, mid-yawn.

"Does Regina have a cousin? Black hair, blue eyes, a lip ring." I scan him for something else specific to identify him, but my eyes keep landing on a black-inked triangle on his hip that disappears below the towel.

"It's Beck," the guy says, "my name."

Beck. I squint, trying to decide if it fits him before remembering it really doesn't matter at the moment. "His name's Beck?"

Eli mumbles away from the phone and then, "Why do you care?"

"Oh, no reason," I say, well settled into my irritation. "I'm just here with him now. He's naked. In a towel."

"He's fucking what?" Eli shouts. That wakes up my dear brother. "Where are you? I'm coming to get you."

"You're not." I look down at my feet, my cheeks heating. "I'm in the Bahamas, at the resort."

"Dammit." A rustling comes through the speaker. "Why the fuck is your cousin in Eden's hotel room in the Bahamas?"

"It's just Becker." Regina sounds half-asleep, like always. "She's not even supposed to be there. It's not my fault."

"The hell it's not," I say.

Eli sighs. "Fuck, let me talk to him."

"What? No, I'm not—"

"Give him the damn phone, Eden."

I set my jaw and shove the phone at Beck, feeling like a child being reprimanded. "He wants to talk to you."

Beck gives an annoyed glare at the screen, bringing it to his ear. "Yeah."

His voice takes on a slight growl, and he turns to the side while listening to what I imagine is a threat, touching his jaw again. Maybe I wounded his ego with my fist, but I doubt I caused much damage otherwise. Very little could from the looks of him. He's solid with hard muscles, which match the roughness of the rest of him.

I follow the tattoos down from his neck. They cover most of his chest, the ink curving over his abs and wrapping around his ribs to his back. Of all the body parts visible right now, the only ones untouched are his face and feet.

"I want ten."

Beck's voice brings my attention up, and he's watching me. His gaze moves down and lazily travels over me. His expression remains indifferent, like at the gate in Chicago, and I cross my arms over my chest. It's unfair. He's the one in a towel, yet I'm the one wishing I could cover up.

"Trust me," he says, his eyes returning to my face, "it won't be a problem." He shakes his head. "I'd love to see you try, man."

He tosses me the phone, and I move out of the way when he rips his bag off the bed.

"What won't be a problem?" I ask, but he passes me for the bathroom and swings the door shut without answering.

I blow out a breath when Eli starts calling my name from the speaker. As if anything could make my day worse at this point.

"I know," I say, bringing the phone up. "I promised I wouldn't do anything crazy, but then—"

"Ashton popped the question to the first thing with tits?"

I drop onto the edge of the bed, relieved I don't need to say it out loud but embarrassed nonetheless. "You saw the pictures?"

"Last night." His voice softens. "You were already gone when I got back to the apartment though."

If Eli had beaten my friends there, he probably would have taken me straight to Ashton's parking garage, slipped the attendant whatever it took to kill the security cameras, and told me to go to town on Ashton's Benz. Baseball bat or golf club, whichever was in Eli's trunk. Then he'd have set the car on fire. He might have anyway, even without me there. When it comes to me, Elijah Monroe would burn the world and dance us through the ashes.

"Are you okay?" He barely pauses before he follows up. "Of course not, but *will* you be okay?"

I shuffle my bare feet against the plush rug, a light blue to offset the white and yellow decor. "I think I just need a few days. And I know I need a few less of Regina's cousins in my room."

"Here's the thing…" The way he always starts when he's about to big-brother me.

"Elijah," I warn.

Before he responds, the bathroom door jerks open. Beck walks out in fitted jeans and a button-down with his sleeves rolled to the elbows. A completely different vibe than the last time I saw him clothed. He throws his bag on the floor inside the closet and stops to adjust the thermostat.

"Hold on." I pull the phone away from my mouth. "What are you doing?"

Once again, he doesn't answer. But he does swing by the bed for a pillow, dragging it with him across the suite. The pillow lands on the sofa, followed by Beck. He stretches out on his back and tucks his hands under his head.

Like he's staying.

No.

I jump to my feet.

"No," I say to him and then again into the phone, "No, Eli."

"It's already done, E. Now, you'll get the time you need, and I don't have to worry about flying down there and murdering anyone if something happens to you. Think of him as your bodyguard."

Regina laughs in the background. "Poor Becker. He thought he was getting a dream vacation, and now, he has to babysit *her*."

As she cackles again, I lose the urge to fight my brother. No need to when she's presented me with the perfect solution to an even bigger problem. Her.

"Fine. I'll get him a room and play nice."

Eli hesitates, cautious of the sickly-sweet tone in my voice. "Great."

"If you dump Regina."

Beck's bicep covers his eyes on the couch, but one side of his mouth turns up, and he lets out a chuckle, low and deep.

"She's going to fucking kill me," Eli says, not sounding all that put out. "I'll pick you up from the airport on Saturday. Don't do anything else crazy until then."

I roll my eyes as the call ends, but no matter how far off the rails my trip has already gone, Regina Cruz will never use my shampoo again. Win.

"You can come with me to the lobby," I say to Beck. "We'll set you up in a room, and then you can forget you know me for the rest of the week."

His elbow lifts enough so that he can see me. "And defy your brother?" You could drown in the sarcasm, and then he gives a *tsk-tsk* of his tongue. "I thought a princess would follow orders better."

"Wrong." I turn to the bed and unzip a suitcase to find more beach-friendly shoes. "A princess gives the orders. So, get your ass off my couch. I don't care what Eli offered you. I'm not spending the next five days, checking in—"

When I glance over my shoulder, Beck's gone. The sliding glass door sits wide open, a warm breeze combating the cold one from the air conditioner. I sigh and flip the lid of my suitcase open. And it's only then, when I look back down, that it finally hits me.

Trusting Drunk Eden with the packing was a *huge* mistake.

Beck

Five days. Ten grand. That's two thousand dollars a day to keep track of Heiress Barbie and make sure any souvenirs she picks up don't have a dick. And a few minutes in, I already feel like I should have asked for more. Maybe added in a car or stocks or whatever rich people trade favors for.

I catch the arm of the first deck chair I run across and scrape it across the concrete to a shaded spot near the pool. Once settled in, I rest my head back and stare up at the canopy overhead, white linen blowing in the soft breeze.

Part of me wants to bail. Go back stateside and find somewhere else to crash until I get the all-clear to go home. Not that any of what happened last week should qualify as *my* problem. For the past couple of months, I've avoided Axel and everything about his little operation. I've put in overtime at the garage and buried myself in classes to speed up the graduation timeline. Exactly why keeping the hell away right now is so important.

I knew the guys Axel had been bringing in were idiots, but now, they've graduated to fucking suicidal. Not only did they try to boost a car from Monte—a dude with such a *Scarface* obsession that it would be almost comical if it wasn't borderline certifiable—but the assholes also got caught. Now, he'll be after Axel and anyone who has ever taken a piss at an adjacent urinal. I'm too close to getting the hell out for my name to fall out of the wrong mouth and drag me back into their bullshit.

Then again, give me a couple of days on princess duty, and I might change my mind.

I reach for my phone to see if Ty has texted any updates. He gave me the heads-up to lie low until Monte gets his ounce of flesh or whatever he feels entitled to. Ty's also the only person I trust to keep my name out of the conversation. The way it's been since kindergarten.

I feel my empty pocket and remember I left my phone in my bag. In the room. Eden's room.

Fuck.

After a while of mentally preparing myself to deal with the likely irate woman waiting for me, I trudge back to the room. I pause outside on the small brick patio. The TV's off. The lights too. Eden's on the bed, just staring at the wall while she chews on her lip.

Her eyes flit to me when I slide open the glass door, but she goes back to gawking at the paint. I cross the room to the closet to grab my bag, and I dig out the phone. Nothing from Ty, and I ignore the multiple texts from Gina. Whatever she did to piss off the princess is her own damn fault. Plus, she screwed me over. Blood or not, she needs to give me time.

When I turn around, Eden's holding out a keycard. I take it, slinging my bag over my shoulder.

"What's my room number?" I ask.

"It's 112."

I arch my brow at her. "This is 112."

"And that's the keycard you left on the bed," she says. I don't back up to give her room when she stands, and her eyes drop to the inch of space between us, narrowing as they return to mine. "There are no other rooms available. Not here or the hotel over."

"Are you sure—"

"I couldn't even bribe them to throw a mattress in a maintenance closet for you." She shoulders past me, smelling like a combination of candy and flowers. A tactic to distract men from the crazy I'm sure lies just below the surface. She stops shy of the bathroom to deliver one last glare over her shoulder. "Sleep on the couch tonight, but I expect you gone in the morning."

The bathroom door slams, and I clench my jaw.

I definitely should have asked for more money.

As much as I'd love to hang around and share another touching moment when she emerges, I throw my bag back in the closet and head to meet Macy. I probably don't need to keep up the show now that my "sister" is pouting in our hotel room, but I need a drink anyway.

By the time I walk up, she's already waiting, her skirt even shorter than I remember. She latches on to me the second I reach her and drags me inside, right past the bar and to the restaurant side.

I slide my arm out of her grasp once we reach the hostess stand. "I thought we were grabbing a drink."

"We're already here, so we might as well eat, right?"

She flashes a smile, and I force one in return. As far as she knows, she's snagged a rich dude. I can't blame her for milking the fuck out of the situation.

"Sure," I say. "Why the hell not?"

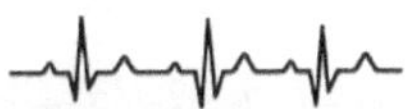

Macy talks a lot. And she's the type of person who sticks her gum on the rim of her glass. I watch it brush her cheek every time she gulps down more of her third vodka cranberry. They cost ten bucks apiece and barely touch her tongue, but at least the rest was on the princess. Macy kindly let it slip that the romance package

Eden booked includes dinner for two every night. Now, I consider us even for the sucker punch earlier.

I scratch at my jaw, where she landed her hit. Not that it hurt, but I'd missed it coming, and that irritates the shit out of me. While Macy continues telling me about a sorority or whatever, I slide my phone under the table and search for Eden Monroe. And there she is on my screen. I scroll through the images, seeing her in every color of dress imaginable. In most of them, she's on the arm of an uptight-looking older dude, easily in his seventies. Anthony Monroe, according to the caption of one. She peers up at him with a gleam in her eye. Daddy's favorite, apparently.

Ashton Weare-Hayes is the other frequent flyer in the pictures. He must be the ex Gina mentioned. Eden stares up at him, too, only he barely seems to notice. If his name wasn't enough of a reason to consider him a tool, the next shot would do the trick. While she looks over her shoulder, showing off the right side of a backless dress, he's checking himself out in a mirror.

I'm following the line from Eden's shoulder down her back when something knocks into my ankle under the table. I move my phone as a bare foot hooks around my leg, and I look up. Macy bites her lip, and then her toes start creeping higher. *Christ.* She hits my thigh without slowing down, so I catch her foot before she's rubbing me off under the table and jut my chin at her empty glass.

"You done?"

She nods, and I tip my head to the front of the restaurant. Then she pops the gum from the rim of her glass back into her mouth.

Once I get her out the door, she turns around in front of me on the sidewalk, sliding my hand onto her waist.

"Are you going to show me your room or what?" she asks.

"Or what." I pocket my phone. "My sister's in the room."

Macy rolls her eyes at the mention of Eden, like my fake sister's existence offends her. "Come home with me then. Missy gets off work soon," she says, her voice low. "She'll *love* you."

Her roommate—and ride—works at a lounge off the lobby. From the pictures she showed me earlier, I doubt I would mind Missy much either.

Macy runs her hand up the front of my shirt. "I'm sure the three of us can find something to do…"

After slamming three drinks, she has trouble pulling off the seductive eyelash batting. And if my disinterest in nailing a drunk chick isn't enough of a reason for a hard pass, I keep thinking about the fucking gum.

"How about you go home"—I pull her hand away, so she stops poking me while trying to walk her fingers up my chest—"and text me all the things we'd do if I were there?"

Her eyes light up, and she pushes onto her toes to kiss me, but it ends up more her smashing her mouth against mine. Before her arms land around my neck, I back away, shooting her a smile, and she squeals, shuffling down the sidewalk toward the lounge. I bet it takes her halfway there to realize she doesn't have my number.

I drag out the walk back to the suite. Tonight won't be a problem since she said I could stay, but when Eden realizes I'm not leaving tomorrow, as ordered, she might lose her shit.

When I finally get back, the room is dark other than the light escaping from around the bathroom door. I strip down to my boxer briefs and rip the comforter off the bed. It already smells like her, and I won't lie; it's fucking hot.

I'm stretched out on the couch when the door opens a few minutes later. The room stays dark, and I roll my head to the side, watching her shadowy figure stumble toward the bed. I could ask *why* she's traipsing around without a light on, but I don't really care. After some zips of a suitcase, the sheets rustle, and she starts fumbling around with things on the nightstand.

Jesus.

I sit up and turn on the lamp beside the sofa, and Eden quickly flattens out on the mattress. She hauls the blanket up under her chin, looking annoyed as I cross the room. I grab my bag, shaking my head on my way into the bathroom.

"Night, princess," I call before I shut the door.

Then I shove her shit to one side of the sink, making room for my own.

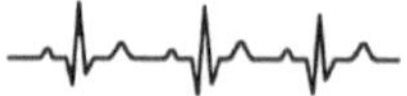

The sun shines through the glass doors in the morning when I open my eyes. And I'm only opening my eyes because someone is pounding on the other door. I throw off the blanket, already annoyed with what I'm counting as my official first day of Eden duty.

I glance at her, sprawled out in the bed. The purple eye mask with black lace around the edges leaves only her pouty mouth and nose uncovered, but it's the beige hotel robe she's sleeping in that receives a raised eyebrow as I pass.

The knocking cuts off when I swing the door open. "What?"

The bulky dude's fist stops midair. He's in a blindingly white shirt and black shorts that you'd expect to see on a dad at a parade, midsummer. The woman next to him looks like a miniature figurine in comparison, her hair pulled back in a tight bun. She's wearing the same outfit, both with *The Grove* printed on the front of their polos. They each hold what looks like collapsed tables, and they smile.

As the guy says, "Good morning, sir," I grab the Do Not Disturb sign from the inside door handle and hook it on the other side. "We're here for—"

I tap the sign before I slam the door.

Eden's already scrambling out of the bed when I turn around. Her cheeks are flushed as she pulls the fluffy hotel robe tighter around her.

"What the hell?" she says, shoving around me for the door. She stays to the side and cracks it open. "I'm so sorry about him. Just give us a minute."

I'm almost to the couch before she grabs my arm and tugs me toward the bathroom. When I don't go willingly, she sets her jaw.

"Please," she grinds out.

Ten thousand dollars—the only reason I follow her.

She carefully shuts the door behind us like they'll hear the click from out in the hall. "I forgot about the couples massage." Her eyes skate over the marble tiles surrounding the tub and the walk-in rainfall shower. They land on me, her chin lifting slightly. "I'll give you a hundred dollars to pretend to be my boyfriend for the next hour."

"Pretend to be what?" I ask but only because she can't be serious right now.

"You don't even have to do that much. Just lie on the table and don't be rude to anyone." She tips her head. "If you can manage."

I should tell her to fuck off, grab my bag, and head for the airport. With my ticket, I can be on the first flight out that has an extra seat. If I stick around, I might end up as the Monroes' trained monkey, clapping and dancing around for cash. Except I can bang the shit out of cymbals for the right price.

Since I don't say no right away, she already knows she's won, and her eyes flit to the other robe hanging behind the door. I scrub a hand over my face, already hating myself.

"Fine," I say, slipping the robe from the hook. "But I get the fucking chick."

I jerk the door open, and Eden rushes to let them in but not before she grabs the comforter from the couch and spreads it over the bed. Right. Because we're such a happy couple.

Rather than pull on the robe, I toss it on the dresser. The man and woman follow her in with their tables and whatever the hell else they need to rub us down. Eden glances over her shoulder at them as she reaches me again.

"Sorry about the mix-up." She pauses beside me, sliding her hand up my arm. "We thought we were scheduled for tomorrow."

The lady's eyes lower to the fingers brushing higher up my bicep, and she gives us a sweet smile. "Not a problem at all. We're sorry we interrupted," she adds with a wink.

Eden tenses beside me, but I don't know what she expected. They walked in to her in a robe and me in my fucking underwear to give us a couples massage.

The man locks the legs of his table into place. "Let us set up, and we'll be ready for you two in just a minute."

Eden's hand falls away the second they have their backs to us. She avoids looking at me, and I can't help but smirk at the flush in her cheeks as she grabs one of her bags and disappears into the bathroom.

By the time she comes out, they've turned on harp music to play in the background. I lie out on the table, watching her try to maneuver the sheet to keep herself covered after she drops the robe. She finally settles in, ready to be felt up by a stranger.

In under an hour, I smell like a candle in a hemp shop. Eden enjoyed it, though, judging from all the sighs coming from her table.

Her process of awkwardly holding the sheet up reverses until she pulls the robe back on. Another knock sounds as she's giving them a tip, and she goes to answer. She directs a woman with a cart across to the patio area outside. Another kid trails them, and rather than stick around to see how many more people parade through, I grab my clothes and head for a shower.

The room has cleared when I come out. Eden's at the wrought iron table on the patio. She slid into a skinny-strapped red dress with flowers on it and looks every bit a part of the crowd around here. Not that I can fucking talk in chinos and another button-down.

I stall out by the open door to check my messages again. Still nothing.

"You want breakfast?" she asks.

I look up from my phone at the spread on the table. Pancakes, waffles, fruit, yogurt. An entire continental breakfast. "Two of us are supposed to eat this?"

Her lips turn down at the corners. "It is wasteful." She taps her bare foot on the red bricks. "Maybe I can see if the staff wants some when we're finished."

I drag out the metal chair across from her. "A real Mother Teresa."

She rolls her eyes, but then they travel over my shoulder. I glance back at a couple walking down the path. The wafer of a woman stares out at the beach, not paying attention, but the guy makes up for it. His focus is fully set on Eden, a grin spreading the closer they get to us.

"Hey," he says as he passes.

Eden bites her bottom lip, smiling back. "Hey."

She twists in her seat to see him, and he does a half-spin to gawk at her a little longer. I'm witnessing a mating dance. Fluffy blondish hair, looks like he spends an hour in front of the mirror and drops a grand while shopping. She has a type.

"You make it a habit to check out another chick's man?"

Her head whips around to me. "You don't know they're together." She checks back one more time before popping a grape into her mouth. "Maybe it's his sister."

"Right. Like I'm your brother?" I pile food on my plate while she glares at me from across the table. "Because I'm pretty sure at least four people on this island think I'm fucking you after our romantic massage."

"Wasn't I kicking you out this morning?" she asks, her voice snippy.

"You were going to try, but your brother asked me to watch out for you. I can't very well do that if I'm not here."

"I think you mean, he's paying you out the ass to babysit."

"Says the chick who owes me a hundred bucks for lying there and playing boyfriend."

As I relax in my chair, picking up a glass of orange juice, Eden pushes hers back. She heads into the room and comes out with a bag over her shoulder. She slaps a hundred-dollar bill against my chest.

"I think I like you less than Regina," she says, walking away.

She heads down the path, peeking over her shoulder to see if I'm following her, but I tuck the cash in my pocket and eat my breakfast. We're at a private resort on an island. There aren't a lot of places she can go.

Eden

Despite the massage, the tension is already creeping into my shoulders again as I reach the front desk to ask that they only send half as much for breakfast the rest of the week. I also double-check for any available rooms but to no avail. Freaking wonderful. Between the unwelcome roommate and my *marvelous* packing job—my sleepwear was clearly chosen with a very specific audience in mind—my relaxing reset of a vacation has so far been more stressful than the reason I came.

On my way out of the main building, I grab my phone out of my bag. My fingers are twitching to log into Instagram so that I can read the reactions on Ashton's proposal posts. Self-induced torture, sure, but there's bound to be at least a couple of passive-aggressive comments to give me vindication. Maybe an *Already?* or a *Wow, that happened fast. Eden's body isn't even cold yet.*

The *fuck Ashton* attitude returns, and I shove my phone away. Refusing to lose any of the day, crying over my screen, I march straight into the spa and slap my credit card down on the counter.

Time of my life even if it kills me. And other than the time Darla passed out drunk in a mud bath and nearly drowned, a few hours of being wrapped, scrubbed, and soaked is hardly life-threatening.

Come mid-afternoon, I'm finally relaxing into the vacation I wanted. I've been pampered to my heart's content and have taken up residence in a chaise lounge on the beach. My toenails are a light pink, my skin all aglow. The kid who carried my bags yesterday, Devon, is working as a server for the beach bar and has been keeping me in alcoholic slushies. With the light breeze fluttering over me, I could never move again.

Serenity.

Even with the umbrella overhead, I notice a shadow cast over me. I expect it to be my refilled drink, so I hold out my hand, not bothering to open my eyes. "Thank you, Devon."

"Is this what you plan on doing all fucking day?"

I tilt my face up to Beck as he looms over the top of my chair. "It's exactly what I plan on doing. Today. Maybe, tomorrow." I bring my chin back down, readjusting to relax again. "Obviously, your services aren't required, so you can disappear now."

The shadow moves, but then the cushion beside me dips. A bit of the spice-and-citrus scent from yesterday invades my space, and I slip my sunglasses into my hair as I sit up, coming face-to-face with him. Well, face to shoulder since he's perched on my lounger. His pale blue button-down hides most of his tattoos, except the ones on his forearms since his sleeves are rolled up, and the star on this side of his neck peeks up over his collar.

When he turns to look at me, his gaze lowers to the tie at the front of my white bikini top.

"See something you like?" I ask, tipping my head to the side.

He smirks and slowly brings his attention up. "I'm a fan of tits all around, princess. But I prefer them attached to someone a little lower maintenance."

I want to disagree, but the four hours in a spa wipes out any argument I could make. "And I prefer dick that's not attached to someone so clearly intimidated by a woman who knows her worth."

Before he responds, I flick my sunglasses down. He drags his teeth over his lip ring. His eyes drift above me, and one side of his mouth curves up. Devon appears beside me, and Beck stands up, swiping my drink from the tray.

"Don't mind if I do," he says as he walks away.

I groan, dropping back on the cushion, already feeling the high-maintenance need for another trip to the spa. Maybe I should see if I could just sleep there.

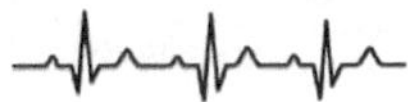

After he stole my liquid sunshine, I don't see Beck for the rest of the day. Not that I'm complaining, but it does leave me glancing around, expecting to see him.

About eight, I decide to take advantage of the dinner plan, and I head to one of the restaurants in the center of the resort. The dining room is set up like a surf shop. The servers wear board shorts and bikini tops, and the entire place smells like tropical board wax.

My server sets down a glass of wine halfway through my meal. I look up, confused. "Oh, I didn't—"

She tips her head to the side. "He sent it over."

When I turn, the gorgeous guy from this morning lifts his glass toward me. Grabbing mine, I raise it in return before taking a sip, the dry white splashing over my tongue.

"I bet he comes over." She winks and moves on to another one of her tables.

He proves her right, abandoning his place at the bar a second later. I take another drink and set it down as he pauses beside me.

"Alone tonight?"

"I am," I say. "And you?"

"My sister prefers room service."

I give a mental, *Told ya so*, to Beck and smile.

He's cute. A boyish charm in his features and swoop to his sandy hair. His slacks are pressed, his shirt wrinkle-free, and he has a slight Boston accent.

As he pulls out the chair across from me, I toss my napkin over my plate, deciding I'm done. Eating in front of someone who isn't quickly becomes a thing—awkward pauses while you chew and they watch, waiting for you to answer them.

"What about your…" He cocks an expectant brow.

"Brother. And I have no idea where he is."

I leave off the, *Nor do I care.*

The guy blows out a breath. "I've never been more relieved to hear someone else brought a sibling with them on vacation." A grin spreads as he reaches across the table. "I'm Hayden Prescott."

"Eden Monroe." I put my hand in his and squeeze as he squints at me.

"The Chicago Monroes?"

I nod, pulling away.

"I knew I recognized you from somewhere. Your father's Anthony." His eyes light up when he mentions Daddy. "The crazy fucker who abandoned an oil empire and invested everything in solar power."

I can't help my smile. For months, I begged him to stop drilling, promising I'd never ask for anything ever again. He sold the company just two weeks before my tenth birthday. Apparently, he'd already been researching the move into wind and solar and slid in on a deal that tripled his investment in under five years. But I like to believe he would have done it even if it'd meant losing it all.

"Your father's a legend in some circles," Hayden says.

"And a crazy fucker in others." I tip my glass up, eyes locked on his.

We talk for a little while, comparing life in Chicago to where he grew up in Boston. His family deals in investments, and we've experienced the same in many aspects of our lives. The private schools and charity events. He recognized me from a gala we both attended a few years ago.

He's funny but not at other people's expense, like so many of the guys I know. He makes eye contact with the server and lets me finish all of my sentences.

Ashton who?

"Shit," Hayden says, checking his phone. "My sister's going to kill me. I told her I was just grabbing dinner real quick."

I glance down at my screen and realize the *little while* has actually been three hours. Rarely do I find a guy in Chicago I can hold a real conversation with, let alone one that involves time-traveling.

Since our suites are close, we head in the same direction. He sidesteps to let someone pass us on the little dirt path and slides his hand to the small of my back, leaving it there.

"We're here until Saturday," he says. "So, if you need a snorkel buddy, I'll be around."

"Just snorkeling?" I ask, and he chuckles.

"Let me broaden it to any activity that involves two people."

His fingers inch lower, and I smile until I look forward again. Beck's slouched in one of the metal patio chairs outside our room, his eyes locking on to mine.

Shit.

He cocks a brow, holding a tumbler to his lips. "Sis."

Hayden slaps on a friendly grin, extending his hand, and I've never been more grateful for my real brother's aversion to fundraising events.

"You must be Eli. I'm Hayden Prescott."

Beck stares at his hand, and then his gaze flicks back to me. "Do we need to discuss curfews, Edes?"

The way he shortens my name digs in nearly as much as his question, and I bite the inside of my cheek, turning to Hayden. "Thanks for walking me back."

He gives my arm a quick squeeze and one last look to Beck before he continues down the path to his own room. Once he's out of sight, I narrow my eyes and swipe the glass from Beck's hand.

"If this is from the basket the hotel is supposed to leave every night, it's mine." I toss back the amber liquid, closing my eyes as the scotch bites my tongue. Licking my lips after I swallow, I open my eyes to see Beck staring up at me, a smirk on his lips.

"By all means, the basket is yours." He leans behind the table and brings it up. "You want a shot of flavored lube next or maybe—"

I blush—my entire fucking body does actually—and I rip it off the table, rushing inside before anyone can see the woven basket full of sex toys and condoms. Beck's laugh follows me inside, and I have to bite back my own smile. The romance package I booked covers all the bases it seems. From romantic boat rides and dance classes to vibrators and a roll of condoms in various sizes. Last night's basket was rose petals, bath oils, and champagne, which I immediately used. I guess they up their game on night two.

While I'm inside, I grab the only other useful thing out of the basket—another tumbler—and return to the patio. Beck takes back his glass, pouring for himself and pushing the bottle across the table. I sit, and after filling my glass, I pull my feet up onto the chair with me.

"Where did you disappear to?" I ask.

He gives me a cautious look, and I shake my head.

"Never mind."

We're not friends. We're not even acquaintances or friendly strangers. But to my surprise, Beck tips back his drink and says, "I went to a party with one of the lifeguards from the pool. He and some of the other employees rent a house not far from here."

"You left the resort?" I sound shocked—to the point that he narrows his look even more—but I've never left the hotel on vacation unless it was scheduled. "Sorry, I just … you made friends with a lifeguard?"

"Are the employees not good enough for you and your ivory tower?"

I roll my eyes, pretending not to feel the lash of his words. "No, I just can't imagine you being nice to anyone." I kick off my flip-flops and go to tuck my feet under me until Beck leans forward. His fingers wrap around my ankle, and he sweeps his thumb over the black and purple on my instep.

He looks up, mouth curved up on one side. "What the fuck is that supposed to be?"

I kick at him so that he'll let go. "A tattoo."

"Obviously." He relaxes back in his chair. "What does it mean other than just being pretty swirls?"

"You think it's pretty?" I ask with a smile.

"Depends on what it means."

I fidget in my chair, avoiding the icy eyes set on me. "I don't actually know."

"Let me guess," he says condescendingly. "You giggled your way into a shop with your friends, flipped through a book, and found something that would look cute with your sandals?"

"No." I finish my scotch and reach for the bottle. Beck watches me refill, twice as much as before, but the scotch tastes so much better than the small sips of wine at dinner. "Not that you actually care, but I walked into a shop, grabbed a pen, and scribbled a bunch of swirls on the back of one of the artist's business cards. He picked the purple and where it went because I didn't care."

Beck studies me long enough that I readjust again. "Why would you do that?"

I look over at the beach and the waves. "Eli came home one night with a tattoo. I said I wanted one someday, and he and my father said no."

"So, you went and got one?"

I nod, turning back to him. "I left right in the middle of dinner."

"Barbie has a rebellious streak." Beck smiles, and it's the first time I've seen it go all the way to his eyes. It's kind of fucking beautiful. He shakes his head, lifting a finger at my foot hidden under my thigh. "I'm surprised the artist picked there though."

"Why?"

For whatever reason, it sounds like an insult. He doesn't have any on his feet—unless they're between his toes or on the soles, which I can't imagine would last long. I got mine at sixteen, and after only five years, the purple has faded, the black losing its edges.

The legs of his chair scrape over the bricks as Beck stands up and shrugs. "Because the feet fucking hurt. Why do you think I don't have any there?"

I smile when he walks away, feeling more badass than I have in my entire life.

Beck

Having polished off plenty of scotch before Eden sauntered up the path with the living Ken Doll, I crash the second she follows me inside. I hear her shuffle off to use the dozen serums and hydrators and whatever other bullshit I had to shove to one side of the counter again.

I'm almost asleep when my phone vibrates. She turned off the lights before she went in, so the screen illuminates the entire room. I roll off the couch and snag it from the desk, where it's charging.

I don't recognize the number, but it doesn't take a genius to figure out who sent the text.

> *Consider this your first daily reminder to keep*
> *your grease monkey dick away from my sister.*

Elijah Monroe. He must have done some research on me. I conducted a little of my own on him while I watched Eden do nothing on the beach for three hours. Her brother looks to be every entitled rich-boy stereotype rolled into one. Always with a cigar or a sports car or a woman he seems bored with hanging on him.

As far as his sister goes, like I told him yesterday, we won't have a problem. Eden's sexy as fuck, but my dick and I have a long-standing agreement about avoiding women with a high potential for drama. Even without her brother's threats, everything about Eden Monroe says she sits at the peak of Mount Everest in that department.

Just have Daddy's money ready, I send.

I drop my phone on the desk and stretch back out on the couch.

Eden finally reemerges. My screen has shut off, so once again, she stumbles her way across the dark room. She must reach her bags because the unzipping starts.

"Christ, woman." I flip to face the back of the couch. "I might not be able to see you, but I sure as fuck can hear you."

"Well, if you would leave, you wouldn't have to worry about—" A *thunk* cuts her off. "*Fuck*," she hisses, her voice an airy squeak.

I blow out a breath and shift onto my forearm, pushing up to switch on the lamp. Eden's on the floor, her face scrunched while she holds her foot.

"You okay?" I ask, trying hard not to be an ass.

"I'm fine. Shut off the light."

I turn the rest of the way over. "How about you get *in* the bed first?"

She hesitates before flashing a wry smile and pushing off the floor. I wait as she plugs in her phone, takes off a bracelet, gathers her hair and weaves it into a long blonde braid over her shoulder. She secures the end with a tie and flips the sheet and blanket down. Just when I think we're about to wrap up the bedtime routine, she spins around, jutting out her chin.

"Are you seriously going to watch me until I get in?"

I raise an eyebrow, and she huffs out a breath. She whips to the bed, and I expect her to ditch the robe, only she climbs straight in, still wearing it.

"There," she says. "Happy?"

"Ecstatic."

As she drags the blankets up to her chin, I almost fall into the trap of asking about the robe, but I think better of it and click off the light.

With the Ken Doll now in the picture, I have a feeling my job is about to become a lot more hands-on. And if that's the case, I need at least eight hours between shifts.

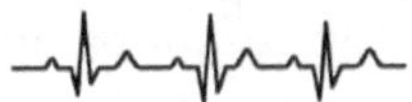

In the morning, I've already showered by the time Eden wakes up. She sits up, pushing the eye mask off, and she scans until she finds me next to the closet. Her face has the same pink tint as yesterday, and several strands have fallen out of her perfect braid.

She eyes me as I button my shirt, her eyes on my chest and then shifting along with my hands when I roll up the sleeves.

"See something you like?" I ask, throwing her question from yesterday back at her.

Her cheeks flush, and she swings her legs out of the bed. She keeps the robe tight around her and rushes into the bathroom, taking her entire bag with her.

While she's primping, room service sets up breakfast on the patio again. They leave far less food today, and given the smile on Eden's face when she sits down across from me, she had something to do with it.

As we eat, I try to figure out a way to get her to tell me what she's doing today. I doubt she'll willingly tell me if she thinks I'll pop up to play bodyguard.

We're finishing up when Hayden and his sister walk by, as if on a loop from yesterday. Only he and Eden have moved beyond the single-word phase after last night.

"Snorkeling today?" he asks with a grin. "Because I'll clear my schedule."

She laughs, her smile showing a slight dimple on one side. "I wasn't planning on it."

"I'll just have to wait and see if you show up on the cruise then." He spins once they pass our room. "That was my subtle way of telling you where I'll be later."

"Noted," she says.

They stare at each other a little longer before he twirls around, and Eden turns back to the table. She hops up then, still smiling, and goes inside while I watch her Prince Charming's head swivel to check out a brunette he meets on the path.

Douche is definitely her type.

I lean forward and swipe the pamphlet she left beside her plate. Relaxing in my chair, I scan the list of everything included in the package she booked, as well as a schedule of resort events. Turns out, Eden has solved my problem for me. Most of the activities she's crossed out, but others have giant circles around them. A boat cruise this afternoon, dance class tonight, a sand-volleyball tournament tomorrow along with another dance class, more beach stuff for Thursday, and on Friday, *snorkeling with Hayden* written to the side in frilly handwriting.

The last one might be a little more difficult to insert myself into than the rest, but I'm sure I'll find a way for the brother to tag along.

When I hear Eden coming, I set the paper back on the table. She steps through the door, still pulling a white cover-up over her skimpy red bikini.

"Another exhilarating day of ordering around waiters on the beach?" I ask.

She makes a face and drags her hair to one side to braid it. "You could always leave and never come back to save yourself the boredom."

"And miss out on the cruise this afternoon?"

Eden's hands stop weaving the strands, her blue eyes popping up. "Who said I was going?"

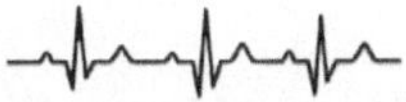

I finish my juice and stand up, giving her a smirk as I slide on my sunglasses. I feel her glare on my back when I walk away. "I guess we'll find out."

And we do, five hours later, when Eden starts to gather up her stuff on the beach. I toss cash onto the bar, and by the time she pops over the small hill leading down to the docks, I'm already leaning against a post, waiting for her.

Two girls dodge her, one of them holding her tits while they pass me, and run down the dock. I turn my head as the other one glances over her shoulder with a smile.

I look back at a huffy Eden, coming to a stop in front of me.

"Looks like you decided to show after all," I say.

"Can you at least keep your distance?" She glances at the first boat, where a bunch of people are already drinking on the deck and a DJ is setting up. "Hayden's a really nice guy, and I don't need my pseudo-brother hanging around. So, grab a drink and have a little fun from at least twenty feet away." She spins, starting backward down the dock. "It is a party boat after all."

She changed again after lying out all morning. The extra straps on her black swim top cross over her ribs, and I really see no point to the skirt tied at her hip since it might cover an inch more of her thigh than the bottoms. A group of guys barrel through, parting to get around her but not before checking her out, and it occurs to me, with her dressed like this and with guys like that, I might be earning a bulk of my money today.

It gets worse as we walk along the side of the boat. Three shirtless dudes up on the deck next to us stop their conversation to enjoy their view of her from above. Not that I can blame them, considering I did the same thing yesterday while she was in the lounge chair.

We reach the woman at the podium in the center of the dock, and all three of the dudes pull off their shades, still focused on Eden.

Fuck. The number of Ken Dolls I need to run interference on over the rest of the week has quadrupled, and we haven't even boarded yet.

I realize how fast this could all go to shit while Eden rattles off our room number.

"We should have spots reserved," she says.

"Awesome." The woman taps on her tablet, and then she looks up at us. "The couples cruise will leave in about fifteen minutes."

Eden glances at me just as I notice the sign next to the podium. One arrow points up the ramp of the boat to The Booze Cruize and another straight down the dock to another boat—The Couples Escape. I smirk at the guys I won't have to deal with now and step closer to Eden.

"Couples?" she asks.

The woman nods, but then she stops and holds up a hand. "Unless you two aren't…" She looks between us, seeing us cozier than a second ago. "I'm sorry. I just assumed. You booked the romance package, which includes the couples cruise."

"Right," Eden bites out.

"Just let me see what I can do." The woman lowers her gaze to her screen, slightly panicked that a guest might not get exactly what they want. "There aren't any spots open on this boat right now, but if you'd like to wait, surely, not everyone will show—"

"No." Eden forces a smile and a quick laugh. "The couples cruise is perfect for us. I just didn't realize there was more than one boat. Thank you."

She rushes around the podium, marching toward my escape from douche duty.

And my afternoon just got a whole lot easier.

It only takes a few strides for me to fall into step beside her, and she looks over.

"I'm not paying you this time. So, add it to my brother's tab."

"We could not go." I wrap my hand around her arm to bring her to a stop before we reach the people gathered around the ramp of the other boat. "You seem less than enthused, and I'd rather watch you sleep on the beach than hang out with a bunch of married people."

"I just…" She pauses, letting the couple behind her walk out of earshot, and then she drops her voice low. "I just want to enjoy my vacation, which is already difficult enough with constant reminders that the guy I should be here with is engaged to someone else. So, if you insist on playing watchdog, then heel."

She jerks away from me and continues down the dock.

I take a deep breath as I check for a text from Ty. It ends up pointless, and I rake a hand through my hair, following her to the ramp.

The lady at the bottom hands us champagne flutes. On our way up, Eden keeps a solid three-foot lead on me, which I don't mind. I am the mutt after all.

Once we step onto the top deck, twelve sets of eyes all turn on us. Six couples are perched on white cushions along the railings. The sulky blonde to my left perks up, and just like in the hotel room yesterday, her hand finds my arm.

I let her lead me around the deck, flitting from one couple to another. Most of them are celebrating their anniversaries with the exception of a corporate lawyer. His busty new bride gives Eden a run for her money on being the youngest onboard—and the least clothed.

After we set sail, Eden settles into a conversation with one of the wives. I'm starting to think I'll get away with not talking to a damn person when the woman turns her attention on me.

"And how long have you two been seeing each other?"

My lips twitch, and Eden's manicure digs into my arm.

"Not long," she says fast. "It's our first vacation together. But I can tell you that I already regret not booking two rooms."

"Oh, come on, baby," I say, sliding out of her hold. "Those sex baskets wouldn't be half as fun if you were using them alone."

The woman, who must be getting the same nightly baskets, bites down on a smile as I walk over to the bar.

While the bartender finishes blending something fruity, I remember what Eden said about her ex being engaged. I could have sworn Gina said they hadn't broken up that long ago, so I pull out my phone and search for her again. I find the picture of them with Eden in the red dress. The site dates the photo as only three months old. When I tap in Ashton's name to search, I pick the first hit for his Instagram. It pulls up, and the first row of pictures are all of him and a brunette with her hand shoved at the camera, ring on her finger.

"Over the champagne?"

I look up to a man in a suit, his elbow on the bar.

"Yeah." I pocket my phone and snag a plastic sword out of the cup beside me. "I prefer something with minimal bubbles."

"I can get on board with that. Bourbon?" he asks as the bartender walks over.

I nod, and he relays the drink order before thrusting his hand into mine. "Brad Sinclair."

"Beck Donovan."

He turns toward the deck and points out a woman who is relaxed in a lounge chair with a wineglass. "That one owns me. What about you?"

Normally, I'd argue with his wording. Except, right now, he's not far off, so I nod my head toward Eden. She happens to pick that moment to pull out her braid and shake out her hair, the sun shining off her fresh tan.

"Okay then." Brad shakes his head as he scans me over. "Now, explain how a guy like you pulls that off."

He grins, letting me know he's fucking with me.

"One strap at a time," I say, chewing on the sword.

Chuckling, he points at me with his glass as I pick up mine. "I like you, Beck Donovan."

My new drinking buddy—a financial advisor from NYC, celebrating his last kid graduating and moving out—launches straight from the basics into a conversation about the divisional playoffs. We argue back and forth about the bracket until his eyes dart to the side.

His wife and Eden are laughing on their way toward us.

"Well, well, well. The little women found each other." Brad lifts his arm for his wife to sidle up next to him as she rolls her eyes at his comment. "Beck, this is Julia."

"Sorry for anything he's said so far." She slaps a hand on his chest. "I typically leave the muzzle on when I leave him unattended."

When Eden inserts herself between my arm and body, she reaches back for my hand, pulling it around her. Her skin's warm from the sun, and the fucking candy-flower scent does its job of distracting from the crazy while she cuddles into me.

"This is Brad," I tell her, moving my hand to her hip. "And this is Eden Monroe."

She smiles as Brad's face lights up.

"Eden Monroe from Chicago," he says, genuinely surprised. "I know your father from when you were still living in New York. I met your brother as well, years ago. He must have been in high school. I was in Chicago and stopped by to see Anthony, and Elijah was interning."

"Well," Eden says, "now, you've met the whole damn family."

Brad chuckles and nods. "And now that I have, I'll expect all three of the Monroes to join me for dinner the next time I'm in Chicago."

Eden's smile goes a little tight as she tenses against my side.

"And Beck, of course." Brad motions to me with his glass. "We'll make a night of it."

I lift an eyebrow. "If you can keep up."

Brad and Julia both laugh, and I earn a side-eye from Eden before she moves the conversation along. Probably because the longer we discuss her family, the more likely our dear friend Brad will be to mention her boyfriend with the tattoos and piercings to Daddy Monroe. Something tells me he wouldn't love the idea of me touching her any more than Eli.

Then again, it's Eden who's doing the touching right now. She holds on to the front of my shirt and tucks her head against me, determined to sell the whole *good girl reforms a bad boy* narrative.

I wait until Brad waves over the bartender to get another round before I move my hand to the nape of Eden's neck and hover my lips by her ear.

"You might sell it better by just climbing on top of me. If you need a boost, let me know."

She sighs, angling her face toward me. "I wouldn't have to try so hard if you were halfway believable."

"I guess I'm just not as experienced with faking it as you are." I slide my glass over for the bartender, and when I turn back, Eden's eyes lift to me.

"Maybe not," she says quietly, "but if this is at all what you're like with women, I'll bet you've witnessed your fair share of it."

I run my tongue over my lip ring, trying to be more annoyed than impressed with the princess holding her own. She looks me up and down, her lips pursed and ready for whatever I fire next, but Brad nudges me before I can.

"You two want to grab a seat?"

He and Julia walk away from the bar, and Eden pulls away from me, going with them without a word. I snag my glass, right behind her.

If she wants to play, then we'll fucking play.

Eden

As Beck trails me across the deck, glaring at my back, I regret not getting another drink at the bar. Maybe this entire mess with him is Karma finally catching up with me for trying to shoplift makeup when I was seventeen. Although, considering all the time I spent crying in the mall security office after turning *myself* in, I hoped she might have a little more chill.

Most of the other couples have congregated around the seating area in the center of the deck by now. Julia and Brad take the small love seat on one side, and Beck wastes no time, sinking into the last empty chair in the semicircle, leaving me nowhere to sit.

I most definitely should have kept the damn mascara.

Beck's lips twitch as he looks up at me. "What's wrong, baby?"

With everyone watching us, I plaster on a smile. "Nothing."

I start to lower onto the arm of his chair, but at the last second, he hooks his arm around me. He pulls me toward him, and I suck in a breath, landing sideways on his lap.

"What are you doing?" I whisper as he readjusts us. He shifts me closer until I'm angled toward him with my legs over the armrest, and the scent I'm growing accustomed to surrounds me.

"You wanted me to be believable." He reaches up, gently pushing my hair back so it stops blowing across my face. "Don't bitch when it happens."

His arm drapes over me, and as much as I want to push it away and get rid of the smug look on his face, he's right. I wanted him to play the part of boyfriend, so I don't get to dictate how much of an ass he is while he does it.

I relax into him instead, and he rubs his palm over my thigh.

"So…" The trophy wife, who is either Bridget or Braelynn— but most definitely born within a few years of me—grins from her wicker chair. "Beckett, we haven't heard much from you."

"Becker," I correct, reaching for his drink.

"Beck's fine." He pretends not to notice, moving his glass to the armrest on the other side beside my legs. I sigh and lean forward to steal it anyway.

"What is it you do?" Bridget/Braelynn asks.

This time, Beck lets me pry the tumbler from his grip but glances up, annoyed as I sit back against his arm. He watches me take a long sip before going back to the question.

"I'm a part-time student for now," he says, returning his arm to my knee. "And I work as a mechanic the rest of the time to save money." His gaze lifts to me again, and he smirks. "That's how I met Eden actually."

I almost choke on the bourbon as he skims his now-empty hand up the back of my thigh.

Oh God.

"Her pricey little car broke down while she was petitioning for owls or some shit." He pushes under my skirt and tilts his face toward me. "Right, baby?"

He stares up at me, daring me to stop him from feeling me up in front of all these nice people and let him return to sulking around the boat. But I refuse to let him win so easily. I scrunch my nose and turn to our audience, not having to feign exasperation.

"By *pricey*, Becker means eco-friendly."

He inches higher, his fingers gliding over my ass.

"And the *owls* I was petitioning to save were one of the two endangered species of bats in the Chicago area." I rush through the end of my sentence when his thumb runs along the edge of my bikini bottoms.

He curves inward, following the fabric between my legs, and I start to grab for his wrist as one of the wives' eyes bulge. "Oh, I've heard about those!"

And with that, she picks up the conversation to talk about an animal-conservation project she's involved in, and everyone's focus reroutes.

Beck withdraws his hand and swipes back his drink.

"You've made your point," I say.

He pauses with the rim on his lips to smirk at me again. "Is that your way of asking me to only be moderately convincing?"

I nod, admitting defeat. "Yes. Please return to being irritated and showing minimal interest in me."

With our performance over, I move to get off him, but then his other arm wraps around me from behind to keep me on his lap.

"No more chairs," he says. "If you stay, I won't have to give up mine."

I sigh and ease back onto his hard chest. "Right."

After a minute, I shift to get more comfortable since I'm probably stuck here for a while. Just as I slump into him, relaxing, his hand slowly drags back in the direction of my ass—over my skirt this time.

I shake my head and can't help myself. "Let me guess … you're a fan of all asses too?"

"Not all." He finishes his bourbon in a quick swallow. "The ones that keep grazing my dick certainly earn my attention though."

He flexes his hips to reposition under me, and I press my lips together, feeling the attention he's talking about.

"Noted," I say, trying not to smile.

Then I scoot over enough that I'm fully on his leg, and I make sure I stay there for the rest of our romantic boat ride.

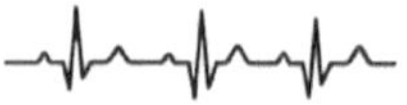

By the time we dock, Beck and I seem to have come to a cease-fire. For the moment anyway.

"We're going to grab supper," Julia says over her shoulder as we follow her and Brad down off the ramp. "A few of the other couples might come along. If you two can stand hanging out with a bunch of parents a little longer, we'd love to have you."

Brad cranes his neck around, his eyes going to Bridget/Braelynn behind us and then landing on me. "Parents and one sorority sister."

He winks before tugging Julia to his side. They get a little farther ahead of us, and I let go of Beck's arm. I'm sure we could both use the space after two hours of being on top of one another. But it only lasts to the end of the dock when Brad and Julia stop to talk to another couple. Beck's hand splays over my lower back, guiding me around them, and then he moves it up to the nape of my neck.

"When and where?" he asks Brad.

"Gateway Cove. Be there at seven."

Brad shoots me a grin as Beck nods and steers me toward our room, away from the others.

"We're going?" I ask, shocked, given his reluctance for everything else. "You haven't had enough of me?"

"From the moment I met you," he says without pause. "But I'm fucking hungry."

I serve some side-eye, and he smiles, dropping his hand to his side.

At our building, he opens the door for me and rolls his eyes. It takes until I step inside and see Hayden by our door to know why.

"Isn't Ken supposed to be on a boat?" he mumbles, following down the hall.

I ignore him, wondering if I've hit the point where the windblown look goes from cute and natural to haggard and not-so-hot mess.

"If you were trying to make me doubt myself by not coming today…" Hayden trails off, scooting out of the way when Beck shoulders through to slide the keycard. Once the door slams, his attention comes back to me. "It worked." He braces a shoulder against the wall. "I spent the afternoon moping around on deck."

"I'm sure," I say dryly. "Moping with a beer in your hand and a dozen other sun-soaked blondes as they dance in bikinis."

He purses his lips and squints. "Yet not the bikini-clad blonde I wanted."

I look away, smiling despite myself. Hayden might not act like the guys circling around in Chicago, but sharks have been confused for dolphins before.

"Come to dinner with me." He rests his head to the side, dreamy eyes imploring me to accept. "Let me impress you with my package's meal plan—wine included."

This time, I laugh, but it cuts off when the door jerks open behind him. Hayden straightens up, stepping beside me as he turns around and clears the way for one irritated pseudo-brother.

"Eden." That's all Beck bothers with, like growling my name conveys his message.

And it does to Hayden as much as to me.

The muscles in Hayden's jaw work under the skin, a brief moment passing between the two of them. Women have similar exchanges—the expressions filled with words. The one coming from Prescott to who he thinks is a Monroe says his family money is worthy of my family money, which means *Elijah* should back off. But it's a pissing match he'll lose because something tells me, Donovans scowl in a completely different language.

"We're meeting an old friend of the family for dinner," I say, pulling on Hayden's arm so he'll redirect.

His features relax, even before he looks at me and moves the arm around me. "I'll just have to stage a bump-in with you tomorrow then."

I nod, feeling him finger one of the horizontal straps on my swim top. He gently pulls on it when he walks between Beck and me in the direction of his room. I give Beck a glare on my way into the room, and he swings the door shut behind me.

Resume fire.

"You could have given me a chance to say no," I say, kicking off my shoes.

I go straight to the closet and look for something to wear to dinner. Brad and Julia chose the most casual restaurant at the resort, and since I won't have time to change before my dance class later, I grab a maxi dress with a slit up the leg. Given the *time of my life* philosophy for my vacation, the two-night class felt fitting. I can thank Darla's unhealthy obsession with late-'80s rom-drams for the *Dirty Dancing* vibe.

"I told you, I'm hungry," Beck says when I spin around. "I couldn't risk you falling for the Ken Doll's line of bullshit."

I shake my head, passing him for my suitcase on the floor beside the bed. "You do a hell of a lot better job of impersonating Eli than my boyfriend." I bend down to find shoes to go with my dress and hear Beck blow out a breath behind me.

"Only if your brother regularly checks out your ass," he mumbles, walking away.

The sliding door opens, and I smile, grabbing a pair of plain black heels.

Beck

The other couples have already settled into a corner booth when Eden and I walk into the restaurant. Brad waves us over first, followed by a grinning Julia in case we missed him. They move to chairs added to the table to accommodate the group. Eden acts like she wants to stop them, but they've already sat when we get there, so she slides in beside the trophy wife.

As soon as we order, Brad and I pick back up our conversation from the bar. Julia has zero interest in being involved and switches seats with him, so he'll quit talking over her. Eden seems to carry on in every other topic at the table, ever the social butterfly. Call it a new bad habit from an afternoon at sea, but when she crosses her legs and bumps me, I move my hand across her lap to her outer thigh. She leaves it there long enough that I've forgotten about it until she grabs my wrist and shoves it away from her. I turn to look at her, but her gaze redirects me the other direction. My head swivels just in time to see Hayden fucking Prescott waltz through.

I look up at the rafters, feeling the crazy hit Eden's bloodstream beside me. She falls dead silent and tenses into a blonde statue until he disappears into the bar area, well out of sight and sparing us the awkward brother-lover scenario we were skidding toward.

Eden lets out a breath and regains enough mobility to take a sip of water.

"You okay?" I ask.

She nods and flashes a half-smile. "Perfect."

No one seems to have noticed our little checkout, and we seamlessly return to our conversations like nothing even happened. But when I put my arm behind her on the booth back, she shies away and checks the bar doors. I rub my jaw, annoyed, knowing I should leave it. Maybe I would if this guy wasn't a complete tool. If I believed for a second he wasn't in that bar right now, groping any chick that let him close enough. And if he wasn't the only true risk I had at losing out on ten grand.

When Eden starts to twist around again, I roll my head toward her. It puts us nose to nose, and her blue eyes pop wide. She's about to pull away, but I slide my hand into her hair and kiss her cheek before moving my mouth to her ear.

"I'll be right back, sis."

She tries for irritated as I get up, but her lips twitch, making it a hard sell. I slap Brad on the shoulder and head in the direction of the men's room, which just so happens to lead straight to the bar. Eden's distracted by the trophy wife and misses me duck inside.

Even in the crowd, it only takes a glimpse of bouncy golden man hair to find Hayden on the opposite side. I move far enough in to see the rest of him. He has one hand on a high-top table and—surprise, surprise—the other firmly connected to a waitress's ass. Blonde, long legs, and I'll just assume she has blue eyes like Eden since the rest of her matches. She sets down her tray, clearly on her break, and his other hand joins in on the fun.

Shaking my head, I fish my phone out in time for them to go at each other. I tap the screen to capture the touching moment. No wonder I'm doing a shit job of acting like Eden's boyfriend. My hands have only been on her this entire time.

I turn to leave but pause, seeing Eden through the dark-tinted windows. She cranes her neck around to look for a dude who is tongue deep in a discount version of her. The flash of disappointment that crosses her face as she rotates back hits me in the gut. And so does the sudden urge to disassemble a Ken Doll.

Before I give in to it, I force myself out the door. I'm about halfway to the table the next time her gaze wanders. Since I block her view of the bar, her eyes set on me instead. I wait for them to flit behind me, but she keeps watching me, even after I sit down beside her.

"What?" I ask.

She shakes her head a little as I finish my drink.

"Nothing," she says. "You just look like you're in a worse mood than usual."

I shrug, not admitting I am or that she has anything to do with it, but I do move my arm back behind her, ready to stop her from looking for Hayden anymore. As of now, keeping her away from him has nothing to do with the money—I'll keep her away from the asshole for free.

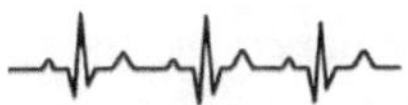

"Please?" Eden says, her voice far too sweet to sound sincere. "I'll pay you again. One hundred dollars for an hour."

I stare at her, not caving.

"Two hundred."

People are walking behind her on the sidewalk, where we've stopped for her to proposition me, and I pull her forward, out of their way. She offers them an apologetic smile before she ups her price.

"Three?"

"I'm not taking a dance class. I'll fulfill my guard-dog duties from there." I point at an outdoor bar across from the gazebo, far enough away that it won't look like I have anything to do with her while she shuffles around to cheesy music.

"Five hundred," she says fast. "Please? Name your price."

One side of my mouth turns up. "Ten thousand dollars, and I'll twirl you around till midnight." I back away when she scowls at me. "Offer expires in three … two…"

Eden flips me off before spinning to the gazebo, and I smile all the way.

Music kicks on shortly after and floats over to the bar. I sip my beer, watching an old basketball game on the TV mounted in the corner. Since my classes won't start up for another week, I'd probably be doing the same thing in Chicago right now. Only there, it would be in a shitty apartment with a cheap beer and a frosted-over window because it's cold as fuck in January.

The game cuts to a commercial, and I look up for Eden. It's been three days since I first saw her in the airport. Three days, and I can pick this chick's legs out of a crowd of couples dancing around. The split in the green-and-white pattern of her dress shows flashes of them and her heels. From here, I can forget the mouth and entitlement that come along with them and just enjoy the show.

"You want another?" The bartender drags me out of a tan-leg trance, and I shake my head.

"I'm good, thanks."

A few minutes have ticked off the play clock when I go back to the game. Can't say I ever imagined dancing would hold my attention more than sports—or anything fucking else for that matter.

Since I've already missed part of a game I watched live four years ago, I finish my beer and head toward the gazebo. The music stops as I reach the steps, and I go up to sit on a bench off to the side. Eden spots me over the shoulder of her dance partner—a woman at least four inches shorter than her, dressed in a modest pantsuit. With the way she shouts out counts and the annoyance aimed at me from Eden, I'd say it's the instructor.

I wipe a hand over my mouth to hide a smile, but it earns me a squint anyway.

The instructor points a remote at the sound system, and the music restarts. She abandons Eden in the center of the floor to correct an older guy's posture. It leaves me the victim of a death glare until she swoops back in, spinning Eden before she starts counting again.

I have my phone out, but I watch them, waiting for the music or barked numbers to stop. That's when Eden's alone, watching me back, while all these people are twirling around with her in the center. She clearly picks up on the steps the first time the instructor introduces them, but she's a good sport, and she smiles along while the woman reteaches her over and over.

When they finish, she hangs around to thank the woman. Then she bounces down the stairs out of the gazebo without me. I catch up with her on the sidewalk as the trophy wife from earlier spots us. The chick slows down, like she wants to stop to chat, and since I've hit my limit on bubbly today—in personality and drinks—I slide my hand into Eden's.

"Oh, hey!" the lady says.

I nod, pulling Eden along with me.

For a second, I think she'll protest, but she moves her hand to my arm and throws out a quick, "Have a good night," on our way by. She laughs, still hanging on to me, her eyebrows raised when I glance over. "You realize you're dragging me, right?"

I slow my strides until the click of her heels sounds less rushed. Eden's hand falls away from my arm, and I let the other go. But at least we don't have to pretend to be shit we're not for the rest of the night.

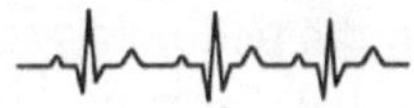

In the morning, I wake to another friendly reminder from Elijah Monroe of all the damage he'll do to me if I lay a finger on his sister. When I collect my money, I probably shouldn't mention my hands were all over her yesterday on the boat.

The only two things on the Eden agenda for the day are the sand-volleyball tournament this afternoon and her dance class tonight. Nothing like spending a day in paradise, playing cockblock to greased-up, shirtless dudes.

I'm pulling the last button-up out of my bag when room service knocks. With Eden asleep, I take the trays instead of letting the guy into the suite, setting everything on the desk. He's still waiting in the doorway for a tip, and I pop a toothpick in my mouth on my way over.

As I flip through bills, watching until he looks satisfied, a door down the hall bangs shut. The employee pries the cash from my hand and is walking away when Hayden waltzes by. He slows.

Fuck.

I see him scanning me. A hint of doubt flashes on his face— like, for the first time, he could be considering the dude covered in tattoos and sleeping in the same room as Eden might *not* fit the description of Elijah Monroe.

And since I personally don't give a shit, I smirk at him and back into the room.

Let him think I'm screwing her. Maybe he'll leave her alone and focus on his waitress.

Eden still hasn't squirmed by eleven. I'm bored enough that I consider waking her up, but that's against my best interest, so I stretch out on the couch and flip on the TV.

I must fall asleep because when I open my eyes, she's not in the bed anymore. The room's also taken on a gray cast. I sit up before I hear the soft *tink* on the patio doors. Massive drops splatter on the brick outside. Then the thunder booms, and the drops become a pour.

A minute later, Eden appears, dressed in a bikini, only to see the rain pelting down on the patio.

"So much for volleyball." I smile, and she narrows a glare on me.

"How did you—" Her eyes dart to the desk, where she left her itinerary open. She pieces it together on her own and huffs, turning around to walk straight back into the bathroom.

I scroll through my phone until she comes out, the most dressed down I've seen her—in a white top that sags off her shoulder and jean shorts. She sinks onto the other end of the couch with the pamphlet.

"Surely, the resort has activities scheduled for when it rains," she says, flipping through until her face scrunches. "Movies and board games? That's it?"

"What were you expecting?" I ask.

She shrugs, rereading, like maybe she missed something, and I glance over at last night's basket, still on the desk. The longer I keep her in the room, the easier my day, so I go over and grab out the bottle of tequila.

"What do you say, princess? Day drinking?"

Eden tilts her head to the side, suspicious of my motives. "Is this just you trying to get out of following me around this afternoon?"

"For the most part," I say, pulling out shot glasses. "The other option is we go to the bar, but by staying here, we'll cut out the step where I carry your lightweight ass back."

The deck of cards at the bottom comes with instructions for how to dirty up almost any card game, and Eden folds her arms when I reach for them.

"So, you're proposing we get drunk and play strip poker?"

I raise an eyebrow at her. "I won't say no to seeing your tits, but I just wanted the cards."

Her eyes roll, and she drops her arms to her sides. "Fine. What are we playing then?"

"Whatever gets us drunk." I toss the cards at her and give her a once-over. "What does it take, three shots to put you under the table?"

Eden slides the deck out, looking offended when I also grab the tumblers and orange juice left from breakfast and set them in front of her.

"Care to wager on that?" she asks.

"I'll put a hundred on it." I roll the desk chair over to the coffee table and sit across from her. "Name your game, Monroe."

She smiles as she starts to shuffle. "Pour the drinks, Donovan."

Eden

Halfway through the afternoon, I'm still only mildly tipsy. We changed games after ordering room service earlier, and ever since my grilled chicken sandwich, I've blamed Beck for my buzz staying steady.

When he moves to crack open the patio door, I steal his glass.

"I knew it," I say after a sip. "You've been skimping on my drinks."

He smirks on his way back. "Considering how terrible you are at a game you picked, it's a good thing."

"If the point was getting drunk, then I'd be playing well, if not for your sabotage." I bring the drink up for another sip, but he pulls it away and nudges mine closer. "Fine, *Eli.*"

"Fine, *Edes.*" He pours more tequila into my glass. "Pick your card."

"Red."

He flips a king of spades, and I take a drink.

"Red."

His lips turn up when he sees the seven of clubs. "So well."

I drink and guess black for the next card.

This time, he draws it toward him, so I can't see. "Shot or question?"

"Seriously?" I reach over and pluck the card out of his hand, and then I toss the six of hearts onto the table. "I'm not even this bad at beer pong."

"Eden Monroe playing beer pong," Beck says. "Now, that I'd love to see."

I take my third sip and reach for the card I threw, stopping when his eyebrow lifts. Earlier, when he guessed three cards in a row, he made a rule that I can't organize them anymore. I also can't sigh or roll my eyes.

Basically, for each card guessed wrong, you sip, and for three in a row, you take a shot or answer a personal question. If either of us manages three correct guesses in a row, we make a rule for the other. The punishment for breaking our rules: a shot or question.

Beck has no rules, and he almost exclusively chooses shots when he guesses wrong, so the most I've gotten out of him is that he's a business major and twenty-two.

"What's the question?" I ask, pulling the deck to my side of the coffee table.

He studies me for a second. "Have you *really* ever played beer pong?"

I squint "Yes. I was vice president of my sorority and dated a frat brother."

"*Was* because you already graduated?"

"Is that a second question?" I cock my head to the side, but it really isn't worth the evasive maneuvers, so I shrug. "I'm taking this semester off and finishing in the fall."

He nods. "Black, red, black."

I turn over the next three cards for him—red, black, black— and he takes two drinks.

"So, what are you doing with your semester off before finishing in the fall?" He picks up the deck and peeks at the top card. "Other than lavish vacations."

"I have fundraisers I help plan every spring, and Eli's still not showing any interest in taking over Daddy's company, so I'm hoping I can—" I stop and resist the urge to sigh. "Why am I still answering questions for you? You chose a shot over telling me if you have any siblings."

Beck checks the second card down, his gaze lifting when I reach up to put my hair in a ponytail.

"My brother also doesn't check out my tits regularly," I say, throwing his comment from last night at him.

"Then don't ask me to be your brother right now." He slowly looks up the rest of the way as I lower my arms. A few seconds pass with the rain hitting the sidewalk. The sound almost echoes in the room between us until his eyes swoop down again to the cards. "Red or black?"

"Red, black, red."

He turns over a heart, spade, and another heart. "Fuck."

Already knowing the perfect rule, I grin. "You're not allowed to look below my neck."

Beck chuckles and nods, running his tongue over his lip ring. "Tou-fucking-ché."

I laugh and lean forward for the deck. We play another half dozen rounds before he misses three in a row, but I barely bother with a question since he never answers.

"Do you regret any of your tattoos?" I ask.

He looks away, trying not to smile. "I used to have the words *break shit* on my left calf, but I covered it up with a lighthouse."

"Why?"

"Why *break shit* or why lighthouse?"

"Either," I say, figuring any answer from him counts as a win.

"Break shit, I have no fucking idea. Some angsty teenage bullshit. A lighthouse is a guiding light. A reminder to stay on the right path." He re-stacks the cards since I can't. "I mean, it's no pretty swirls, but..."

"Black, black, red." I watch him turn the cards, and when he smirks, I wince.

All of them wrong.

"Why did you and the ex break up?" he asks.

I snort out a laugh. "Nope. This is an Ashton-free zone." I take my shot before grabbing the cards and sliding the discards under the pile without thinking. "Shit."

"I believe this belongs to you." He pours another tequila shot for me, and I make a face, letting him call and draw his own cards while I toss it back. He sips from his mixed drink for one missed card and waits for me to guess.

I blow out a breath, blinking through the burn in my throat. "Black, red, black."

He checks all three and chuckles, showing me red, black, red. "So fucking bad at this game."

My lip pouts out as I hand him my empty glass to refill, and he snatches up the bottle.

"If I weren't here, would you have broken out the sex basket?" He finishes pouring and looks up to add, "No one else is here either. Just Eden Monroe and a whole lot of ways to get off."

I narrow my eyes at him. "You take some long showers. Maybe I already have."

"You haven't—but that wasn't my question. Would you *truly* be enjoying your vacation solo?"

It only takes about half a second for me to reach for the shot, but Beck wraps his fingers around the glass, shaking his head.

"This would be your third in a row." He slides it back to his side of the table. "I think you should answer."

"Pick a different question then."

"And you'll answer?" he asks. "No matter what it is?"

I hesitate before I nod, and his mouth perks up on one side, making me instantly regret it.

Beck barely even thinks about it, leaning back in his chair. "How often do you actually have to fake getting off with a guy?"

"What?" I laugh out.

I think he might be fucking with me, waiting for me to turn red and go hide in the bathroom, but he holds my gaze, and my pulse spikes. Looking away for a second, I lick my lips.

"Simple question, Eden. How experienced are you really when it comes to faking it?"

I glare at him, but he's unfazed, as always, so I blow out a slow breath. Beck's grip tightens on the shot when I lean forward for it, but he lets go and tips his head to the side as he watches me take it.

After I swallow, I wipe my mouth with the back of my hand. "Very experienced."

I send the glass skating across the table, and Beck catches it without taking his eyes off mine. Then his gaze drifts lower. Past my neck. Breaking my rule, he brings his shot to his lips while he scans what feels like every inch of me. He looks up again, and the air buzzes, the humid breeze blowing through the door where he slid it open.

"Pity," he says before taking the shot. He pours another and drains it without flipping a card. "I'm cutting us off."

He twists the cap onto the bottle and pushes off the floor. I consider arguing just to argue but decide that's the tequila, and I gather the deck into a neat pile. Beck shuts and locks the patio door. I'm reaching for the last cards when he crosses in front of me and smirks.

"What?" I ask.

"I put the basket on the shelf in the closet. If you need it."

My brow lowers, and I have no idea what he means until he disappears into the bathroom, and the shower turns on. I laugh, dropping my face into my hands as the door shuts.

The last shot reaches my head when I stand up. I sway a little, and my knee bumps the table, sending half of the cards cascading to the floor on the other side.

"Fuck."

More slide off, but I leave the mess for later and crawl into bed. I drag Beck's comforter over me, opting out of life for a bit. At least rainy-day tequila is better than security vodka. More fun and less tears.

I'm all but asleep when someone knocks on the door from the hallway.

"Come back later," I call, pulling a pillow over my head.

But they keep pounding, and unless I'm mistaken, it takes on an irritated rhythm.

I sigh and get up to answer.

Swinging open the door, I start to smile, but it fades the second I see the girl from reception on the other side. Macy's expression flattens at the sight of me too.

"Oh," she says.

She still has on her uniform—if you can call it that. I wait a beat, slightly panicked since I bribed her the last time I saw her. When she doesn't say anything, I swallow and straighten my shoulders, slapping on my confidence mask despite the buzz.

"Can I help you?"

She juts out a hip, curling her lip, as if I'd insulted her cheap spiked heels out loud. I cock my head to the side, and she huffs.

"Is Becker here?" she asks.

I blink at her, confused. "Beck?"

She nods. "Uh, yeah. Your brother?"

It takes a second for me to push through the tequila, and then I realize she would have been the one who let Beck in the room when he got here. "Right. He's—"

I glance over my shoulder when the water shuts off. My eyes stick on our playing cards, our half-empty tequila bottle, and the shot glasses. The morning and afternoon linger in the air, but the suite's taken on a heavy undercurrent.

"He's what?" Macy says, and I bring my head around.

She shook out her hair recently—the dent from her hair tie still visible—and her makeup looks freshly reapplied. And then I know exactly what she's doing here, and before I can stop myself, the lie comes pouring out.

"Not here." I pout my lip and push out a hip of my own. "You *just* missed him."

She scans the room behind me before giving me the thinly veiled smile all girls know secretly means *fuck you*, throwing in an eye squint that adds on a *skank*. "Tell him I stopped by."

Not a question, but an order.

Macy digs in the bag she has slung over her shoulder and pulls out an empty gum wrapper and pen. "I'm off tonight, and Missy only works until eight, so…" She scribbles on the wrapper. "We can finish what we started the other night."

The words knot around the liquor in my gut, and I catch myself before I repeat the last part as a question. Whether she thinks I'm his sister or not, I doubt Macy would hold back with her answer, and I'm really not interested in knowing what started between her and Beck *any* night.

I can't say I'm surprised though. Drunk Eden planned to fuck her way around the resort, so why wouldn't Beck have the same expectation for his trip? And with incredibly low standards, if *Missy* has a shining personality anything like the check-in girl.

Macy holds the wrapper out for me, and I pull it from her fingers, not bothering with the fake-ass niceties anymore. As I walk away, she tries to check the room again, and I throw the door shut behind me. I barely glance at her number before I toss it on the table with the other remnants from the afternoon. Beck can figure out the heart is supposed to be an *A* on his own.

I grab my keycard and walk straight out the other door, not feeling so buzzed anymore.

Beck

The afternoon took an interesting turn with my stupid ass basically hitting on Eden, so I shouldn't be surprised when it zags in the other direction without warning. I leave her unattended for twenty minutes and come out of my shower to an empty suite.

I glance around for any signs of abduction, but if someone broke in here and didn't at least toss her expensive luggage, they had no idea what they were doing.

A bunch of the cards have fallen to the floor, and I run a hand through my hair, going to pick them up. I get dressed and clean up the rest of the mess before Eden waltzes through the door. She sips on a drink, barely acknowledging me on her way in.

"Where'd you go?"

"Food," she says dismissively. She kicks off her shoes and tosses her sunglasses on the nightstand.

I prop my shoulder against the wall and watch her pick shoes out of her bag and a dress from the closet, cold-shouldering me so much that I almost smile. She grabs the rosy-pink ball left in last night's basket, which claims to make you and your tub smell like heartbreakers.

"Taking a bath?" I ask.

"Yep." She pops the P, and as she turns for the bathroom, I straighten up. When she tries to dodge me, I move enough so that she can't. Finally, she stops the avoidance to stare me down. "What, Becker?"

"Any reason you're acting like a stuck-up princess again?"

"I didn't realize I'd ever stopped."

"Maybe not fully, but you at least put it on mute for a second." I pull the ball from her hand to sniff it, and she swipes it back, her eyes drifting to the side to the coffee table I cleared off.

"May I please attempt to relax in the bath? You can reattach yourself after."

She straightens her shoulders, lifting her chin, and I step aside, gesturing toward the bathroom. Either she'll get over whatever the hell has her acting like day-one Eden, or she won't.

"You missed the stuff under the table," she says.

The door slams shut behind her, and I'll need another shot to deal with her mood. The cool shower to remind my dick of our agreement about high-drama chicks destroyed my buzz. If only it'd fulfilled its original purpose half as well.

I pour and set down the bottle, seeing a scrap of paper and balled-up napkin I missed earlier. I bend down to pick them up as Eden marches out, her attitude still on. She grabs her phone and pauses at the end of the bed, her eyes tracking me through the suite.

"Don't worry," I tell her. "You won't earn any demerits from housekeeping."

I shoot the trash into the basket from where I stand, and she picks at her phone case.

"Thank you," she says after a second. "For cleaning up the mess."

A hint of the chill Eden from earlier bobs to the surface, and I nod, still curious what the hell I did in the first place. I reach down for my shot, but before I can even straighten up all the way, she steals it out of my hand.

"For this too." She holds the glass over her head and disappears again.

A song starts playing a minute later through the speaker in the bathroom ceiling, and I twist the lid onto the bottle. Eden probably did me a favor. My dick and mouth have already proven untrustworthy around her on tequila. And that ball thing smelled really fucking good.

Eden could win an award for her ability to soak in hot water. The music finally cuts off two hours after I come back from grabbing something to eat.

I look up from my phone when she surfaces. She hooks in a hooped earring and then lifts her foot to slip on a heel. My eyes stick about halfway up her thigh, where the hem of her red dress brushes over her skin. I've spent the last three days with her in a bikini, but this fucking dress. The back sits low, the front pushes up, and I might not understand the point of the tie on the one side, but it has my full approval.

"Dance class?" My voice is gravelly as hell, so I swallow while she puts on her other shoe. "They develop a dress code since last night?"

Her gaze flicks to mine. "No. I thought I'd ask Hayden to go with me. They treated me like a pariah last night without a partner, and you have no idea how embarrassing it was to have to dance with the instructor."

"You could just not go," I say like it ever works.

She stops in front of me on the couch. "And hang around the room all night, trading jabs with you?" She delivers one hell of a sarcastic smile. "I'd rather tango with Giselle."

As she walks away, I watch the curves of her ass. It reminds me of Prescott pawing the waitress's, and I pull up the picture I snapped. One glance from her, and I'll guarantee a Hayden-free existence for the rest of the trip.

I stand up and follow her out the door. She's already halfway down the hall, but I bring her to a stop before she reaches his room. I might not be able to pull him off if he sees her right now.

"Hold on, princess."

"Why?" She jerks her arm away and squares up with me in her fucking heels. "Were you wanting me to beg you to come with me again? Offer you a thousand dollars to be sulky?"

"You get the sulk for free. It's a part of my charm." I smile at her, and her stance relaxes, but our standoff continues.

"Will you please move?" she asks.

She crosses her arms, and I tighten my grip on my phone. One look, *poof* goes Hayden, and smooth sailing to my money. Except I can't shake her face from the restaurant last night. This douche wasn't worth the disappointment she showed over him then. And he sure as fuck isn't worth it again.

I rub the back of my head and sigh, shoving my phone in my pocket. Time for the dancing monkey to dance.

With another sweep over Eden's dress, I point my chin toward the exit behind her. "Come on."

"What?" she asks, not having the decency to hide her shock. "You're going with me now?"

"Why not, right?" I walk around her, so she spins the direction I want her to go. "What the hell else am I going to do other than track you around?"

Eden has a set to her jaw, a defensive guard up. "You could take the night off. I'm sure you could find something better than entertaining your fake sister."

"Fake girlfriend," I correct. She gives me a look, and I shrug. "It lessens the chances of people questioning the placement of my hands."

I smile, and she glances over her shoulder at Hayden's room one more time, only mildly resisting when I tug her down the hallway. She thaws more once we get outside. Her pout fades by the gazebo, and we flip to her pulling me. At some point, while introducing me to people I'll never again see in my life, she threads her fingers with mine. I don't even notice until she pries them loose to hug the woman from last night.

"Eden, my beautiful partner, have you replaced me?" Her head draws back as she scans me over, and I'm fairly certain my mother wears a similar dress to every funeral.

"Giselle, this is Becker," Eden says. "He wasn't feeling well last night."

I nod. "Highly allergic to most group activities."

Giselle gives me an up-and-down with her disapproving gaze and then pats Eden on the arm. "Let me know if you want me to kick him out of class, baby."

Eden purses her lips together to hide a smile as Giselle walks off. She shouts instructions, reintroducing a step they learned last night before she hits the button on her remote to start some music.

Everyone shuffles around, and Eden turns to me.

"Think you can keep up?" She moves my hand to her waist while grabbing the other. "Otherwise, I can call back Giselle. I'm sure she'd have no problem—"

I spin her and then pull her into me, her surprised eyes meeting mine.

"You can dance?" she asks.

"I did watch an hour-long class last night."

Eden pushes off my chest to put more space between us as the music stops, so Giselle can give us more orders. It's another step she taught them in the first class. All the steps she pauses the music to announce are, and we do the same thing for the next fifty minutes—reset from the beginning, add in something they already know, and listen to Giselle tell us we're marvelous.

Our chief claps her hands at the end, congratulating us for mastering nothing. "Brilliant. All of you. Now, before we go, I want you to find a new partner and show them what you've got."

Far too many women shift their eyes to me in that moment. *For fuck's sake.* I feel like the new pool boy on the block.

I tighten my grip on Eden. "We've found my line. If you expect me to stick around for the rest of this, you're not trading out for a housewife."

She skims over the other couples as they switch around. "Don't see anyone you like?"

I shake my head, not exactly the real answer, but the one she's going to get. A feisty look hits her eyes, and I really hate how sexy she looks when she smirks.

"A hundred dollars, and I'll stay."

I drop my arms away from her. "No deal. I'll be fantasy fodder."

She laughs. Or cackles—I'm not really sure, but it's fucking intoxicating. I touch her without thinking, brushing my hand over hers before I lift it to my shoulder. She glances at the couples still pairing off and Giselle restarting the music, and then she sighs, slipping her other hand into mine.

"So rebellious, Eden Monroe," I say, moving my arm behind her.

She sways along with me, her face tilted up. "Thank you for coming tonight."

I shrug, slowly moving us away from the other couples as they bump into each other. "I told you, there wasn't much else to do."

Her lips press together, and I have to stop myself from pulling the bottom one out. For some fucking reason, I want to know what she's not saying. Why she went all brat on me earlier after our game.

"My mom's Puerto Rican."

She looks up. "What?"

"You asked about my family earlier. My dad was born in Ireland, but he's been in Chicago most of his life."

Eden smiles, and I'm about to keep going, but Giselle, dancing with herself, twirls by and plants an elbow in my side. "Spin her."

This fucking woman.

"As for siblings, I have a baby sister." I spin Eden, my hand landing lower than before, where the back of her dress starts. "Grace. She's eight, so fucking dramatic, and I'd murder someone just for making her cry."

"You sound like Elijah," she says, tipping her head to the side. "Are you sure you're not my pseudo-brother right now?"

"Do you want me to be your brother right now?" I ask, gliding my thumb under the material above her waist.

When she stares up at me, I realize I might have falsely accused tequila earlier. Right now, the only thing in my system is her, and my mouth keeps going, my thumb rubbing over her skin.

The song stops then. The other couples start applauding for Giselle or themselves, and one of the ladies announces that she wants a group picture. Eden's brow crumples, like she thinks it sounds as lame as I do, but unlike me, she goes over to join them.

I wait at the bottom of the gazebo stairs, taking out my phone. A text came through about halfway through the class, and I expect it to be Elijah, early with his daily warning to not touch his sister. Because I've been doing a fantastic job of that so far. Only, when I check, it's the name I've been waiting to see pop up all week.

Ty.

All clear, my dude. Call me.

I go to tap Ty's name but stop, seeing Eden bounce down the steps. "You finished campaigning for the title of Miss Grove?"

She marches straight by me, sticking her nose in the air, and I shove my phone in my pocket, following her.

Back in the suite, I scan over the mess on the bathroom counter. I've stopped attempting to maintain any separation between the sides and dig until I find my toothbrush, and then I give up entirely and use her toothpaste. Three days on Eden duty, and she has me housebroken.

We slip by each other, trading spaces. The shower turns on as I bring a different comforter to the couch than last night. Housekeeping must have been here after we finally left and changed the bedding. Eden marked for them to only come once over the week—saving the world or some shit.

I toss the blanket to the end and sit down to call Ty. Only I end up staring at his message instead. I have no idea how long I blink like an asshole at my screen. Long enough that I miss the water shutting off.

"No," Eden shouts from the bathroom. "No!"

My phone lands on the cushions, and I'm reaching for the handle when the door flies open. Eden's wrapped in a towel, her wet hair clinging to the skin on her neck while she frantically searches the room. "Where are the robes?"

"The fuck?" I say. "You're screaming about complimentary robes?"

She nails me with a glare and practically pushes me out of the way to check the latest basket. As if they'd micro-folded the robes and tucked them between the chocolate-covered strawberries and fingertip vibrator.

Once she's thoroughly tossed the hotel room, she starts stomping back toward the bathroom. I hook her arm and spin her around, tired of this shit.

"What's with the robes at night?" I trap her face in my hands when she tries to turn it away again. "Tell me what's going on in that psycho little head of yours."

With a huff, she says, "I packed drunk, okay?"

"I have no idea what that means."

Her cheeks flame beneath my thumbs. "I was drunk and mad and…" She pushes my hands away, chewing a hole in her lip before she looks up at me. "I only packed skimpy lingerie to sleep in."

My eyebrows draw in. "Like lace and crotchless shit?"

Every inch of visible skin—and I'm sure the rest of it—pinks. "Ew, not crotchless."

I chuckle, scrubbing a hand over my face as she retreats to the bathroom. She locks the door, and I lean beside it, crossing my arms.

"Are you planning on sleeping in there then?"

She doesn't answer, and I rest my head against the wall.

"You've traipsed around in bikinis all week, Eden. I can't imagine whatever you packed shows more skin than those."

"It's different," she says, her voice quiet, just on the other side.

"Hardly. Just turn the lights off and stumble around in the dark, like you usually do. I'll never know the difference."

She goes quiet again, so I straighten up, heading for the desk. If she won't come out or talk to me, then she can flip shit when I pick the lock.

"Beck?"

I stop, waiting for the rest.

"Shut off the lights before you lie down."

As soon as I strip to my boxers and plug in my phone, I hit the switch on the lamp. The door creaks open a little later, and then Eden's figure rushes through the room and dives onto the bed. I chuckle, stacking my hands behind my head.

"Night, princess."

She mumbles something back and starts screwing with stuff on the nightstand. I'm about to pull the pillow over my head to drown her out when my phone buzzes on the desk. I turn my head, not thinking. Then the screen lights up the entire room, and any agreement between me and my dick is gone the second my eyes land on Eden kneeling on the bed.

All I see is lace and skin. She has her bottom lip between her teeth, her thighs slightly parted, and blonde hair over her shoulder. Which leads me straight to her tits, practically spilling out of the low-neck, lace-lined whatever the fuck she's wearing.

When she looks up, her eyes meet mine. Neither of us moves other than her chest rising faster and my gaze lowering over her again.

"No different than a bikini," I rasp.

It's not even a believable lie with the way I'm staring at her. And I'm too hard to go shut off my phone. Fuck, if I got off this couch right now, I wouldn't even make it to the desk.

In a few seconds, the screen dims on its own and then darkens completely. As soon as she's a shadow again, I roll my head back on the pillow.

I thought not seeing her would help. I was wrong. She shifts on the bed, and I imagine the way her body moves, how it would line up with mine. The room falls silent, the air with a pulse, and something tells me I won't be sleeping tonight.

I lie there and stare at the ceiling. Anytime I close my eyes, I think about the thin sheet separating me from everything underneath. Then I get hard, remembering the feel of her soft skin, smooth when my hands ran over her.

Fuck.

Eden hasn't moved in an hour, so I toss off the comforter and grab my phone. Sliding the glass door open, I check over my shoulder, making sure she's still asleep before I step through. The bricks cool the bottoms of my feet, and I breathe in the ocean air.

Ten thousand dollars.

I bring up my phone, shaking my head at Elijah's text.

Don't even look at her.

Well, he blew that out of the water himself. His *sweet dreams* text is the reason I can't go a full minute without imagining sleeping with his sister.

I refocus and call Ty.

He answers right away with loud music pulsing in the background.

"Hey, B!" he shouts. "We're at Axel's. When you getting here?"

"What happened with Monte?" I rub the back of my head, hearing someone else start talking to him. "Ty, fucking focus."

"Right." He must go outside, and the music fades out. "Monte and two of his guys were picked up for fucking speeding, man. Cops found enough stolen shit in the truck that they sent half the department over to search his garage."

My brows lower. "Sounds convenient."

Ty laughs. "It sounds like, problem solved. One of his other guys even dropped by earlier. Monte's out of commission. Now, get your ass here."

"Not in the city yet," I say.

"Where are you? I saw Gina yesterday, and she almost ripped my fucking head off when I asked."

"I'm staying with a friend."

Enough light reaches through the glass that I can see the blankets curving over Eden's body on the bed.

"Well, when you plan on getting back? Tomorrow?" he asks, and someone calls his name.

"Maybe." I tear my eyes off Eden's form. "I have a chance to make some cash on a…" The word *job* tastes fucking bad in my mouth, and I leave it off. "I don't know, man. I'll be back sometime between tomorrow and Saturday."

"All right," Ty says. "Hit me up when you get in."

After someone starts shouting, the line goes dead. I lower the phone, and instead of going inside, I pull out one of the iron chairs. And I'm all too aware that I pick one facing the goddamn door.

Eden

Beck's not in the room when I wake up in the morning.

I'm relieved to slide the mask off my eyes and not see him on the couch after he basically saw me naked. I don't buy his bullshit about the lingerie not being any different from a bikini either. For one, my swim bottoms usually consist of more than see-through lace. Also, I've caught Beck checking me out at least once in each of my bathing suits, but last night, his gaze raked over me until my skin burned. I couldn't even move, giving him every second of light to look at whatever he wanted.

My cheeks heat, even without him here, and I hike the sheet up to my chin, pulling until it untucks from the bottom. Call the wrap dress I create out of it linen chic.

One of the couples at dance class said they rescheduled the volleyball tournament for noon, so I change into a suit and cover-up for the day. By the time I finish my hair and makeup, Beck still hasn't surfaced. I glance around the empty suite, wondering if I should be concerned. Never having had a bodyguard go missing, I'm not exactly sure of the protocol.

Room service knocks before I land on a decision. I hold the door, stepping out of the way to let the kid push his cart into the suite.

"You want it inside or out?" he asks.

"On the desk is fine."

While I wait for him to unload everything, my eyes drift to the closet. Mentally running through my dresses, I happen to glance down to the closet floor, and my brow draws in. Beck's ugly green canvas bag isn't there anymore. I start to go check if he moved it when the cart rolls in front of me.

"You're all set, miss." The kid stops in front of me on his way out. "Anything else I can do for you?"

Shaking my head, I hand him his tip and force a smile. "Thank you."

Once he and his cart leave, I open the other side of the closet. The bag isn't there either. It's not on the shelf or in the bathroom. Not anywhere.

Beck's gone.

Sometime between when I went to sleep and woke up, Beck grabbed his bag and left.

I sink onto the bed as the realization twists through me, surprisingly cool and hitting a few sore spots along the way. I can't decide if it stings because I'm now officially alone on a couples trip or the timing of his middle-of-the-night departure. I've asked Beck to leave since we arrived, and he ignored me every time. The fact that he bailed less than ten hours after seeing me in lingerie feels insulting.

Tempted to throw on the blue lace baby doll and flaw-search in the mirror, I push off the bed, reminding myself that he was never supposed to be here anyway. With him out of the picture, I can finally enjoy my vacation the way Drunk Eden envisioned— on the beach with a bunch of hot guys.

My eyes fall on the empty carpet inside the closet again, and I sigh. I'll just have to figure out a way to push everything Becker Donovan out of my mind first.

After I pile the nightly baskets, liquor bottles, shot glasses, tumblers, and the comforter in the closet and close the door, I eat and head to the beach, ready for a day in the sun. In two days, I'll be back in Chicago in the dead of winter. I need to store up all the serotonin I can to last me until spring.

A crowd's already formed around the nets when I get down there. I find a semi-clear section of sand off to the side and scan faces. Sand volleyball feels like something Hayden would be interested in with his muscles and athletic build, but I don't see him as the first match starts.

I only make it through the first set before the bulkiest dude on the beach plants himself in front of me. I sigh, about to move, when a set of hands grips my waist from behind. Before I can jerk away from whatever asshole thinks they can manhandle me, I s

Beck.

My heart lurches, and I smile as his arm encircles me, his chest against my back. But then I remember he made me feel like shit by disappearing, and I shove his hands away, spinning around.

"You think you can just—"

The rest cuts off when Beck's fingers slide into my hair like at the restaurant the other night, and in the same breath, his lips press to mine. No part of me dares to move for the second he kisses me. When he pulls back, his eyes drop to my mouth, and it's like a shot of adrenaline. I draw in a breath, my skin burning again. He sweeps his thumb over my cheek and looks up.

"Look who found me, baby."

Just then Brad and Julia pop up beside us, and my eyes dart to them. Whatever function I lost, I regain and immediately lean into Beck as he slips an arm around my waist, tucking his thumb in a hole in my cover-up.

"We hijacked him from the bar when he said you were down here," Julia says with a grin. "Brad played volleyball in college. We needed to come watch at least one game to let him relive his glory days. Back when he could jump straight in the air and not hurt his back on the landing."

He shakes his head, chuckling. "My wife, the comedian."

With them in the lead, Beck and I trail behind to an empty spot on the sand to watch the set. It doesn't take long for Brad to zone in on the game, entertaining Julia with his reactions and running commentary.

"I told them I was meeting you later," Beck says after serves.

I shrug. "Could have found a different way to warn me they were right behind you."

His lips turn up on this side. "I wasn't sure how else to shut you up before you ripped out your boyfriend for touching you."

Brad shouts at one of the players, and Julia cackles.

"Your bag was gone this morning." I try to sound like I didn't notice even though I'm the one bringing it up. "I thought maybe you had gone home."

"I was doing laundry. Not all of us brought three outfit changes for each day, princess." Beck pauses and then dips his head down closer. "If you didn't have so much shit on the bathroom counter, you might have noticed *mine* was all still there."

Until this moment, I didn't even realize he had anything on the counter, but I still refuse to admit he has a point. "Maybe you were in a hurry."

He turns to look at me. "Just laundry."

I nod, and he goes back to watching the game.

After the first match, Julia wins the argument with Brad that mimosas have no limit on vacation, and she drags me along with her to the bar.

Everyone goes for drinks between matches, so Julia and I avoid the beach bar and try our luck at one of the restaurant bars. On our way back from getting what ends up being a glass of champagne with a splash of orange juice, I finally catch sight of the face I was looking for earlier. Hayden's tucked in the back corner of the beach bar. I smile when he looks over, and he pushes his sunglasses up, biting his lip when he grins.

"Hey," I say, hanging back a little from Julia. "I'll catch up."

She doesn't even look back, just waves a hand over her head while she sips from her flute, probably trying to get rid of the evidence before getting back to Brad. I stop on the sand, waiting for Hayden to slowly saunter over.

"You are one hard woman to track down, Eden Monroe." He comes to a stop in front of me, and I smile.

"I'm here now."

"Yes, you are," he says.

He reaches up to run his thumb over my cheek, and I can't help but look over at the volleyball match starting. Everyone's facing the nets, but I still shy away enough that his hand falls to his side.

"I keep trying to guess where you'll be, but so far, I'm always a little off."

"We could just make plans, you know?" I tip my head to the side, and he chuckles.

"We could." He reaches in the pocket of his board shorts and pulls out his phone. "So, I'm thinking dinner tonight, the snorkeling you've been teasing me with tomorrow, Saturday, we can—"

I laugh and shake my head. "You're leaving tomorrow, and I'm leaving Saturday."

He nods. "I know. That just means we'll have to get creative until I come to Chicago to visit. Or you can come to Boston, but we should probably start with watching a movie together over the phone."

He flips his phone around, so I'll give him my number. I start to reach for it as he glances over his shoulder toward the bar. And I stop, seeing the fresh hickey peeking out from under his bright blue polo shirt.

Shark in the water.

I expect more of a gut punch, realizing he's no better than any of the other spoiled fuckbois buzzing around my orbit on any given day. But after an initial twinge, it turns to irritation, and I pull his collar away from his neck. His head jerks around while I stare at the rest of the iceberg that was lurking below the surface.

"Jesus," I say. "How were you planning to explain that when you talked your way between my legs?"

Hayden rubs a hand over the bruised skin once again hidden by his shirt. "Eden, it was just some waitress." He lowers his voice, looking at me like I should understand. And I do because I've heard it before—only in Ashton's case, it was *just some TA*. Then *some barista*.

"It was a stupid, drunken hookup that shouldn't have happened," he continues. "She was completely meaningless."

I roll my eyes. "And you're completely pathetic."

Hayden lets out a hushed, "*Fuck!*" as I walk away, but I'm sure he'll find someone to lick his wounds for him within twenty minutes.

Beck's on the outskirts of the crowd, his arms crossed when I reach him. "How's the Ken Doll on this fine day?"

"Fake and most likely without genitals."

"Most likely." He looks over, a smirk forming. "But I could have told you that on day one."

Julia pushes her way toward us and grins, stopping in front of us. "Brad decided to get closer."

When she points to a gap between two girls, Beck ducks down to my level to see Brad all the way at the front on a knee, loudly coaching one of the teams.

"My man." She giggles and starts back the way she came.

Beck shakes his head and sighs. "I guess we're getting closer."

He laces his fingers with mine, pulling me behind him.

I would have gone willingly, but I'm starting to like his way better.

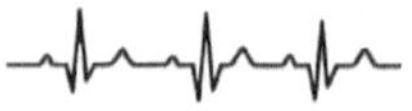

We spend most of the afternoon watching the teams play through the bracket. At the beginning of the final game, I decide the body can only store so much serotonin at a time. I plan to abandon Beck on the beach with Brad and Julia, but when I tell him I'm going back to the room, he taps Brad and hooks his head, indicating we're leaving.

"Dinner after this?" Brad asks him. "I have car questions."

Beck shrugs. "I charge a hundred an hour."

I smack him in the chest, and he catches my wrist, smirking.

Before Beck can give a real answer, Brad jerks his head toward the net and shouts at one of the teams.

"You can stay," I tell him.

"You don't want to go to dinner?" He gives a long look at something behind me.

"Not really. I'd rather hang out in the room. Maybe order something."

Hayden winding up being an asshole might not have broken my heart, but it still reminded me of Ashton. Most everything on this trip has, aside from Beck—the anti-Ashton if there ever was one.

Beck returns my hand to my side. "You want me to walk you back?"

"I've been walking on my own for over twenty years now," I say, turning. "I think I'll manage."

Once I get all the way around, I see Hayden by the bar, his eyes on me. I must have thought his name too many times and summoned him out of his hole. I'd change my mind and bring my bodyguard with me if I hadn't just made a big deal about going on my own.

"I'll see you later," I call over my shoulder.

My gaze ices the closer I get to Hayden. He stays put like a smart man, not even looking at me. Once I clear him, I glance behind me and see why. Beck's where I left him on the sand, every part of him threatening Hayden. Or maybe daring him to move.

At first, I let it go as Beck being Beck, but as I swipe my keycard for the suite, I remember I didn't tell him about what had happened earlier. So, the warning for Prescott to stay away or die had nothing to do with the hickey and Hayden being an asshole.

I think about Beck's mouth on mine, and I touch my lips, wondering if he wants Hayden to stay away from me for another reason.

The door swings shut behind me, and when I pass the closet, the door's open. Beck's bag sits on the floor inside. I scan the rest of the room, my cheeks heating. Everything I shoved away—

attempting to out-of-sight, out-of-mind Becker—is *exactly* where it had been when I woke up this morning.

So great.

Since the basket from last night is back on the floor beside the couch, I scoop it up and dig through for the mini spa kit. If I have to be mortified, I might as well do it while wearing a hydrating face mask, sugar scrub mitts, and revitalizing booties on my feet.

I squeeze as much tranquility as possible out of the next hour and forty minutes, hanging my legs over the ledge of the empty corner whirlpool tub and watching *Dirty Dancing* on my phone, balanced on the faucet. As the credits roll, I have the fleeting thought of calling Darla but quickly bury that one along with the memory of Beck finding my reminder-stash in the closet.

I haul myself out of the tub and rinse off my feet. Walking into the main room, I jump. Beck's sprawled on his back on top of the comforter, his shirt riding up and abs peeking out.

"I didn't think you'd be back until later," I say.

He sits up and runs a hand through his hair, leaving it messed up. I finally noticed the extra toothbrush and comb while I did my makeup. And by noticed, I mean, searched for them.

"I thought maybe you'd want to do something tonight."

"Together?" I ask, and he gives me one of his irritated looks.

"Yes, together."

I study him, trying to figure out his angle. He hasn't mentioned the closet or even smirked at the missing basket from the floor yet, both of which I'm bracing myself for.

After a second, he groans, falling back on the bed, and covers his face with his arm. "You're already making me regret asking." But he sits right back up, getting to his feet. "Put your fucking shoes on."

"Where are we going?"

He stops short of the patio doors. "A party."

Eden

I roll my window down in the back seat of the cab. The night air feels even better, blowing across my skin, than the sun-heated ocean breeze. We ride for probably ten minutes before the car stops. Music beats from a small house across the street. It reminds me of the drawings all children make—a simple square with one window and a door and a slanted roof. I wouldn't be surprised to see a stick dog running through the strip of grass out front, serving as a yard.

As Beck pays the driver, I climb out and glance around. Most of the other houses look the same—square shapes and a line of grass. Other than this block, very few cars line the lamplit streets, with even less vehicles in the driveways.

The car pulls away, and I spin around to Beck, stepping off the curb.

"Where are we?"

He tips his head toward the music. "A party."

I squint at him and march across the street without him. But by the time I reach the sidewalk, he catches my hand and turns me around to him so that my chest bumps his. I start to step back when his other hand presses to the small of my back, keeping me there.

"We're together when we walk through that door." His gaze dips momentarily to the sweetheart neckline of my top before locking on my eyes again. "You don't leave my sight, and you don't drink a goddamn thing unless I put it in your hand."

I check over my shoulder at the house, then I set my jaw and look up at him. "I've been to parties before. Probably with worse people than anyone in there. A lot happens inside penthouse apartments and VIP sections at clubs, you know."

He nods, his eyes searching my face. "I'm sure it does. And I'll bet every one of those assholes knows exactly who will come after them if they lay a finger on Eden Monroe." He moves the piece of hair blowing across my face. "Don't expect the same in here." There's a softness to his tone, not usually there, and I nod.

Beck lets me go, and we climb the steps to the house. With our first step inside, his arm snakes around my waist. His palm flattens against my stomach as he tucks me against his side, maneuvering us through the large group of people dancing in the living room. It flows into the kitchen off to the side with more room to move and breathe, but he keeps me close until we reach a surprisingly familiar face.

The cab driver from the airport stops mid-conversation with someone when he spots us. "Fucking Tourist." He lets out a laugh, grabbing Beck's outstretched hand and pulling him close enough so that he can clap him on the back. "You found me."

Beck tips his head to me. "Eden. Winston."

Winston looks down at me and then away, so he can give a dramatic double take. "She Lives!" Then he's throwing both arms around my middle and lifting me in a hug. "Gucci for da win."

I have no idea what the last part means, but I smile along with him. Beck's hold reengages again as soon as my feet touch the floor.

"Yeah, calm down," he says, curling his hand around my hip.

Winston holds up both palms in mock surrender. "All right, no touching. Can I at least offer her a drink?"

"You can." I deliver a squint to Beck, which goes ignored.

He loosens his hold when Winston hooks his head toward a counter covered in booze and leads us over. While they argue about the legitimacy of mixers, I watch a guy carrying a fan into the kitchen. He balances his joint on the edge of a counter and then proceeds to set the fan on the floor in front of the open refrigerator door, facing it toward the living room. Once he plugs the cord into an empty outlet, he nods as he takes a puff off his joint, clearly proud of his solution for cooler air.

Beck lowers his brow, checking out the stoned thermodynamics expert.

"What's in it?" I ask when he hands me a cup.

"Rum and whatever cherry shit this guy keeps going on about."

Winston gives him a scowl before he winks at me. "Don't listen to him. You'll love it."

Beck rolls his eyes, sipping his drink, and Winston knocks the rim of his cup to mine. His brows lift as I take a cautious swallow, my eyes bulging.

"Oh my God," I say, pulling the cup away. "That's the most dangerous thing I've ever tasted."

I pick out the cherry floating on top and bite it off the stem. Vanilla and rum hit my tongue, twisted with the cherry, and I moan, nodding my approval.

He chuckles and sends a pointed, "See," to Beck. "Told you she'd love it."

"And what *exactly* does she love?"

I'm still chewing when a girl appears beside Winston, folding her arms over her chest. She has on a tight black dress with her raven hair in loose curls down to her shoulders. And a glare on him that only comes from an irritated girlfriend.

"I leave for five minutes, and you get a drink with the first random white chick you see?"

Winston doesn't even look at her before he reaches to pull her over to him. "So we're clear," he says, leaning close, "she's the second one I saw."

I laugh, and her pursed lips slowly lose their seriousness. He gives her a kiss as she relaxes against him, swinging her attention to Beck and me. It flashes between us, and answering her unasked question, Beck moves his hand to the nape of my neck at the same time as mine runs over his abs through his shirt while I angle closer.

"Tourist," Winston tells her, nodding to him and then motioning to me, "and his girl, She Lives."

The nicknames earn him another look, so he tries again.

"Beck and Eden." He lifts his cup to his mouth. "But my names are better."

"Hardly," she says, sliding the drink from his hand.

Not missing a beat, Winston grabs another from the counter behind him. "This is Sasha."

"Love of his life. Even if he acts too cool to admit it in front of his friends."

Winston winces, and she swats at him with her free hand. They're sweet together, playful and teasing, but the way they move around each other so intuitively shows the deeper connection. How well they read each other without even being conscious of it, shifting and readjusting seamlessly.

It only takes a drink for Sasha and me to turn on Winston and Beck, deciding we're much better company for each other, and after two, she lunges for me.

"We are dancing," she says, looping her arm through mine.

Shockingly, Beck lets her pull me away from him and toward the living room.

"I'll bring her back," she calls to him, and I add, "Eventually."

With Sasha as my guide, we hold up our cups and force our way into the middle of the group of people. She's shouting stuff at me and laughing, but I can't hear a word. A haze hangs over the room, the skunky smell of weed all around us. It's far from the club scene I'm used to, but somehow, it's exactly the same. Most of the women seem content with dancing with each other while guys try to creep their way in.

A couple of songs in, Sasha's gaze flicks behind me before her eyes roll, and she leans into my ear. "Incoming in five."

But it only takes three for someone to brush up against my backside. I spin around to the guy laying claim to my waist. A joint hangs out one side of his mouth, and I can't say the mustache helps his case much. I coolly shake my head to the music, backing away until his hands fall away.

Sasha laughs as she catches me and shouts in my ear, "Winston's glare's got nothing on your man's."

Her hand peeks around me, finger pointed to the other side of the room. Between the bodies, I glimpse Beck, stone jaw clenched and his stare on me. I rest my head back on Sasha's shoulder.

"I'll be back."

She gives a little push when I start in Beck's direction. "Cheer him up, yeah? And tell Winston to get his ass out here."

I dodge people until I reach the edge of the living room. Cool air hits me almost immediately from the fan set up in front of the open refrigerator door. Beck crosses his arms as I approach. He's not in one of the button-downs he's been wearing around the resort, but a plain black T-shirt, like the one from the airport. The real Beck. Not-my-type Beck, but right now, he's supposed to be all-my Beck.

He lifts an eyebrow when I stop in front of him. "Finished getting groped?"

I shake my head, emptying my drink, and then I trade it for his beside him on the counter. The one he gave me was way weaker, but I fight off the burn in my eyes and the back of my throat.

He yanks the cup away after a few gulps. "Take a breath, princess."

I lick the last of the cherry flavor off my lips, turning my head to Winston. "Sasha says for you to go dance with her."

"She does, huh?" He claps a hand on Beck's back, straightening up. "Then I guess I'm going to dance."

Beck watches him walk off behind me, then he brings his attention back to me. While he stares me down, I slip my fingers over his wrist and pull it toward me until his cup hovers in front of my mouth. He lets me steal another drink, a smirk appearing.

"You just can't fucking listen."

I shake my head. "Rebellious, remember?"

That gets a laugh, and I officially like this Beck. His shoulders rise in a deep breath, his gaze searching around the living room behind me. "Fuck it," he says.

He throws back the rest of his drink and sets the empty cup on the counter. I smile when he nudges me backward to the living room, and as I turn, he grips my sides. He guides me until Sasha jumps at me. She does a little wavy thing with our arms and laughs, crashing her head back onto Winston's shoulder behind her. He wraps his arms around her as they move to the music.

Beck pulls me to him, my back to his chest while his hands skim down to my hips. It's nothing like last night. No instructed steps or pausing to reset and try again. Just the music and the high and him. I close my eyes to feel more of all three. Somewhere between the beats of bass, the stubble on his jaw grazes my temple. Sasha's laugh breaks through, only to fade a second later when fingers inch up to my ribs on one side. I loop my arms up around his neck, resting them on his shoulders. My head leans to the side as he scrapes his jaw farther down to my neck. The roughness rubs against my skin, his hard leaving a mark on my soft.

One song blends into the next. When the tempo changes, Beck turns me around, pulling my wrists behind his neck again before reclaiming his hold on me, his arm cinched tighter this time. Face-to-face with him, I forget the high, and the music blurs. I barely have to tug for him to press his forehead against mine. My hands run over the back of his neck and into his hair.

"What are you doin', crazy?" He says it like I shouldn't be touching him, but he's touching me, too, finding places to be skin to skin. His fingers glide over my shoulder and down my arm, his thumb sweeping over my collarbone, and then the other tucks under the bottom hem of my top.

"Fan of skin as well?"

Beck nods against my forehead. "So it would seem."

My pulse drums faster when he traces my strap down to my neckline. His gaze drifts lower to watch his thumb following the curve inward. He looks up, hesitating to see if I plan on stopping him but I don't. His hand starts to move, but then someone nudges me.

Everything bleeds in at once. The song and smoke and people. And Beck's hand falls away.

I look at Sasha and Winston beside us again. Fuck, they might have been there all along; I really can't say. She still has her arm stretched out toward me.

"You two are adorable together," she says over the music.

I force a smile, noticing the distance Beck's put between us.

"You're making me look bad, Tourist," Winston shouts with a grin, and he jerks his head toward Sasha. "She'll want me acting all dopey when we're out now."

Sasha slaps at his chest, and Beck chuckles at his joke, but I think the rum hits because I feel sick. Hot and weak, and I want to be anywhere but here.

Pushing Beck's hands away, I sneak around Sasha and Winston.

"I'll be back," I say in her ear, and she nods.

I avoid looking at Beck, ducking under someone's arm and sidestepping my way through the bodies packed together. I need space. A minute away from him and whatever act we're putting on.

Because that's what it is … or supposed to be.

We just might have been too convincing.

By the time I get away from all the people, my lungs burn. The air is too warm, and even passing the fan and fridge, I need more cool. I burst through the door off the kitchen and into an enclosed porch or pantry. It looks like it might be used for both with shelves of canned food on one wall and furniture along the other. A couple of people are sitting on the couch, the whites of their eyes shining in the slight glow of light passing through a gap in the shades over the windows.

I take deep breaths, my head spinning. It doesn't take long at all for the door to open and shut behind me. It's Beck. I don't need to look. I close my eyes instead with the first creak of the floorboards. Each one is a little closer until I feel him. His hand brushes along my side until it reaches my stomach, and then his breath reaches my ear. "Come back inside."

I open my mouth to argue, but his fist bunches in my top.

"Now." He jerks me with him, and when I start to fight, he flips me around and traps me with his arms. "Sorry."

It doesn't sound like he's talking to me as he backs to the door. He rotates us, so he can open the screen, and I glance over at the people on the couch. My heart lurches in my chest. The shadowy outline of a gun rests on one of the guy's knees—pointed at us.

Once we're in the kitchen again, Beck lets me go to ease the door shut. The latch barely clicks, and he spins to me. Then he's grabbing my face and pushing me through the kitchen until my back presses against the side of the refrigerator. We're blocked from the living room, and no one else is in the kitchen with us.

"I told you not to leave my fucking sight."

I swallow, my eyes frantic as they bounce around the room. "I just needed some air."

His jaw ticks, his grip on my cheeks tightening. I feel the constriction edging into my throat, the tears welling. Before they fall, he runs his thumbs under my eyes.

"Then let's get you some air."

Thirteen

Beck

I pull Eden along behind me through the other door in the kitchen. It leads to the backyard and not straight into a fucking drug deal. People have been cycling in and out of that door all night. I should have just hauled her ass out of here when I first noticed instead of expecting her to stay the hell away from it.

Once we're outside, I let go of her and walk into the grass. I need some space to calm down after seeing a fucking gun on her, but I don't let myself get too far away from her before I stop, hands on the back of my head.

"What the hell, Eden? Were you trying to—" I turn around, ready to storm back to her, but she's right there, colliding with my chest. She hides her face in her hands and then buries even deeper in my shirt.

Fuck.

I let out a breath and close my eyes. "I'm too fucking pissed to be hugging you."

But I wrap my arms around her, tucking her head under my chin and doing it anyway. We stay there for a minute until her breathing slows and I can manage a relatively civil conversation.

"What the fuck was that in there?" I ask, my voice low.

When she doesn't answer, I curl my fingers under her chin, bringing it up so she looks at me. The string bulbs hanging from the awning over the deck highlight her face, as if she cut a deal with them. It's unfair. One change in lighting, and my anger slips.

I skim my hand up, sweeping the hair away from her eyes. The light catches her lashes then, her lips pressed into a slight pout. Just like that, I'm lost in a blur of candy flowers and crazy. The way I was last night and again inside while she danced with her hands on me.

And just like in there, I can't keep mine the fuck off her.

"Why did you bolt, Eden?" My palm slides from the back of her neck, following her spine down, and she swallows.

"I told you, I needed air," she says.

Her fingers graze the front of my shirt, and I shift enough so that they press to my abs on the other side.

"No more air in the middle of a drug deal than in the living room, princess." I watch her lips, waiting for them to move, but they don't, and I flick my gaze up. "So, you needed air. Why couldn't you tell me?"

She hesitates, turning away, but I bring her face right back. "Why?"

"Because you're the reason I needed it." She rushes through the words, and the steady beat from inside counts off the silence as she stares up at me.

"Do you need air now?" I rasp.

Her eyes shift between mine until she slowly shakes her head. "No."

I skim my fingers across the strip of warm skin between her top and skirt, feeling her hands creep up my chest. She has my fucking head so warped and deep in Eden World that I'm starting to think I might have permanent damage. I have no idea why else

I'd push my hand into her hair, dying to kiss her when it could easily cost me ten thousand dollars.

Ten thousand dollars.

A shot of cold water streamlines straight into my veins as Eden's hands hook behind my neck, pulling me down to her.

And then I do the stupidest thing I could.

"We should go," I say, less than an inch away from her gorgeous lips.

She freezes, her face somewhere between shock and confusion. "What?"

Already hating myself for it, I pull her wrists away from the back of my neck. "I shouldn't have dragged you out here. Or even brought you in the first place. I'm sorry if I…" I leave the end for fill-in-the-blank, not having a clue how to finish that fucking sentence.

"If you what?" she shoots back. "Were all over me? Because you were, and you didn't seem terribly concerned with going anywhere a second ago. And inside—" Shaking her head, she takes a step back, pulling away from me. "Why'd you bring me tonight, Becker? If you don't want me, then why am I here?"

"I thought you could use a night away from the resort."

A mostly true answer, the rest being that I thought, away from the resort, I'd see her uncomfortable and judgy and remember why I couldn't stand chicks like her. Obviously, it backfired. Her unease faded almost immediately, and she barely batted an eyelash at the house or the people in it.

"And last night?" Eden asks. "Why did you take me to dance class?"

Fuck.

"That's not a simple answer," I tell her.

"Then make it simple. Tell me why you changed your mind and took me."

"Leave it alone, Eden."

"Answer the question, Becker." She steps closer, and I feel my cool starting to slip. She wants to fight in a stranger's backyard, and the harder she pushes, the closer I am to giving her what she wants. "Tell me why you chased me down the hall instead of letting me go with Hayden."

"Because I was trying to keep you *away* from him," I snap.

Fuck, I can't keep my shit together when it comes to her.

Eden doesn't even flinch. "But why would you do that unless you—"

A look of realization washes over her, and my gut clenches the same way it did over her disappointment.

"Elijah?" she asks, her voice cold. "Is that it? You're supposed to be keeping me away from guys while I'm here?"

"I told you, it's not that simple."

Eden stares me down. "Was it a part of the deal?"

I nod, and she lets out a brittle laugh, fast-forwarding from hurt to pissed.

"Of course it was." Her arms fall to her sides, and she backs up. "Screw you, Beck. And you can give Eli the same message when you collect your cash."

"Eden, wait." I try to stop her from storming off, but she jerks her arm away.

"Call a fucking cab," she says, not even looking back as she stomps up the steps.

⎯⎮⎯⎮⎯

As our cab makes its way back to the resort, the silence stretches between us. Eden stays plastered to the inside of the car door on her side, all of her smiles and mischievous glances from earlier gone. She stares out the window while I stare at her.

It terrifies me how close I am to saying *screw the money* and dragging her across the seat to me. But I already know where every fucking penny of that money is going. Credit card payments, overdue bills, rent. And I can't give it up over a chick I've known a few days. Even if every mile of not touching her is slowly driving me insane.

Eden doesn't wait, scrambling out once the car stops. Her door slams, and I drop my head back on the seat, looking up at the ceiling.

"Shit," I whisper.

It only takes me another second to realize I'm being a fucking idiot. I send a quick text, and then I'm throwing money at the driver and climbing out after her. She's already across the lobby when I push through the doors, her heels clicking across the sidewalk.

"Eden," I say, hooking her arm.

She rips it away while turning around to face me. "What, Becker?"

"What happened in the backyard—"

"I get it." She might be keeping the volume conversational, but the rest of her is yelling at me. Her arms cross, and she juts her chin up. "This started as a free vacation and turned into an opportunity you couldn't pass up. I'm a job to you. A fucking paycheck for you to collect."

"You know, if you'd stop talking for a second—"

"Why? So you can try to make me feel better about it? Act like you actually give a shit about me and not the money waiting for you at the end of this?"

Eden licks her lips, her chest rising and falling under her tight top. Even in the middle of her giving me a verbal lashing, all I can think about is how hot she looks right now.

She opens her mouth to say more, and just before I pull her toward me to shut her the fuck up the only way I think will work, her eyes dart to the side.

"Perfect," she says, letting her hands fall away from her hips.

I have no interest in what she sees, but what she sees has an interest in me. Macy stops beside us. Although she might as well have walked straight between us and shoved Eden out of the way.

"Hey, I was hoping I'd see you again before you left." She jerks at my arm. "Want to grab drinks again?"

"I'm kind of in the middle of something," I grind out, not taking my eyes off Eden.

"You're really not," Eden says.

We end up in a staredown with Macy remaining completely oblivious.

"I realized I didn't get your number the other night." She slides my phone out of my hand. "Luckily, I have plenty of pictures saved for you."

The screen is still unlocked, and I glare down as she starts putting her number in. I figure the fastest way to get rid of her is to just let her, but when I look back at Eden, a hurt smile appears before she marches off.

"Eden." I reach for my phone, and Macy turns away with it.

"Hold on. I'm getting yours, so I can send the—hey!"

I swipe it out of her hand, already on my way after Eden. She's made it all the way to the pool closest to our room when I catch up.

"Would you quit acting like a fucking brat and talk to me?" I ask, coming up behind her.

She whips around. "What do you want, Beck? Permission to go fuck the check-in girl? Well, you've got it."

I groan, rubbing the back of my neck. "That's not what I want."

"Then what? Because you made it perfectly clear tonight that you don't want *me*. Hayden apparently doesn't want me. Ashton doesn't—" She cuts off, tears in her eyes while she looks around.

Then, out of fucking nowhere, she grabs my phone out of my hand.

And throws it in the pool.

Fourteen

Eden

I threw his phone in the pool. Right in the center of the deep end.

But I'm half a second away from crying, and I needed a getaway. His phone is the poor, innocent bystander I riddled with bullets—or drowned or whatever—for a distraction.

"Fucking seriously, Eden?" Beck shouts.

When he turns his shocked face toward the pool, I take off for the room. I hear a splash behind me and pick up my foot to drag off one heel and then do the same with the other, so I can run down the path. As I sprint through the hallway to our suite, I bite my lip, trying to fight off the tears, but I lose out to them.

I'm not supposed to cry over Beck. I'm not supposed to *anything* Beck.

But by the time I lock the bathroom door and slump against it, a sob bursts out of me.

Because I *a lot of things* Beck.

I glance up at my reflection in the mirror and have a flashback. My mascara is running, my cheeks flushed and eyes red-rimmed. Drunk Eden would be so disappointed.

Wiping my cheeks, I strip out of my clothes and walk into the shower. The water hits my face, mixing with the tears as I scrub off my makeup. I let the stream run over my head and into my eyes, over my ears. For a minute, the water mutes out the rest of the world.

The shower door jerks open, and I jump. Beck is standing on the other side, his clothes dripping wet and the scent of chlorine competing against the roses from the bouquet on the sink. I'm still processing him standing there when he walks straight in. With nowhere to go, my back presses against the cool tiles as he closes the distance between us. I open my mouth to ask what he's doing, but he wraps his hand around the back of my neck and slams his lips onto mine. His other hand skids over the wet skin of my side, grazing my breast on its way to my neck. Mine run up his chest and into his wet hair. He teases his tongue across the seam of my lips, and it still tastes like cherry when I open for him.

Suddenly, he grips my face, and when he pulls away, I'm out of breath. Beck stares down at me, the heat in his icy eyes burning through me as water streams down our faces.

"I. Want. You," he says, low and raspy. He drops his gaze to his thumb, sweeping over my bottom lip. "God, do I fucking want you."

The metal hoop digs in when he kisses me again, and I shove up his soaking shirt, frantic for his skin. He drags it over his head and lets it fall to our feet. I barely get a breath before his mouth crashes right back into mine. My arms wrap around his neck as he grabs the backs of my legs, lifting me up the wall. They hook around his waist, and his abs rub against me. I moan, which makes him kiss me harder. This kiss is savage and brutal. It's like he's punishing me for making him want me. But I want him to hurt me, to kiss me like he has no control. Like he means it.

I barely notice we're moving until the chill of the tiles leaves my back. Then it's cool air while Beck carries me out of the shower.

"Wait," I mumble into his mouth. "The water."

Beck growls, and I think he's going to ignore me, but then he reaches back, and the shower cuts off. I smile against his lips as he walks us across the bathroom.

"Thank you."

He answers with an, "Mmhmm," sucking on my tongue until I whimper. When he finally releases me, he raises a brow. "Now, with the planet saved and shit, can I get back to fucking you?"

The way my core clenches at his words, I'm starting to think I've never been fucked—at least, not the way he plans on fucking me. I nod, lowering my mouth onto his, and I tighten my thighs around him.

The suite is still dark, the only light from the bathroom as he lowers us down on the bed. My back touches the mattress before he stops, hovering over me. I try to pull him the rest of the way, missing the warmth of him on my wet skin, but he won't budge.

"Do you have any idea how hard I was last night?" He tilts his head and watches the finger he's dragging down my neck to my chest. "Lying on the couch with you over here, in whatever the hell that thing was."

"A baby doll," I say, not recognizing my own voice.

He lowers his head and pulls my right nipple between his lips, sucking as hard as he did my tongue. My back arches, my hands on the back of his head to keep him there.

"Scraps of lace," he whispers, moving to the other side.

He bites down before he soothes the spot with his tongue. I lift my hips, seeking any sort of contact between my legs, but Beck trails down, kissing and nipping at my skin and then dipping his tongue into my navel. Once his mouth reaches my hip, he crawls backward off the bed. His shadow casts over me as he unbuttons his jeans. They hang low on him from the water they've absorbed, showing most of the triangle tattooed just inside the cut of his V line. The denim hits the floor, followed by his boxer briefs.

"You threw my phone in the pool," he says.

I nod, sitting up. "You hurt my feelings."

His knee hits the mattress, and he leans down, bringing his mouth back to mine. "Let's see if I can fix that."

He brushes his lips over mine, leaning forward until I fall back on the mattress. His hand skims up from my ankle, pressing my knee to the side and gliding higher. My eyes flutter shut as he grazes over me and dips his head down. My breath shallows when his hits my inner thighs.

"Gorgeous," he says against my skin before his eyes rise to mine.

He settles between my legs, and I sink into the mattress, his tongue dragging against me, over me, through me.

"Beck," I say his name like it's air, leaving my body automatically.

"No faking it, Eden." Every word vibrates through me as he slips a finger inside me. "Not that I'm giving you the chance."

He seals his mouth over me, and nothing even makes sense anymore other than the way he feels. His smooth lips, his skin on mine, the rumble in his throat when my hips move with him. My hands slide through his hair, and he groans, pushing another finger in with the other. It has me aching, pulling at him for more, and he lets me. I tug at his hair and grind into him, his arm wrapping my thigh and holding me to him.

Just when he drives me to the edge and I'm one flick of his tongue from falling, he moves back to kissing my inner thigh, his fingers staying in me but not moving anymore.

"Beck." I rock my hips, trying to bring his mouth back to me. "Don't stop."

Beck's eyes meet mine while he gently sucks at my skin. But not where I *need* him.

"Why shouldn't I stop, baby?" he asks. His thumb starts rubbing against me, too light. "I want to hear you say it, so I know every sexy sound you're making right now is real."

I moan, his fingers stroking me higher again, tortuously slow. "Yes," I breathe out, my gaze never leaving his. "It's real. All of it. Now, please make me come."

He smiles before his mouth is on me, his fingers thrusting, none of it slow anymore, none of it gentle. I climb higher, my nails digging into his scalp. I'm moaning so loud that I know it travels through the walls, and I grab above me for a pillow. But as I pull it over my mouth, Beck swipes it away. He throws it across the room.

"I want it all," he rasps.

My back lifts off the bed the next time his tongue touches me. His fingers curl inside me, and I don't care that I'm screaming, my legs trembling. Beck sends everything else falling while I stay still. A blur of light and sound, the world moving around us, but him keeping me there with him. It has my mind pulling apart, wanting it to never end even as it becomes too much.

By the time everything slows, Beck's working his way up my body. I feel him hard against my thigh and then between my legs, and his lips finally reach mine. He kisses me, his hand grabbing my ass and pulling me against him like he can't *not* touch me. He can't *not* feel me anymore.

"Jesus, Eden," he groans, grinding between my legs before he's off the bed, heading to the closet.

I push up onto my elbows, my eyes raking over him. He grabs the strip of condoms from the basket on the shelf, ripping one open with his teeth on his way back, and I get distracted, following his hand as he rolls it on.

"Thank you, sex basket," he says, pushing my legs apart.

He hovers in front of me, but he doesn't kiss me. Instead, he brings his face almost to mine and pauses less than an inch away. The air tingles in the space he leaves, a pull between us like even the gap knows his lips should be on mine.

"Kiss me," I say. I don't wait though, pressing my mouth to his and mumbling the words this time, "Kiss me."

Beck drops the rest of the way down onto his elbows. His lips slide over mine, and he sweeps his tongue between them. He pushes my arms above my head, holding them with one hand, and glides the other up the back of my leg, pulling it higher. The thrust comes fast and hard, so deep and unexpected that I gasp into his mouth. His fingers flex into the back of my thigh, and he's dragging almost all the way out and then sinking all the way back in. He drives into me harder then, his mouth all over me.

"Yes," I cry out, not in control anymore.

He groans against my throat. "Fuck, is there anything not hot about you?"

I want to touch him, but his fingers thread with mine, keeping my other hand pinned to the bed above us. With every roll of his hips, he goes deeper. His lips return to mine when I moan, my eyes crushing shut so I can feel every second. He licks and grazes his teeth over my skin, coaxes my body where he wants it, pushing into me and pulling me apart.

"Beck…" I open my eyes to see him watching me.

He keeps his gaze locked on my face, and when he speeds up his rhythm, I completely lose myself. Beck lets me pull my arms down this time, and I run my hands over the rippling muscles of his back, desperate for an anchor. He growls and pumps his hips harder, rough and relentless, and I drop so fast, I barely see it coming. My body shatters for him. I quiver and clench around him, his jaw tightening.

"Perfect." His breaths grow rapid, his movement near frantic. "So fucking perfect."

Then he hikes my legs higher. He thrusts and pulls me against him over and over until he groans. His muscles twitch as he buries so deep inside me that he has nowhere to go. He's still tense when his mouth lowers to mine, still pushing inside me.

We don't move, kissing as he slowly trails his hands over me. Everywhere he skims, my skin tingles, then burns, and then soothes.

"All better?" he asks.

I nod up at him, and he smooths his fingers over my lips before sucking on my bottom one.

"Pity," he says. "I thought maybe I'd get to play with that little vibrator in the basket."

He drops his mouth to my shoulder and bites me, making me squeak.

"Beck!"

With a chuckle, he gently kisses my skin and then grins up at me. "Did that hurt?"

I nod. "Yes."

"Fuck. I wonder how I can make that up to you."

He rolls over, bringing me with him, and his mouth finds mine again, everything more right than it's been since I left Chicago as I smile against his lips. I can't even remember why it was all that bad before—other than he wasn't there.

Beck

From the first moment my lips hit Eden's to when I'm slinging my bag over my shoulder is thirty hours. We stayed in the room all of Friday and destroyed the sex basket. By Saturday morning, I've fucked her on every feasible surface in the suite. And the taste of her has had my head in an Eden-induced haze every minute of it.

"Let me find you a ticket," she says, wrapping her arms around my waist.

"I have a ticket." I hook my fingers under her chin and tilt her face up. "You leave this afternoon?"

She nods, big blue eyes blinking up at me. Fuck, she's hard to say no to. I brush my lips over hers, curling my hand around the back of her neck.

"I'll call you," I tell her. "Eventually."

Her mouth turns up, and she pulls away from me. She crosses the room to the leftover shit from a week's worth of baskets and comes back with an oversize marker, popping off the cap with a determined look in her eyes. I don't even fight her when she tugs my arm to her, flipping it over before switching to the other one.

She smiles, finding a relatively empty space on the underside of my forearm. "No excuses."

I shake my head as she kisses the spot and then writes her name and number. By the time she finishes, it bleeds into the script already there, and they could use it to test someone's vision from across the room.

"Think anyone will find it weird that I have my sister's name all over my arm?"

She shoves my hand back at me, but I pull her closer with my other arm, kissing her until I glance at the time.

I push her hair back. "See you in Chicago."

"See you in Chicago."

I press my lips to hers one more time before I leave her in the suite, out the sliding glass doors. It feels almost more surreal to be leaving The Grove than when I conned my way in.

When I walk out of the lobby under the bronze arches, a familiar taxi driver pushes off the side of his car.

"Fucking Tourist." Winston grabs my hand and pulls me in, slapping me on the back before I throw my bag through the open window to the back seat and get in the front.

We worked out logistics for him driving me to the airport *before* my phone took a swim the other night.

"You two ducked out quick the other night," he says.

I nod, not offering much else as we pull out onto the highway. It doesn't take long, and we're stopping at the curb at the airport. He throws the car in park, and I slip off my shades, pulling the handle for his glove box. I lift my eyebrows at everything else tourists have left behind.

"You realize you have a couple of grand in there, right?"

He shrugs. "I sell it off once a month."

I toss the sunglasses on top of the collection and flip it shut. "You ever come to Chicago, let me know. I'll chauffeur your ass around."

Nodding, Winston chuckles. "All right, all right. And the next time you play the rich douche, I'll have a warm beer waiting. But bring She Lives with you. We like her better."

"You got it, man." I catch his hand again and then reach into the back seat, swiping my bag off of the seat.

"Take it easy, Tourist."

I give him a nod, shutting the door. As he speeds off, I turn around to the airport doors. My eyes drop to my arm, to Eden's name and number in fresh black ink. I walk up the sidewalk, my jaw already working, the fog clearing with reality only a plane ride away.

I told her I'd call her. I also told myself I'd be leaving with ten thousand dollars waiting for me. Only one of those things knots in my gut as I go through the doors.

A lot changed the last time I stepped into an airport.

It makes sense it all starts to shift back when I walk back in.

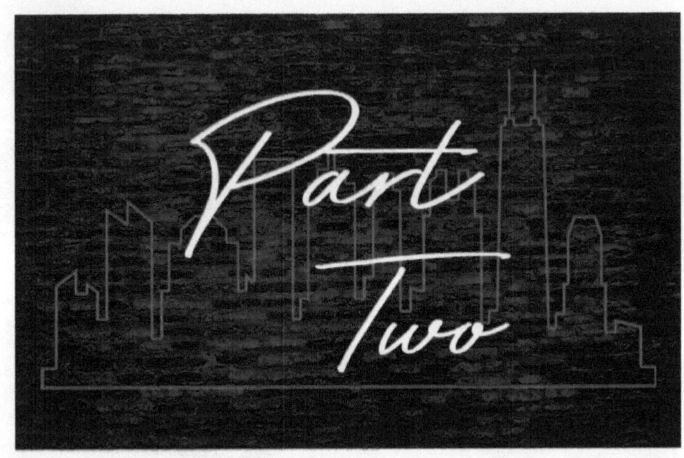

Part
Two

Eden

When I get off the plane in Chicago, Eli is waiting for me in the terminal, as promised. He holds out his arms for me, and I swing my carry-on straight into his chest.

"Fuck," he grunts, catching it and then groaning behind me as I walk away. "Come on, Eden. You can't still be mad at me for sticking you with Regina's cousin."

I spin around and cross my arms, waiting for him to stroll over with my bag casually swinging in his hand. And once he reaches me, I tip my head to the side and smile.

"Should I be mad that you paid him to keep me away from guys all week instead?"

Eli pushes a hand through his blond hair. "I guess I didn't specify for him *not* to tell you." He gives a disinterested glance to someone passing us. "You were hurting, Edes. We have a habit of feeding into it. Shit, we throw it a fucking dinner party. I wanted you to have a chance to heal the right way instead of losing it to another jackass who will never deserve you."

Elijah Monroe—one hundred percent genuine, forty percent of the time. The other sixty ranges from completely full of shit to a mixture of the two. And right now, we're in the forty.

"You practice that speech the entire ride here?" I ask.

One side of his mouth curves. "Only part of the way. The rest I spent in a very productive text exchange with a redhead from the bar last night."

I sigh, and he tugs on my arm, pulling me into a hug.

"I missed you," he says, and my grip tightens on him. He presses a kiss to the side of my head and pulls back. "So, since Becker Donovan texted me to fuck off the other night, can I assume he won't be coming to collect?"

"No need," I say, turning toward baggage claim. I pause then, and I look over my shoulder. "He already came multiple times."

Eli's entire face hardens. "Tell me you're fucking joking, Eden."

With a shrug, I head to get my luggage, smiling when he shouts, "*Fuck!*" and it echoes through the terminal.

I'll tell him I'm kidding later, so he'll pay Beck—even if he did text Eli to fuck off—but for now, I want my brother to suffer.

We find my luggage, and I trail Eli through O'Hare as I turn on the notifications on my phone for the first time since I left. I swear it vibrates without stopping until I've settled into the back of the town car.

As the driver pulls away from the curb, I chew on my lip and open my missed texts. I look for anything that might be Beck, only to reach yesterday's messages without seeing anything.

"Everything okay?" Eli asks, glancing up from his own screen.

I nod and push the phone deep in the outside pocket of my carry-on. "Perfect."

He quirks one side of his mouth up, and I smile. His attention lowers again as I set the bag between us on the seat. I watch the busyness of the airport turn into the expressway out the window, already feeling the doubt spread like wildfire.

But it's only been twenty minutes since I walked off the plane. Only hours since I marked him up and felt his lips on mine. I have no reason to think anything has changed between the heart fluttering in the Bahamas to the heaviness in my chest now. Becker said he'd call.

I just wish I could convince all of me that he meant it.

Eden

One Week Later …

"**W**e hate him."

I sigh, sinking further into the couch cushions. "We don't *hate* him."

Strongly dislike right now, yes, but Layna Owens either loves you or hates you—there is no in between. And when she loves you, she's vicious.

"No," she says through the speaker. "Get on this train with me. The guy crashed your vacation, made you fall for his unworthy ass, and then vanished into thin air when you touched down in Chicago? We fucking *hate him*, Eden."

She started the conversation the same way when she called. Then she launched into a lecture about how I don't get to just send a random text about leaving the country for five days and then shut off my phone. Never mind that she's the one who drunkenly encouraged me to go.

We've been best friends since the world started. At least, that's what we say, joking our worlds started turning after I transferred from New York in the fourth grade.

The line falls silent once she finishes, both of us pausing a beat before I say, "You done?" at the same time as she says, "I'm done."

We laugh, and she lets out a frustrated breath. "Okay, sweetie. Don't leave the country, and I'll kidnap your ass from your daddy's building this week for lunch."

"See you soon," I tell her before tossing my phone down the couch.

By day three, I'd given up on Beck calling. I told myself to swallow the sting, remember it was a week on a tropical island. Nothing there was real. Not us being in a relationship or the touches and looks.

Only it felt real as hell. And the sting that's slowly turned into a wound feels real too.

I reach for the remote and hit play on a movie. Something loud and uninteresting, but it fills the silence. The apartment door swings open about halfway through, and I sit up, glancing over my shoulder as Eli tosses his keys on the entry table.

He has on a blue button-down, rolled up to his elbows, and a pair of navy pants, so he must have gone into the office today. Daddy's been trying to get him to take his future seriously, pushing him to learn the company.

"Did you earn any gold stars today?" I ask.

He jumps over the back of the couch and lands with his shoulder leaning against mine. "Yep. I sat in a conference room, nodding at people all afternoon. Can we fill in my chart before bed?"

I roll my eyes as he gives me a cheesy grin. We used to get the star stickers for finishing our homework and whatever lessons we were taking, and I might have to bring the practice back.

"You might not care now," I say, "but—"

"I will someday." He readjusts, pulling his phone out and tossing his wallet on the cushion beside him. "You back yet?"

I lean over and grab my phone. "Been home for a week."

"But not *really*. You've buried yourself in helping with that fundraiser coming up for the children's whatever it is, and otherwise, you've watched Darla movies, which always means you're sorting through shit." When I don't answer, he asks, "Do I need to ruin Ashton's car again? Jones said the dealer just dropped off a new one yesterday."

I squint at him, not a fan of his friends encouraging his deviance. "I think putting a nine iron through the windshield after practicing your drive on the rest of it was plenty."

"Nah. The guy's getting off easy because we run in the same circle."

Like I need the reminder.

"I'm just readjusting to January in Chicago," I tell him. "I miss the sand and sun."

Partly true. It hasn't hit thirty degrees since I touched down. Eli's right though. I've been off my game the past week, acting more like Darla than myself.

And that is not something I take lightly.

My brother groans, standing up. "You want a drink?"

I nod as he walks around the couch, and then my eyes dart to his phone, where he left it beside his wallet. Earlier in the week, I went through Elijah's contacts for Beck's number, deciding I would take matters into my own hands, but Eli must have already deleted the texts without saving it. I have one more number I can look for though. Then I can track down Becker Donovan and set his car on fire.

Metaphorically.

I crane my neck around, waiting until he disappears into the kitchen before I dive across the couch for his phone on the cushion. Dragging it back with me, I scroll through his contacts and head straight for the Rs.

If anyone ever thought of Eli as a saint, they only need to check out the naming scheme he uses for women based on the reason he quit texting them and the danger level of screwing them again. I usually tell him to just delete their number, but for once, his assholery serves a greater purpose.

When the name *RC Eden Low* appears, I want to give Elijah credit for his reason, but then I see his danger level and snort. I quickly copy the number into my phone and glance over my shoulder. Ice clinks in glasses, and a cupboard shuts in the kitchen. Since I have time, I change the *Low* danger level to *High* before tossing his phone down the couch again.

Regina Cruz might not be a clinger threat for Eli, but if I ever find her in my bathroom again, I'll lose my shit. And with this in mind, I send a message that requires zero back and forth, speaking a language I know she understands.

Becker Donovan's number for $50.

I flip the screen facedown on the cushion beside me. It only takes seconds for her to answer, and I turn it over to Beck's number. And a list of different ways to pay her, of course. Because I'm a good person, I send her the money I promised, and after another Eli check, I call the number.

My heart barely has time to thrust around before an automated message tells me the caller is unavailable. *Shit.* I try it one more time, like it will make any difference, and am about to hit pathetic with a third when a drink appears over my shoulder.

I look up to Eli and then at the martini in his hand. "Where's the olive?"

"You hate olives," he says.

"Then why did you make me a martini?"

I smile sweetly, and he shakes his head, bringing the glass up and then drinking it halfway down.

"Whiskey?" he asks, walking away.

"Straight, please." I push up to check he's gone and then slump into the cushions.

Address? I send. *Another $50.*

$100.

Regina fucking Cruz. I groan but can't honestly say I'm surprised. It took all of three minutes to figure out her favorite thing about my brother—the size of his trust. Unfortunately for her, I'm Eden fucking Monroe. And I do *not* negotiate with anyone who I've witnessed scratch their ass with a one-hitter.

$40.

Eli rounds the couch, and I drop my phone like it caught fire. "Here you go, princess."

"Don't call me that," I snap, swiping the tumbler from his hand.

He crashes onto the sofa beside me. "Duchess? Royal Highness? M'la—"

I clamp my hand over his mouth, and he grins, pulling it away. After a second, he reaches for his phone, and I resume my movie from earlier as mine vibrates on my lap. I sip my drink and nonchalantly peek at Regina's response, my belly flipping when I see the address.

Holy shit, it worked.

She sends another text seconds later, asking why I haven't paid her yet.

I roll my eyes, as over her as I am her cousin. Although I only plan to call one of them out on their shit, and it isn't Regina.

But if Becker Donovan thinks he can screw me and never talk to me again, then I'll gladly prove him very, *very* wrong. Eden fucking Monroe–style.

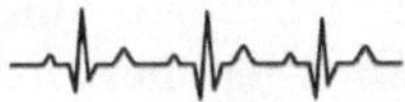

As the driver pulls up to the gray stone building, he glances back at me. "You sure this is where you want to go?"

I give him a pointed look, very in touch with my man-hating side at the moment.

"Want me to wait?" he asks.

But the second I shake my head, his shoulders relax, and I try not to roll my eyes. Worried about his Audi, I'm sure.

Climbing out, I glance up and down the street. Lights on the corner leave the rest of the block dark, and I pull my coat tighter around me on my way to the concrete steps leading into the building. A couple of men look up, but I pretend not to notice their quick handoff.

The inside of the deteriorating building is an experience from the first step. The carpet running the halls and stairway is brown, except for the glimpses of the true pink color along the walls and where no one's trekked. Thin walls let me know more about the people on the other side of them than I care to know. Babies crying, game shows blaring, a couple fighting.

The light on the second landing is burned out, leaving the turn of the steps in shadows. I walk faster when I pass someone in the corner, not unclenching my fists until I reach the third floor. I knew Beck lived in a rougher part of the city, but it only sinks in what that means halfway down the hallway when I glance back to see the guy following me.

I stop at Beck's, and he stops too. I'm braver with Beck on the other side of the door and turn to face the man. "Can I help you?"

He shifts, picking at his bottom lip, his brown coat worn at the elbows and at least three sizes too large. "You a social worker?"

I shake my head and knock while he inches another step in my direction.

He squints, nodding toward the door. "He doesn't like visitors. Maybe you should—"

The door jerks open, a familiar glare on the other side. Beck's brow lifts, the sweatpants hanging off his hips and the white tank top tight on his abs. Somewhere between the Uber and stairwell, my *I am woman, hear me roar* lessened to a growl. And damn it if the second he smirks, it doesn't dissolve to a meow.

He runs a hand through his hair and props a shoulder against the doorframe. "Slummin' it tonight, princess?"

I stick my chin higher, reclaiming some semblance of an upper hand. "Forget how to use a phone?"

Instead of answering, he backs inside and waits for me to come in. I glance at the guy still hovering by the stairwell, dilated pupils on me, before Beck's gaze follows me through the door.

I walk into the living room. A dark kitchen sits just off to the side of the door with tall cabinets and mostly bare counters, short of a microwave. Considering the noise in the hallways, the apartment is quiet. No evidence of TVs or stereos from the surrounding ones.

The door shuts behind me, and I spin around. Beck reaches around the corner into the kitchen, his hand reappearing with his phone. "Hasn't turned on since someone threw it in a fucking pool."

"Oh." I bite my lip, embarrassed by the tantrum. "It's been a week. I thought you'd have gotten a new one by now."

He tosses it back on a counter and moves closer. My muscles tense, every inch of me warm as he slides one hand into my coat, the other undoing the large button on the front pleat.

"You're staying," he says, backing me farther in.

I nod like it was a request even though he's already thrown my coat onto a recliner.

Upper. Fucking. Hand.

Other than the chair, the room's barely furnished. Floor lamps bookend a black leather sofa with a gaming system on the wooden floor in front of the TV, mounted on the harsh white wall.

"Not what you expected?" he asks, his eyes raking over my dress. The way his throat bobs in a swallow, maybe I'm more in control than I thought. When I don't answer right away, he pushes his hand into my hair, bringing his face close enough that his breath heats my lips. "Say whatever's going on in that sexy fucking head."

"How can you live here?" I hear how terrible the question sounds and shake my head. "I mean, you have a box for a table."

"Crate," he corrects. "And it's cozy." His arms wrap around me, his lips grazing my cheek. I've missed his mouth on me. His hands, his eyes, his breath. Him. He brings his mouth to my ear. "Plus, no one lives on either side, so you can scream as loud as you want."

I melt into him, circling my arms around his neck. "I'm not sure if that's a threat or an invitation."

"A challenge maybe." His breath is hot, sending chills across my skin. "Or a premonition."

I smile, burying my face in his shirt. His hold on me loosens, and he tucks his fingers under my chin and lifts it up so that I'll look at him. He lowers his head, so our noses touch. Our lips brush, the distance wedged between us since he left the hotel room vanishing. Or maybe it was never there. His hands slide over the curves of my hips, mine up the back of his neck. He tugs my bottom lip down with his, and I trace the tip of my tongue along his top one. Not kissing, but waiting for the other to cave. I close my eyes, just wanting to feel him. His eyebrows are drawn together when I open them.

"I was going to call," he whispers, studying me with a cautious look. "You believe me?"

Everything about him is gentle in the moment as he pushes my hair back where it fell forward. And I give, nodding while I crush my mouth to his.

"About damn time," he mumbles, already nudging me backward to the couch.

He turns us and pulls me down on top of him, so I straddle his lap. I moan at the feel of him between my legs again. When his mouth dips to my neck, my head falls back, but then the notebook beside us distracts me. Small, blocky letters in black ink cover the page, a laptop and Econ book stacked on the next cushion over with a pair of glasses on top.

"Were you studying?" I ask.

His fingers flex over the front of my thighs as he licks my skin. "Paper due tomorrow."

I lean all the way over to snag the glasses, Beck and his mouth moving with me. He pulls me upright while I slip them on him. He glares up at me through the thick black frames, annoyed at my interruption, his hair mussed up from my fingers, lips slightly parted.

Professor Fuck Me at your service.

Beck goes to take them off, and I slap his hand away. "Leave them on."

"Your tits will be blurry."

"I don't care."

"I fucking do." He swipes them off his face and dips me back to toss them on the crate-table thing. I'm more than ready to argue as he brings me back up, but when we're face-to-face again, someone starts pounding on his door.

"Fuck off," he shouts.

"Get fucked," a voice answers. "It's freezing out here."

Beck's forehead falls forward onto mine, slowly rolling back and forth. "Any chance you'd wait in my bed if I asked?" I narrow a glare at him, and he sighs. "Didn't think so."

Then he's sliding me off his lap and onto the couch. He stands up but bends right back down, his hand in my hair when he kisses me. I think it's going to be quick and sweet until his tongue sweeps into my mouth, all the momentum from before returning. I grip the front of his shirt, tugging him down as I lie back, but he growls, forcing himself away.

Shaking his head, he grabs his books and laptop. "Close your legs, princess."

Beck

I wasn't going to call her. The decision was made when I walked into the terminal. Final.

Except black permanent ink is a bitch to get off, and even after the mark of her faded, I could feel her on me. The *E* and the *D* and the fucking *EN*.

Five days. No money. And her name was an invisible tattoo I'd never wanted dug into my skin.

I put off getting a new phone, giving myself time to work her out of my system. I would go back to life before her, and she wouldn't have to deal with any of the shit in it.

Then I realized I've missed a total of four people in my entire life. My parents, the first time they went somewhere overnight without me. Grace, when I go too long without seeing her. And

Eden fucking Monroe, before I even got on the plane to come home.

I planned to pick up a new phone tomorrow, and then I was going to call the number I'd memorized on the flight.

But I guess I should have stopped for a phone tonight.

Ducking into my room, I toss Eden's coat on the bed along with my computer and schoolbooks. As I pull the door shut, Eden sits up on the couch, her lips swollen and face flush.

"Christ, you're killing me, woman."

She smiles, and I'm fucking glad her impatient ass couldn't wait another twelve hours. Of course, if she had waited, Ty wouldn't be banging down my door right now.

I blow out a breath, scanning her over. A dress I've wanted to peel off since she walked in the door, hot as fuck heels with red bottoms, and a gold bracelet, dangling from her wrist.

"How much does that all cost?"

Eden's eyebrows pull in, and she dips her chin down. "My outfit?"

"Ballpark estimate." I pull her to her feet. "More than my rent?"

She presses her lips together, the wall suddenly fascinating as she looks away from me. "I don't know how much you pay," she says, her voice small.

Whether or not she meant for her response to answer my question, it does.

I haul her against me and bring her face back to mine, not wanting her to think I give a shit how much she spends on her clothes. "You are fucking gorgeous, and I can't wait to strip you out of this dress. But I won't handle it well if anyone on the other side of that door looks at you like they want to fuck you and then sell your clothes. So, for the sake of my sanity, will you please go into my room and find something ugly to wear over it?"

One side of her mouth turns up, and I kiss her, dragging her with me while I back us to my bedroom. She laughs when I spin us at the door and push her the rest of the way in.

"I'll put on ugly clothes if you wear the glasses later."

"Not happening, princess." I flip on the light, and Eden's eyes hit my nightstand, dresser, and closet in one sweep, so I decide to save her the trouble. "The condoms in the nightstand are rarely used—none since you. I don't have a stash of porn anywhere or kinky shit in drawers. And in the closet is a box of pictures my ma sent with me last time I was there. Any chicks in them, I haven't talked to since high school."

She gives me a look, and I grab the knob, pulling shut the door and leaving her to go through my shit in peace. Because we both know she will, so we might as well get it out of the way now.

Ty pounds away as I recheck the living room for anything I might have left out that I prefer not to have people touching—other than the sexy blonde in my room. I set my glasses around the corner in the kitchen before I jerk open the apartment door. After a quick scan of the group in the hallway, I zero in on Ty in front of me, rubbing his hands together.

"Invitation?" I deadpan.

He laughs and throws his arms around me before slapping me on the back and walking around me to the living room. "I'm sure it got lost in the mail, right? I mean, your best friend—"

"You're not my best friend."

He is, but I could hang him from the window right now and not feel too put out if he slipped.

I move aside, so five chicks I also didn't invite can file in, and then Lee and Milo follow them through. Milo gives an apologetic raise of his eyebrows on his way by, the only one to bother reading the room.

"Your *best* friend," Ty continues, "has to hear from your mom that you've been back for over a week?"

He shrugs off his coat and throws it in a corner, everyone else's landing on top of his.

"My phone isn't working," I tell him.

Lee points at the sound system, and I nod. Within seconds, he has music on, and he adjusts the settings until the bass kicks through the speakers. For a guy who's only been here once before, he wastes no time in making himself at home, stretching out on my floor. He started hanging around Axel a little over a year ago, and Ty picked him up from there.

Milo went to school with us. His grandma lives in the house behind my parents', but I haven't seen him since we graduated. He sets a case of beer in my fridge and hands me one on his way to the couch, tossing another to Ty and dropping a can to Lee on the floor.

They boot up a video game, and the girls perch around the living room. One climbs on Lee's back to watch him play, and I shake my head as Ty stops beside me.

"If I told you this wasn't a good time, would you leave?" I ask, already knowing the answer.

"Nah." He rolls the bottom of his stocking cap, so it sits above his ears. "We've been barging into each other's places since always, B. All times are a good time."

Cracking open his beer, he notices mine unopened. He pops my tab before he goes to collapse in the recliner, pulling one of the girls into his lap.

When I decided to call Eden, I played out how this moment would happen—how she would meet Ty. Them both showing up, unannounced, with Ty bringing a goddamn harem with him wasn't what I expected, but it's the scenario we've entered.

The bedroom door opens then. Eden pads out, barefoot, in my shitty gray hoodie, hanging down to her thighs, and I have a serious *what the fuck* moment, seeing her in it. She's just as hot in grease stains as designer. And even without the dress and heels, the princess looks utterly out of place in my shithole of an apartment.

She swallows hard as she looks around the now-crowded living room, and someone pauses the video game.

"Uh, Becker?" Ty says. "Did you abduct a lady?"

I flip him off and stride over to retrieve her. She tenses as I reach around her to pull the door shut, running the knuckles of my hand holding the beer across her stomach.

"Find anything to be annoyed about?" I ask.

Eden blinks up at me. "Not in there…"

Her eyes drift behind me, flashing with insecurity, and I immediately know what she sees. I talked her into baggy rags, only for her to walk into a room full of women dressed for attention.

Fuck.

I nod, raking a hand through my hair before I turn around and step behind her. "This is Eden," I say, gripping her hips as I walk her all the way into the room. "Ty, Milo, and Lee."

Ty and Milo nod at their names, and I catch a small smile from her, licking my lips to hide one of my own. Little Miss Congeniality, even when she's uncomfortable as fuck.

I set my beer down by the couch and bring Eden straight down onto my lap.

"Nothing out here either," I tell her. I yank a blanket from the back cushions and throw it over her legs, covering what the sweatshirt over her dress fails to. "We have different definitions of ugly."

She bites down on a smile as I readjust her and slide my hand over her thigh under the blanket. Most of the room's attention returns to the TV once Lee restarts the video game, short of Ty and the girls in and around the recliner with him. When his eyes finally fall to his phone, Milo's goes off. Milo quickly glances at it and tosses it down to me, going straight back to the game.

Eden leans forward for my beer while I read Ty's message.

My phone would be broken too.

I bring my arm around her to tap out a response.

Keep looking at her, and it won't be your phone that breaks.

He chuckles from across the room and sends, *You talk like she's a steady ride.*

A pair of blue eyes flit away when I look up, Eden's cheeks turning pink. I reply but make sure I wait until she sneaks another peek before I hit send.

She's whatever the fuck she wants to be.

I delete the messages off of Milo's phone and hand it back to him. When I slip my other hand under the blanket with Eden, she still has tension to her.

"You didn't introduce me to the girls," she says quietly.

"Stella, Rachel, Sophie, Emily…"

Her face falls, the more names I prattle off, so I stop, and she glances down at me.

"I have no idea what their names are," I tell her.

Her mouth turns up at the corners, and while she might still look out of place, she certainly feels fucking perfect right where she is. She relaxes, settling in with me.

But then someone knocks. I look over at Ty, irritated he has more fucking people coming.

"Oh, come on." He lifts the chick on his lap to the arm of the chair as he gets up. "We all missed you, B."

My eyes track him across the room, and I'm about to go back to Eden when he answers. Axel stands on the other side of the door, and my jaw clenches when Ty welcomes him with open fucking arms. The guy walks in, and the entire mood of the room shifts. Lee pauses the game, the girl on his back scampers off the floor, and Milo, down the sofa, sinks into the cushions.

Axel's the type who has a *need* for respect, not that he deserves it. And he doesn't expect just the decent amount a human should give another. He wants more respect than anyone else in the room, and if he thinks he's not getting it, he resorts to accepting fear as an alternative.

The guy gets neither from me. I think he's a loose fucking cannon, and I've only tolerated him because of the cash he pays, and he knows it.

Axel grins on his way over. "Becker Donovan returns."

I reach up, so he can slap my hand before he goes to drop into the recliner, which leaves Ty to trudge back through and sit beside me on the couch.

"Where have you been hiding?" Axel asks, cracking open the beer Milo went to get him.

He drops one off for me, too, since Eden's taken mine over. I nod him a thanks and shrug in response to Axel. Not that he pays much attention for the answer, already pulling one of the girls that was on Ty down to him.

Ty gives me an eye roll as the game on the TV resumes, and then he narrows his gaze at Eden. "So, you're the reason my best friend has been avoiding me?"

"Ignore him," I say. "He's not my best friend. I'm not even that attached to him."

"Ha." Ty takes my beer before I even get a drink, and I shake my head.

Eden smiles a little, warming up to Ty despite everything about him. "He's been avoiding me too. If it makes you feel better."

Ty thinks it over for a second and nods. "You know what? It kind of does."

He knocks his can on hers and gestures for one of the other girls to come over. She rightly chooses to squeeze in between him and Milo, and he angles toward her.

I steal back my original beer from Eden and take a drink, and then I lean forward to set it on the table. Sitting back, I glide my fingers up the side of Eden's neck and kiss her, sick of not having my mouth on her. She tenses for a second, but when I wrap my hand around the back of her neck, she moves into me.

My lips trail up her jaw to just under her ear. "Stay tonight."

Eden traces my abs through my shirt under the blanket. "Don't you have classes tomorrow? And work?"

"I'm feeling sick." I skim my way back down. "Fever maybe. Definitely a twenty-four-hour thing."

"Yeah?" she asks against my lips, and I nod, slipping my tongue between hers.

Between the music and video game, not even Ty can hear me groan when she pushes under my shirt. I've spent a week trying to remember exactly how it feels to have her skin running over mine. A week of telling myself I was exaggerating about how crazy it drove me.

I wasn't.

The hem of the sweatshirt slides up under my palm, dragging the bottom of her dress higher with it. She smiles and moves my hand higher to her ass, but then she stiffens. Her gaze is over my shoulder, and I look back. Axel's watching us despite the chick grinding on him, his attention on the gold bracelet hanging on Eden's wrist.

His eyes return to the TV, but Eden nudges my hand away and fixes her dress under the sweatshirt.

"Your friends seem…" She lays her head on my shoulder, like if she can't see them, they can't see her.

"Ty's my friend." I trail my fingers over her skin, lower down her thigh. "The others I deal with when I have to."

The last time I even saw Axel was two months ago. He paid me for a job, and I walked away. As much as I could. But with my parents and Grace only two blocks from his house and the garage a few in the other direction of him, away isn't far.

I haven't let myself think about the money from Elijah since I texted him to fuck off in the cab outside the resort. I decided Eden was worth it, and she was. She is. Choosing her just set me back to my original time frame. I'll graduate in May and find a job that pays well enough so that I can save for first and last month's rent and a security deposit for a two-bedroom that gets my parents and sister out of their shitty neighborhood.

"Maybe I should go," Eden says, twisting at the fabric of my shirt. "You said you have a paper due tomorrow anyway."

I press my lips to hers, about to carry her into my room, throw her on the bed, and say fuck every one of these assholes. But since she's waltzed in here, I've already thought about blowing off school and work, forgotten about my paper, and seriously considered shoving my best friend out a window.

"We'll deal with the dress another time," I say.

She nods, and I catch her chin when her eyes start to move behind me again, not wanting her to care about anyone else in this fucking room.

"Tomorrow. And it doesn't matter if it's this dress or fucking sweatpants, I'm stripping it off you."

Eden smiles. "Only if you call me."

"Oh, I'll call you." Then I add, "Eventually."

It only takes about ten minutes for her car to pull up outside the building. I warn Ty that I'll blame him if anyone touches my shit while I walk her out. Eden latches on a little tighter when we pass Phil by the staircase, where he usually hangs out. He only chances a glance at her before staring at his hands.

Jesus. Eden Monroe hunted me down to this hellhole in her heels.

"How'd you find me anyway?" I ask as I open the main door for her.

The annoyance on her face answers before she does, "Regina. Or Gina or whatever. Eli still had her number in his phone, so I paid her off."

"Here's where I'm torn because she sold me out for a little cash—"

"Ninety bucks," Eden corrects.

"Right. She sold me out for less than a hundred bucks, which is a huge fucking problem." I glance up and down the empty sidewalk as I follow her down the stairs.

"But…" Eden spins at the bottom, and I pull her against me.

"But it was to you, and I fucking missed you," I admit.

Fuck. I really missed her.

I kiss her and leave my forehead on hers for a second. "I'm calling you tomorrow."

"I believe you," she says.

When I let her go, she backs to the car. I wait until she's safe in the back seat and the taillights have disappeared around the corner.

I look up at the building, thinking about the people upstairs, the bullshit politics and being around them for the rest of the night even though I couldn't care less.

Instead of going inside, I walk down the street. I duck into the convenience store a block over and grab a burner phone, tossing it on the counter. On my way back to the apartment, I set it up.

Then I call the number I memorized on the flight home. The one I can still feel on my arm.

Eden

When Beck follows me into my apartment, his eyes scan around the entryway. He stalls out, barely even inside, and I have to pull him the rest of the way. As I do, I spare a quick glance at the entry table to check that Elijah's keys are gone.

I lead Beck into the living room, his eyes still crawling the walls.

"And you keep wanting to sleep at my place because…" His hands glide over my hips when I turn around, and I drape my arms over his shoulders.

"It smells like you," I admit, only mildly embarrassed at how obsessed I've become with the scent of him. But for the past few weeks, I've breathed it every chance I've found.

It's not enough, if you ask me. Between his work schedule and school and all the time I've spent finalizing the details for next week's fundraiser, those chances usually come at night, in his bed. Not that I'm complaining. I happen to like his bed.

A lot.

For the first time since I stormed into his apartment building, we both have the entire night free. Shockingly enough, Becker Donovan is not the date-night type, so I've quelled any anticipation of flowers and being whisked away for dinner, settling on ordering in.

"I smell like me." Beck wraps his arms around me, and I fall into him. He kisses me, moving us backward until my back hits the couch. "Now, I want *you* to smell like me."

I smile as he drops his mouth down to my neck, but then his lips slow, and I realize he's looking at something behind me. When I glance, I see his eyes set on the TV and sound system.

"Am I going to lose you to the surround sound?" I ask.

"Not if you keep me entertained." He bites down where my shoulder meets my neck. "A tour of flat surfaces should do the trick."

I only get to show him one though. Beck scoops me up and climbs over the back of the couch with me in his arms. He lands with me straddling him and pulls my face to his. I'm laughing against his lips, but it turns into a breathy sigh when he pushes the bottom of my skirt up.

"Do you own fucking jeans?" he asks.

"Yes." I sit back a little, and he watches his hands traveling up, slowly exposing more of my thighs. "Do you not like the dresses?"

It almost sounds needy, like I'm seeking approval, and I try not to cringe, hearing it. That's a reflex from Ashton, his comments always carrying more weight beneath the surface. *Is your hair different? Do I need to get you a new necklace for your birthday? You only wanted a salad, right?* The hints at what he didn't approve of— picking while maintaining innocence and deniability.

"*I never said I hated the necklace your father gave you. I just asked if you'd like a new one.*"

As much as I'd love to say everything Beck has replaced everything ex, it bobs to the surface out of nowhere sometimes.

"You think I give a shit what you're wearing?" Beck asks, shifting us so my back touches the cushions. He hovers above me, his hand running down my side and his hips settling between my legs. "Wear a fucking parka. I'll happily strip you out of anything."

I smile. "Careful. You might end up with a girlfriend who lives in sweats if you're that easy to please."

He pulls back more, studying me. "Girlfriend, huh?"

Realizing what I said, I start to shake my head. "I didn't mean to … if that's not what this is—"

"I meant what I sent Ty the other night," he says, caressing up my thigh. "You're whatever you want to be."

Beck kisses me and then *really* kisses me. I push up his shirt, and he drags it off, tossing it over the back of the couch, before he crashes back into me. It never feels like enough with us. I need him closer, need him on my skin and inside me.

He tugs down the straps of my dress, and I'm so lost in every sensation he is building inside of me that I completely ignore the sound of the door. The sound of the keys landing on the entry table.

"Don't mind me," Elijah says from above us, and my entire body stiffens. "I'll just eat my Chinese in my bedroom since we apparently fuck on the couch."

And now, my entire body flushes.

Beck, not seeming nearly as bothered, kisses me one more time and then sits back on his knees, grabbing his shirt off the back cushions. He and Elijah are immediately locked in a tense staredown, and I scramble up off the couch, pulling my straps back up to cover my bra.

"I thought you were gone for the night."

"Just working late," my brother grinds out. "And the dude who thinks he can put his hands on my sister is…"

Beck's eyes cut to mine then, a slow smirk spreading, and I will time to rewind or for an asteroid or something to spare me from what happens next.

"You keeping me your dirty little secret, princess?" Beck asks, amused.

I shake my head, not wanting him to think I was *purposely* not telling Elijah about him. I mean, I was, but more because of the look of murder on Eli's face right now.

"Princess, huh?" Elijah says. My brother has a memory like a vault, everything locked down and ready to access as needed. It makes him dangerous and brilliant, piecing the tiniest things together. "And the peasant is…" He trails off as Beck pulls his shirt on, his eyes scanning his tattoos before his jaw tightens. "Becker Donovan."

"Elijah," I start, but he takes a step back and turns to toss the takeout bag onto the kitchen island.

"I'm really fucking glad I didn't pay you," he says to Becker as he pulls out his phone.

"You did in a way." Beck stands and snakes his arm around me, hauling me to his side, and Elijah's eyes flick up from his screen, his nostrils flaring.

Oh my God.

When Elijah pockets his phone a second later, I raise my eyebrows at him, questioning who he just messaged. I'd rather not have to go to battle with him tonight, but if he just asked one of his friends to help him deal with a situation, then ring the bell.

"I ordered more food," Elijah says. His attention focuses on Beck. "I take it, you're sticking around?"

Beck nods. "Not planning on going anywhere."

It's a revisit to the relationship conversation we just had, only in code, and I'm not the least bit involved in this one.

"And you can't be persuaded?"

"Elijah," I snap.

He holds his hands up in resignation. "Just feeling this out. What kind of brother would I be if I wasn't looking out for you? Especially since the last time money was involved, he jumped on it."

Beck's jaw twitches, and I can see the effort going into not responding.

"Food should be here in about twenty," Elijah says, backing toward the kitchen. "Until then, I'll be in the kitchen, drinking and trying to forget what I walked in on. Then we can have an incredibly awkward and aggressive dinner together. Plan?"

"Sounds great," Beck says dryly.

I scowl at Eli until he vanishes behind the kitchen wall. When I look up, Beck's still glaring after him. He might be the first guy to outright challenge my brother when it comes to me. Most bail, deciding it's not worth the torment, and the ones who stay usually roll over and show their bellies, taking whatever he doles out.

"You can run, you know?" I say. "Get out while you have a chance."

His eyes shift to me first, and then his head rolls in my direction. "Not exactly the duck-and-run type, princess. Plus, you promised me food."

⎯⎪⌐⎺⎼⎪⎺⌐⎯

The dinner veers more toward the aggressive side than awkward five minutes in when Elijah slides the glass of whiskey across the island to Beck.

"So, how long have you been fucking my sister?"

"Jesus, Eli," I say, earning me a shrug from him.

Beck just relaxes back on the stool, moving his hand to the back of my neck. "You got my last text message, right?"

Eli shakes his head. "I take it, you're the reason she was miserable when she got back?"

"*She* is right here," I remind him. "And how is any of this your business? I don't interrogate your girlfriends."

"No. You just make me break up with them when you don't like them."

I bite my lips together. Regina might not have been the only one I made a deal to get rid of, but I stand by every one of them.

"No one has answered my question yet." Eli points between us. "Either one, I don't care. I just want to know if he's the reason you were upset."

When I look away, I feel Beck's hand flex like he wants me to look at him instead, but I don't.

"That's what I thought," Eli says.

Beck's hand moves down to my leg, tracing smooth circles on my skin.

"So, I'll put this out there right away." Elijah has his hands braced on the counter, the cool look of intimidation I've seen directed at so many etched on his face—like he couldn't care less if you listen to him, so long as you're doing as told. "The next time you hurt her, I'll destroy you. Your life, your reputation, anything you love is fair game."

"You have a habit of threatening me," Beck bites back. "Maybe that's how you're used to working with whatever douche bags you usually hang around with, but not me. I have no plans on hurting her, but you can fucking bet it has shit to do with you."

He punctuates with a smug smile that falls off his face just as fast as it appeared, and he downs his whiskey, shoving the glass back at Eli.

The tension radiates between them, and maybe it's because no one ever fights for me, but I revel in it for a second longer than I probably should before I sigh.

"If the pissing match is over, I'd love to eat now."

Eli taps his finger on the counter while Beck's thumb rubs my thigh. After a few tense seconds, Eli swipes the bottle off the counter beside him, refilling Beck's tumbler.

"Saw Dad today," he says, and my eyes lift to him. "He put Wilson in his place over him wanting to get back into oil. Then he told him to get an eco-friendly car by next week, or I'd kick him out of his swanky executive office."

"You plan to hold Wilson to it?" I ask.

Elijah nods. "Wilson will be in the basement next Monday unless he rolls up in something electric."

I smile, mostly because the head of Daddy's acquisitions team drives an Aston Martin, which is terrible for the environment, but also because Wilson's a douche who drives an Aston Martin into the office every day. He needs to be taken down a few pegs, and if Eli can be the one to carry out the orders, then it'd set an excellent stage for him to take over.

Even if he still acts like it might kill him.

We make it through the rest of the takeout without more threats. The sniping between my brother and Beck levels out, and by the time we finish, they seem to have settled into a mutual agreement to scowl at each other without talking.

I'm throwing the empty cartons away when Elijah walks into the living room on his phone. When I turn around, Beck grins on his way over.

"You got dinner out of me, but if you think I'm hanging out with your brother tonight, we need to have a conversation about expectations."

"Thank you for not waging war," I say. "Elijah can be—"

"A fucking prick," he finishes.

"Misguided in his attempts to protect me."

Beck tips his head to the side and lets out a sigh. "I hate that I get it. I'll probably dismantle the first asshole who hurts Grace." His face goes even more serious then, his hands sliding into mine. "Fuck, he should be pissed about the week I didn't call."

"But you were going to," I say.

He nods, pulling me closer. "I was going to."

He kisses the top of my head, and I snuggle into him, sighing.

"So, my place?" he says, the words vibrating in his chest. "I hear it smells like me."

I nod against him, and he pulls away.

We walk into the living room, and Elijah glances up from his phone, not seeming all that bothered to see Beck heading toward the door. I hang back, waiting until he steps into the hall before I nail my brother with a glare.

"He doesn't get a free pass just because he doesn't have a trust fund," he says coolly.

"Just remember, Eli." I grab my phone off the table in front of him. "I can fuck with your life too. I just choose not to."

He rolls his eyes and tips back his glass as I walk toward the door. "He's just a mechanic, E. I can get you a new one by the fundraiser if I need to."

I flip him off, not looking back, and he chuckles.

"Love you," he calls after me.

Even if he can be an elitist ass, I sigh. "Love you too."

The door slams behind me, and Beck looks up from his phone. My eyes drag over him, every sculpted inch, his biceps stretching the fabric of his T-shirt and the black ink on his skin.

"See something you like?" he asks, bringing my attention up to his smirk.

I do. And I think I'll like it just as much in a tux.

Beck

One day, I'll figure out how to say no to this woman. In just over a month, she's managed to get a couples cruise, dance lessons, and now, a black-tie fundraiser out of me.

But no matter how irritating I find the tux and the shiny fucking dress shoes, not a damn complaint will make it out of my mouth after I see Eden's dress. Black and sleek with enough skin showing that I almost forget I'm about to spend the next several hours in a ballroom, bored out of my mind.

I tuck her against my side in the elevator, slipping my fingers under one of the straps. She fights off a smile when I slide it over and press my lips to the bare skin of her shoulder.

"Remind me why we're in a hotel and you're not under me right now?" I ask, pushing it even lower on her arm and moving my hand to the front of her dress.

She lets out a shaky breath, like I might be making ground and getting out of this. "Children in the foster care system need advocates available to speak for them in the courts."

Fuck.

I push her strap back up. "Way to kill the mood."

She wrinkles her nose at me, and I pull her face to mine just as the elevator stops. My lips brush hers before the doors open, and Eden grins up at me.

"You ready to be nice to a bunch of people all night?"

I run my thumb over her lower lip. "Not even fucking remotely."

"Not even if you can do whatever you want to me when we're done?"

My eyebrow arches as she walks off the elevator, and I start making a list of what all those things will be when I get her the hell out of here.

As we walk down the hall, I hook my arm around Eden. She rests her head against my side for a second before she smiles at the guy checking names at the door.

"Miss Monroe," he says. "Everything looks amazing."

She thanks him, beaming even brighter, and in a second, I understand why. The entire ballroom has been transformed into an indoor garden. Flowers and ivy drape down from the ceiling, and shrubs line the room. There's a fucking cherub fountain in one corner.

"You did this?" I ask, scanning around.

Eden nods, biting down on her smile. "I hated the idea when they came up with it—for obvious reasons." She points her chin toward the stage at the front of the room with a banner that says, *The Children's Advocacy League Garden of Eden Gala.*

"Wow," I deadpan. "You threw a party with your name in it."

She rolls her eyes, and I run my hand up to the side of her neck, leaning in to kiss her.

"It looks incredible, baby."

Her lips turn up again and then press to mine.

"And you're already all the fuck over my sister."

I consider reminding Eli what that really looks like, but … the children. Not that there are any here, just a bunch of people in tuxes and gowns with drinks in their hands.

Eli hooks his arm around Eden's neck as I back up. He kisses her temple, and she shakes her head, looking up at him.

"You showed up?" she asks, surprised.

"I might have had something to do with that one," a guy says. He has on a black-on-black suit, his jacket already off and a mostly empty tumbler in his hand. "You said you needed Lust for the Seven Deadly Sins auction, so I thought what better than an evening with this asshole?"

Eden laughs, slipping away from Eli and back to me. It only takes a second for her to drag my hand around her, like she did on the boat in the Bahamas. I curl my fingers around her side, not missing the way Eli's jaw tenses. His friend watches, too, but he plasters on a grin.

"You must be Becker." He extends his hand to me. "Ezra Jones."

We shake, and Eden sinks even closer to me. "Jones and Eli have been friends since we were kids."

"Most of our group has," he adds, pulling his hand back. "And Eden's like a sister to every one of us." His voice loses the friendliness at the end despite the smile still on his face.

Great. Another guy to get on my dick every time I touch my girlfriend. And there's more of them apparently.

"Speaking of the other two," Eden says, "since I asked for four sinful items—"

"We're all on the auction block." Jones nods to two more guys by the bar—both with dark hair and boredom etched on their faces. "A night with one or all of us. Whichever you think will bring more cash."

She looks up at me. "We'll go separately. We don't need to expose any of these people to the Four Horsemen."

Elijah cracks a smile on that one. "No fucking fun." He swivels his head to me. "We getting you a drink? Something tells me I'll like you better with more booze in me."

"Something tells me that's not true," I mumble. I press my lips to Eden's head. "Drink?"

She nods. "Champagne? I need to check on a few things."

I wink at her as I follow her brother and Jones toward the bar. He and Elijah go straight for their friends, but I have little interest in meeting the rest of their group. The four of them blend together once they all lean side by side. Fuck, their hair creates a gradient with the way it transitions from Elijah's blond to black on the one at the end.

"Ryker," Jones says, pointing a finger to him before he orders a scotch.

Ryker takes over then, as if they've rehearsed it a time or two, lifting a shoulder to the guy between him and Jones. "Puck."

The brunette looks up long enough for a casual nod and then goes back to staring at the dresses and suits.

None of them say another word to me, which I can't say that I mind. No offense to Eden, but I doubt the five of us are going to be trading friendship bracelets.

I grab my drink and a glass of champagne for her before I head back to where she's talking to a couple. The woman has her claws sunk into Eden's arm, the man nodding along to whatever they're talking about. I get a quick look, her eyes the only giveaway of how uninterested she is in whatever they're saying.

"But really, it's tacky as hell," a chick says on her way past me.

Both she and the girl with her are wearing tight gowns with high slits in the legs, her gaze lingering on me.

The other girl has her focus on Eden. "Everyone is going to notice."

"And I bet the other ladies had nothing to do with the theme. It's such an attention grab."

They stop off to the side of me as I realize they're talking shit, and I swing my attention in their direction. The first one starts to smile until she realizes my interest isn't something she wants. I'm about to show her how much she doesn't want it when I feel someone stop on the other side of me.

"Oh, thank God."

I turn just as a chick tries to take the flute out of my hand. My grip tightens, and her manicured brows shoot up high. She has her dark hair gathered low on the back of her head, and the dress she's wearing stops just above her ankles to show off the studded heels.

"We'll try this one more time," she says, wrapping her fingers around the top of the glass. "I say, *Oh, thank God*, and you give me the alcohol."

"And why would I do that?" I ask, irritated I'm dealing with her in general.

"Because, otherwise, I'll lose it all over one of these people and ruin Eden's gala," she simply says.

This time, I let her slide the flute from my grasp. She sighs before taking a sip. Her eyes drift around before they land on me, giving me a once-over.

"You blend in better than I thought you would."

"Why were you thinking about me at all?"

"I'm Layna," she says.

"The best friend," I mutter.

Tonight just keeps getting better and better.

"I hear you don't like me."

Her head bobs as she hands me back Eden's half-empty drink. "That's an understatement."

"I have no idea why. You don't know me."

She turns to me then. "I know you tried to ghost her after spewing shit at her in the Bahamas."

Everyone seems to be holding that one against me, myself included. After Elijah said something, I realized I wasn't the only one going through hell while I tried to stay away from Eden. So fucking pointless when I think about it now.

"Didn't exactly work out that way," I tell her. "In case you missed me standing here. Or all the times she's ignored your texts lately."

We stand off a few more seconds before Layna shakes her head, clearly bothered I'm not quivering and bowing.

"You really are the *don't give a shit* type," she says.

I shrug. There's exactly one person I give a shit about in this building, and she's smiling and still trying to get away from the old couple.

Despite the common theme of hostility between me and everyone else in Eden's life, I've dealt with worse than the next hour. It reminds me of the boat cruise with Eden beaming and introducing me to couples. Except these people tense a little when looking me over. Even with most of my tattoos covered and having left my *I'm lower class* sign at home.

I'm not the only one who gets that reaction though. Every once in a while, someone will cast a nervous glance in Layna's direction. She catches them more often than not and rolls her eyes.

"You always so popular?" I ask her while at the bar.

She's been staying close to Elijah and his friends. The more people I meet, the more I understand their looks of boredom. Puck sighed so loud at one point that I think the entire ballroom heard him.

"Ever since my parents started parading me around," she says, only mildly annoyed with me this time. "You don't walk into a room filled with hoity white people as the only Black girl and *not* be noticed." Her eyes flit over me, asking the question for her.

"Half Puerto Rican," I answer.

Her attention fades, and I chuckle, grabbing my glass and turning around.

Eden fills the space between us a second later. She doesn't even hesitate to steal the drink out of my hand, and I'm so used to it at this point that I barely even resist.

"Oh my God," one of the girls from earlier squeaks, rushing over. She's holding out her hands and grasps on to Eden's arm once she reaches us. "This is amazing, Eden."

The other one pops up then. "Garden of Eden. It's *such* a cute idea."

Jesus Christ, they're laying it on thick. My annoyance hits a peak as I listen to them go on about the details they were so quick to trash earlier. Their plastered smiles falter a little when they notice me with my arm slung around her, but they keep prattling on.

At least Eden seems well aware of how full of enthusiastic shit they are, her grin forced and her hand fisted into the back of my jacket.

She eventually introduces me, but I don't pay attention. The other guys seem only mildly more interested, barely even acknowledging their existence as they flirt their way down the line.

"Friends of yours?" I ask Eden.

"What gave it away?"

Her lips curve as she sips my whiskey, and I take back my glass.

"We have what," she says, pulling my phone out of my pocket to check the time, "twenty minutes until dinner?" She checks the screen but then shakes her head, quickly handing it to me. "Sorry, I thought it was mine."

I shove it back at her. "Mine tells time just as well."

"I wasn't sure if you wanted me to see the missed text," she says.

My eyes lower, seeing the notification. "If you were anyone else, I might care, but that's mostly because of all the naked pictures you send me."

She squints. "I don't send you naked pictures."

"Then start."

It earns me a smile as she puts the phone back, but when her eyes move to the side, she goes rigid.

I glance over to see Ashton Weare-Hayes in all his douchey glory. The brunette on his arm I recognize from the pictures, and I'm sure I'd recognize the rock on her left hand if it were shoved in my face like it was at the camera.

"Fucking kidding me," Elijah says.

With his first step toward Ashton, Layna's hand shoots to stop him, but he jerks his arm away, stalking through the ballroom.

"Shit." Jones hands off his drink to Layna and rushes after him. The other two calmly set theirs down on the bar behind them before splitting up and going in from each side.

Fucking choreographed.

Eden tugs on me when I start to follow them. "Beck."

I don't stop. Call it hardwiring or macho-caveman bullshit, but the sight of this dude is enough to set me off. I know little about him or the details about his and Eden's relationship—and never plan on learning more—but what I do know is, a minute ago, my girlfriend panicked because she looked at my phone, and I'll bet it's because of him.

By the time Elijah reaches Ashton, the chick with him has wandered off to talk to someone. I can't tell if that's to his benefit or not when Eli marches straight into him, getting in his face.

As the other three guys reach the door, they essentially make a wall, blocking the oblivious donors from what could potentially turn into a homicide if the corded muscles in Elijah's neck are any indication of his feelings. I'm not far behind them, stopping beside Ryker. For the first time all night, he and Puck both look interested, their sights zeroed in on Ashton.

"Invited," Ashton says to Elijah. "Just like everyone else in here."

He has a smugness to his tone, but the nervousness floods off him. I feel a hand slip into mine, not needing to check to know it's Eden, staying behind me and her brother's friend.

Elijah waits for a couple walking in the door to pass before he cocks his head to the side. "Of course you were, asshole. You're a Hayes. And the fact you showed up makes you a fucking idiot."

Ashton's eyes search the room, flashing over me before they stop at the gap between me and Ryker.

"Edes," he says, relaxing once he finds her. "Clear this all up for me. Tell them you want me here, sweetie."

I make it a step before Ryker grabs my arm, and Ashton swiftly steps back, not expecting it. He looks between us then, more confused when Eden pushes Ryker out of the way and stops beside me. In case he's having trouble with the math, I pull her against me.

"I don't want you here, Ashton," she says. "But I also don't care enough to let my brother waste his time throwing you out. So, stay. Enjoy the party. And thank you *so much* for your donation. I'm sure it will be well worth it."

Ashton's mouth sets in a straight line, but he doesn't say anything—like a semi-intelligent person, given the five glares narrowed in on him. His jaw tenses when she tugs on the front of my jacket before she slips back between Ryker and me. Once she's out of sight, he looks back at me. It seems like he's ramping up for a comment that will end with me hurting him, but Elijah steps forward again.

"That donation is going to match the highest donor, *sweetie*."

Ashton's head tips back a little. "It is, huh?"

"No," Eli says, closing in more. "You'll double it. And if you even look at my sister while you're here, Puck will remember your girl's phone number."

"Don't have to," Puck interjects. "She still calls."

Elijah grins when he glances back, and Puck shrugs. The way his lips twitch, I can't tell if he's serious, but the look on Ashton's face says he believes it.

Since they seem to have it under control, I turn around and follow Eden. She's on her way back to the bar, and when she glances over her shoulder, I have a flashback to the restaurant, her face when she was looking for the Ken Doll. It taps into a level of irritation I'm not used to, thinking she wants to see the ex again, but then she smiles when she sees me.

"Looking for someone?" I ask when I catch up with her.

She nods. "You."

"Right here."

"Good," she says. "You and my brother had a similar look in your eyes, and the cost of insurance on these events is terrible. It would be very expensive if one of you throttled my ex."

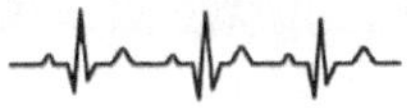

By the time dinner is over, I've ignored another two texts, but when my pocket vibrates for a fourth time, Eden glances down between us. I drag my arm off the back of her chair and fish out my phone. All the messages are from Ty. We're not the chattiest people, so I check them.

Remember that time I saved your ass from juvie for breaking into the school?

Or the time I told your old man I pushed you off the roof when you broke your leg, so he wouldn't find out about your motorcycle?

What about when I took the fall for the weed in junior year?

Do I need to go on?

I shake my head as I answer.

So, you need something?

He replies, *Junior still owe you a favor?*

Shit.
"I'll be right back," I tell Eden, getting up from the table.

I take the wide, open staircase at one end of the ballroom up to the second floor. From the balcony, I can see Eden below, and as always, when I'm above her for any reason, I enjoy the fucking view.

Ty answers on the first ring.

"Please tell me that asshole owes you," he says.

He does, but there's no way in hell I'll admit that without information first. Last year, I "hid" a car for Junior until the owner gave up the search.

"Talk," I tell Ty.

"He's valeting over at the Williamson Hotel now."

I wait for the rest, and Ty blows out a breath.

"I need a car, and he's working tonight. You know he's not going to let me near it after I fucked his sister last year."

"Shouldn't put your dick in every pussy that lets you." I run a hand through my hair, realizing where the fuck he's going with this and wanting him to just stop right now.

But he doesn't.

"B, I need you to get this car for me. I'll consider us even on everything I've ever done for you."

"Everything, huh?" I say dryly. "That's cool, except if we tally everything up, I'm pretty sure you owe me more than I owe you."

"Fuck, come on, B. You know I'd do it for you."

He would. No questions asked.

I lean on the railing over the balcony, over all the rich assholes who are so out of touch with what they're even doing. Chances are, they've never even *met* a kid in the system. And if they have, they sure as hell have no idea what they need.

"Yeah, give me twenty minutes, and I'll be there."

"My fucking brother. Yes. Thank you, B."

I scrub a hand over my face as I put my phone back in my dress pants. I'm about to go from sipping champagne with Chicago's elite to boosting a car in under half an hour.

What the fuck even is my life anymore?

Eden

When I glance over my shoulder for Beck, I see him on the balcony above. He pushes through his hair, leaving it tousled and wild, a tattoo creeping out from under his dress shirt up the back of his hand.

"I'll admit, he's gorgeous," Layna says, not even checking to see if I'm staring at him. "But—"

"But you still don't like him," I finish for her.

She lifts a shoulder, which in Layna speak is almost a blessing. Almost.

On the other side of the table, Puck, Ryker, and Elijah are all on their phones. This is not where any of them would choose to be on a Saturday night, but we've all been bred to deal with what's expected of us. Schools, events, balls. Puck was my escort when I was a debutante.

I'm the only one floating right now, needing a breather to figure everything out. Layna's president of her sorority and interning this summer for a lawyer. Elijah and his friends will all take over either their own family businesses or a friend of the family's empire.

My brother fights that future more than the others. Jones has accepted it the easiest. Puck and Ryker Devereaux, on the other hand, are dangerous when they're bored and destructive when they're driven, so they'd act the same whether they wanted the life they were being guided into or not.

While our circle runs broad, the five of us and Layna have always stayed the closest. As Beatrix and Gretchen proved earlier with their feigned praise, so many of our friendships run surface level. We can drink and party and have every photo op imaginable, but most of them wouldn't hesitate to peel our skin off if they thought it would serve them.

That's not to say everyone is fake, but we all understand trust isn't on an even plane. It has different depths. The people at this table are at the murky bottom with each other—for better or worse. Which is why they're all here now, ready to be auctioned off, the guys as Lust and Layna as Pride, where she'll give a complete wardrobe overhaul.

Beck's not on the balcony the next time I look, and I see him descending the staircase. He's like a magnet, pulling at me when he's in the same space. And right now, he's a broody magnet with his brow furrowed.

"Keep these assholes in line for me?" I ask Layna as I stand.

She snorts. "Asking for a lot."

I get a warning look from Jones and follow his line of sight to Ashton over by the stage, but I'm going the other way. Even if I wasn't, this is my domain. I meant what I said earlier; I don't care if he's here. The scar tissue's set now.

I'm about halfway across the ballroom when I meet Beck.

"What's wrong?" I ask.

"Nothing," he says. He grasps my wrists, hanging them around his neck. "But I have to go."

"So, something is wrong."

Beck's face has no give, all hard and locked down, and whatever he's not saying is twisting in my belly. I glance back at the table and then around the ballroom before I settle on him again.

"Fine. If you won't tell me, then I'm coming with you."

He smirks. "No, you're not. I'm going to help Ty out with something, and you're going to stay here." His lips hit my forehead, and he starts to walk away.

It stings, having him leave me in the ballroom, and my face must show it because when he looks back, he stops. His eyes search around like he's trying to figure something out, and then he's stalking back toward me. I don't have a chance to ask why before his lips cover mine. It's rough and quick, like he needs it.

"You're driving," he says. Then he walks away again.

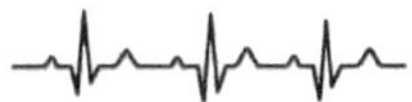

I narrowly avoid the inquisition by choosing Ryker as the messenger everyone will shoot for me leaving. He gives me a look when I corner him in the hallway on his way back in from getting high with Puck. And since he's on his way back inside after getting high with Puck, I put all the instructions in his phone for him.

"You owe me," he drawls as I shove his phone back in his jacket pocket.

Probably not though since I don't bother adding that to what he needs to remember.

I've finished most of my official duties for tonight other than tipping the service staff and overseeing the auction items, but even a stoned, unimpressed rake like Ryker can handle those things.

"Is this because of the mechanic?" He cranes his neck around at the sound of the door as Puck walks back in from outside.

"His name is Beck," I say with a sweet smile. "And since when do you inquire about my love life?"

"Since the last guy ended up being such a douche," Puck answers. He drops his shoulder against the wall, just behind his brother. "We've decided to take a more active role in your happiness."

"Ew, please don't."

Ryker chuckles, and I leave them in the hallway to entertain themselves.

Beck's already waiting with my BMW, the passenger door open when I step out of the building. He leans against the side, his jacket off and his sleeves rolled up. He puts his hand on the small of my back, guiding me in. He shuts the door and jogs around. Once he slides into the driver's seat, he looks over.

"What?" he asks.

"I thought I was driving." I reach for my seat belt, and he peels away from the curb.

"You will. After we get there." He speeds down an alley that I wasn't even aware existed behind the hotel. "Unless you think you can get us to the Williamson in five minutes?"

I shake my head. At least, now, I know where we're going. To help Ty at another hotel.

"What does Ty do?"

"Hmm," he says, his voice low. "You don't want the answer to that, princess."

"I wouldn't have asked if I didn't."

Beck shifts his eyes to me and then back to the road. "Ty's in collections."

The way his mouth turns up at the corner makes me sigh, and I slump deeper into the leather seat.

"Maybe I shouldn't have come."

"You shouldn't have," he answers quickly. "I shouldn't have let you."

"Then why did you?" I ask.

"I'm wondering the same damn thing, baby."

With Beck driving, it only takes a couple of minutes. But when he slows down, we're still a block away from the hotel. Ty's not far ahead of us on a bus bench, his hoodie pulled over his head and his hands shoved in the front pocket.

Beck cups my chin, turning my face toward him. "Ty will tell you where to go." I open my mouth, but he presses his lips to mine to stop me, his eyes amused when he pulls back. "He'll lie if you ask questions, so save yourself the trouble."

"Will he lie about everything or just what you're helping him with?" I whisper.

He considers the question for a second. "Probably everything. But I'll tell him not to if you ask about me."

I start to smile when he kisses me again. My seat belt clicks, and then I gasp against his mouth as he wraps his arms around me and pulls me over the console. In the same motion, he opens the door, sliding from under me until I'm in the driver's seat and he's outside of the car.

"What are you doing?" I ask.

He whistles, and Ty's head jerks our way, his jaw going slack at the sight of my car. My eyes shift between them as Beck bends down again, his standard irritated look in place.

"I have a hard time saying no to you," he tells me. "*That's* why I do stupid shit like let you come with me tonight. And it pisses me off."

I, however, am perfectly fine with it.

The door slams, leaving me to watch them with the engine idling. Beck hops up the curb to meet Ty, and their hands lock. The two of them barely even talk to each other before Ty strides toward the car, and Beck heads down the block, away from us.

Ty drops into my passenger seat, his head shaking before he's even all the way in. "Fuck. This is the car I should have gotten tonight."

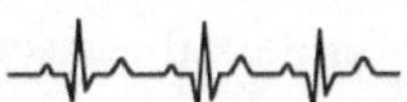

We drive for several blocks with Ty giving me directions over the music Beck left playing. He's on his phone most of the time, looking over at me every now and then. Even without conversation, he has an entirely different vibe than Beck but with something similar underneath. It's below the surface, one of those threads that makes us who we are that they must share.

"And we're off," he finally says, dropping his phone into the cupholder. He immediately starts screwing with my presets, pulling a face anytime it changes and trying another. "So, you had Beck at a fancy dinner?"

"A fundraiser." I turn when he points down another street. "We're raising money for child advocates for kids in the foster care system."

"How much you make? Turn left at the next light."

"I'm not sure yet. We kind of left in the middle, but we were only three thousand away from paying off the event, so—"

"I thought you guys charge for a plate or whatever."

I take a left when the light turns green, not really sure where the fuck I am anymore. "We do, which pays for the food and space, but we still have other costs."

He nods, directing me up another road, this one darker and more residential. "So, you spend a shit-ton of money, ask other people to give you a shit-ton of money, and then use their shit-ton to pay off your shit-ton. And anything left over goes to the kids' advocacy or whatever?"

The way he says it has an undertone, like he's trying to trap me into making his point for him.

"Essentially, yes," I answer, rather sure I know where he's going with the question.

"Wouldn't it make more sense to just give both shit-tons instead of a song and dance and then fancy dinner with everyone bragging about how generous they are?" he asks, smug in his question.

He relaxes back in his seat, watching me as I drive.

"It would." I shrug. "And I wish it were like that. But a lot of these people won't give unless they have a reason to, which is shitty but the way they work. I try to remind myself we're not just giving to the charity. We hired caterers and servers and rented decorations. We might not be giving as much as we should to the advocacy program, but we put cash in about a half-dozen small business owners' pockets and hopefully help feed their kids for the week."

We is me. I would never tell the ladies on the committees I help plan with that the caterer isn't a five-star chef from one of their approved vendor lists. They would melt down if they knew the one for tonight also runs a food truck during the summer and her training came from her grandmother's kitchen and not an institute in France.

His gaze stays on me, and I feel fidgety, judged.

"B's losing it over you," he says, switching the music back to what he originally started on.

"Why do you say that?"

"Because we usually don't bring chicks along for a job."

Ty nods to a group of people standing about half a block ahead of us on the side of the street. A car pulls up from the other way, parking and leaving the lights on. The driver's door opens, and Beck crawls out.

My attention shifts to Ty beside me. "Whose car is that?" I ask.

"Mine," he says, not missing a beat. "Beck was just getting it washed for me."

Right. He lies.

"Stop here," Ty says.

I pull to the curb across from the half-dozen guys, all of them turning their heads as I shift into park.

"Well, Blondie, this is my stop." Ty clicks his tongue at me and winks.

After he shuts the door, the interior light fades until I'm in the dark again. He slaps Beck on the back once he reaches the group, and Beck checks over his shoulder to the car. It only takes another second before he's on his way over.

He took off his tie, and his jacket is still in the back seat, leaving him in just his black dress shirt, the top few buttons open to show the script on his chest and part of the ship's wheel in the center.

When he climbs in the passenger side, he barely shuts the door, leaning straight over to kiss me. It doesn't stop with just a quick one though, and his fingers curl around my neck to keep me there. Almost as if he has a point to prove. His tongue dives into my mouth, and I think he's about to drag me over the console to him again when he finally breaks his lips away from mine.

"Hey," he says, an inch away now.

"Hi." I sound a little drunk, but I guess I am. "What was that for?"

"You look hot. Also, I needed to make sure you remembered that, while I might steal cars every now and then, I can make you wet with little effort."

He grabs the seat belt then, and I swallow hard.

"You just…" I look across the street again, seeing Ty crawl into the sporty little car Beck got out of a minute ago. "You *stole* that?"

He lets the seat belt retract, and he comes back over the center. Our mouths collide, and he kisses me hard, his lips demanding and tongue teasing mine. I want to ask him a million questions, but that would require him to stop, and I really don't want him to.

He does, though, when someone knocks on the passenger window. I jump, pulling away from him, so his hand is still suspended in the air. His eyes slowly open, studying me like I might run before he looks over at the looming figure outside the car.

They lean down as Beck rolls the window down a crack, and I realize it's the Axel guy from his apartment a few weeks ago. His eyes flit over Beck to me, and I sink back into the driver's seat. The first time he was around, I felt the same way, like I needed to sink away, become invisible. No one else has ever made me feel like that—at least, no one I didn't immediately dismiss or put in their place.

Something tells me Axel wouldn't exactly scamper away if I turned up the bitch though.

He studies me for a second before he glances around the rest of the car. "We all good?"

"Car's here, isn't it?" Beck responds. "Ty came through for you, like he always does."

"*Ty* came through, yeah." Axel straightens up, and I reinflate a little. "Like always."

He walks across the street, nodding to the others, and they all dash off to different vehicles. Axel gets in with Ty, and they take off along with everyone else.

Once it's just me and Beck and a dark, empty street, he drags my hand across to him, kissing the backs of my fingers. He looks up, his lips soft and breath hot.

"What are you thinking, crazy?" he asks, studying me.

"That you're not playing fair."

"No?"

I shake my head. "You can't just steal a car and then seduce me into forgetting about it."

He smirks, dragging his tongue over my skin. "Let's go to my apartment and test this theory."

His teeth graze one of my knuckles, and I already know the results.

Beck

I have to dodge Axel's texts for a while after helping Ty get the car from the Williamson. It's easier to avoid him since I've been putting in more hours at the shop, and I took an extra class this semester, so I wouldn't have one left over the summer.

And then there's the fact that I've spent every other minute doing what I can to breathe, eat, and fuck Eden. Sleep's supposed to be in there somewhere but not when she's within reach of me.

Lately though, she hasn't been with our schedules not lining up. She finished the gala and slid right into planning another event with a different organization. I've stopped trying to keep track of them, but it sounds like some of the board seats she holds for foundations she recently took over from her dad.

I'm working late on Thursday night at the garage when a stern face appears on my screen for a video call. I balance my phone under the hood of the Honda I'm saving after the guy decided to DIY the install of his cool air intake before I answer.

"Why does it look like I'm in trouble already?" I ask.

My sister sighs, dramatically pushing her dark hair away from her face. "You were supposed to be here for dinner tonight."

"No," I tell Grace. "I was supposed to be there last night."

Which I missed, but I've already gotten the lecture from Ma, so I don't need a follow-up from an eight-year-old.

"I wanted to show you my song."

"Sing it now." I look up when she doesn't respond, and she's killing me through the screen. "I'm serious. It's just me in here."

Grace shakes her head, and I shrug as I turn the wrench. It's probably a song she made up while dancing around the backyard, like she's on one of those shows with the celebrities making asses out of themselves for the enjoyment of the viewers.

But I really don't fucking care if she wants to sing the ABCs.

"How about I pick you up from school tomorrow, and you can show me then?"

She's smiling when I glance up. "Deal. But you'd better have a good excuse for not coming tonight."

I nod. "I'll make one up by then."

Her mouth falls open, and I grin at her, ending the call.

Even if she hadn't called, I would have seen her tomorrow when I stopped by my parents'. My dad hurt his back a few years ago on a construction site, and since their worthless landlord doesn't repair anything, I'm their guy whenever a project involves climbing or crawling.

It's around nine when Jorge emerges from the office in the back. He sighs, taking inventory of his garage, like he does every time he's getting ready to leave. I can't blame him. When you have to work like hell for something, you appreciate it more.

"You good?" he asks on his way by me.

I nod. "Half an hour maybe."

He hits the button to close the overhead door to the shop and then kicks the bolt over at the bottom to keep it from being pried up before he heads out the service door.

Any other guy, and he'd hang around until they finished, but my dad taught him to turn a wrench when he was a teenager, so he gives me full rein of the place. It makes me feel guilty, how badly I want the fuck out of here, but not guilty enough that I'd consider staying a second longer than necessary.

I have my back to the front of the shop when I hear the door again a little later. I look over my shoulder and catch sight of a set of legs I'm frequently between in one way or another. Eden's cautiously walking in as I turn around.

It's interesting she's walking in at all since she's never been inside the place before. She didn't even know where the hell it was until I left my school bag in my locker one night. I stopped by, popping the lock on the service door and grabbing it while she stayed safely locked in my car.

"Fuck." I wince, wiping my hands on a rag. "I ordered a redhead for tonight."

She scrunches up her face and tries stopping a few feet away from me. Greasy hands or not, I reach for the back of her neck, pulling her the rest of the way until my mouth covers hers. It's been almost a week since I've seen her. A fucking week since I've touched her.

"Tell me you missed me," she says, her lips never leaving mine.

"So fucking much."

And I did. It's unhealthy to obsess over someone this much. To have your entire brain dedicated to one person.

"Now, why the fuck are you here?" I ask.

She purses her lips, not sure if I'm serious or not. "You said you were working late."

I nod. "I am."

"So, I wanted to see you." She gives a half-shrug, her fingers twisting in the front of my shirt. "I can leave if you want me to."

Her eyes lower like she thinks I'll really kick her out.

She squeaks when I spin her around and set her up on top of the tool chest. I step between her legs when they part for me. The bottom of her dress hikes up, and I slide my thumbs under as my mouth works down her neck.

"This is why..." I graze over her panties, and Eden sucks in a breath.

"Why?" she asks, breathy and running her hands up the back of my head.

"Why you haven't set foot in this fucking shop." I nip at her skin before I drop my hand to the open drawer for a screwdriver and back away with a smirk.

"Tease," she says.

"Only if I don't put out in the end." I turn around and try like hell to focus. Because, right now, I don't give a shit if this dude's car runs or not if I can make her come.

Unhealthy.

Once I turn on music from a speaker another guy keeps around, I stop hearing her shift around on the cart behind me, and it doesn't take me long to reassemble everything I tore apart to fix the owner's mess. She sighs as I straighten up like she's been waiting on me for hours instead of ten minutes.

I look back, and she's taking out her hair tie. She watches me as she shakes out her hair, pulling it over to one side. My eyes don't leave her, following her hands when she lowers them down her neck. Then she's spreading her legs apart on top of the metal, dragging her dress higher until I see the barely there lace. *Fuck.*

"What are you doin', crazy?" I ask.

Her fingers brush over her bare skin, tempting me. "Why do you call me that?"

"What? Crazy?" I push up the hood to set the prop down and then let it drop shut. I still need to test the intake, but fuck it. Nothing else is happening until I've touched her all the ways I've thought about since she walked in the door.

Eden nods as I walk over to her, and I set my tools back in the drawer and close it, so I can stand between her legs.

"You really think I'm crazy?" she asks.

"Nah, baby. I call you that because you're *my* crazy." I suck her lower lip into my mouth, taking care of the slight pout she had aimed at me. "Until you, I was completely sane, but since you"— I shake my head, feeling my way up the backs of her dangling legs—"everything about you sends me over the edge. The way you smell, your laugh, this perfect mouth. I have no fucking clue what I'm doing half the time because all I can think about is you."

Eden's eyes dart between mine, and she swallows. "Good answer."

She's barely finished when she crushes her lips to mine. Her hands slip up my shirt, pushing the bottom over my abs, and I unbutton her coat with one hand while the other jerks her forward. I toss her coat to the smooth concrete by the cart, and I yank my shirt the rest of the way off before sealing my mouth over hers again.

"You're dangerous," I mumble. I rub my hard-on against her, and she whimpers. "Hazardous. So fucking sexy."

I kiss down her jaw, hooking my thumb in her panties and moving them out of the way. My mouth skims down the material of her dress and up her thigh. As my tongue drags over her, she pushes her hands into my hair.

"Beck."

When I look up, Eden wraps her legs around my waist, and I hitch her up, lifting her off the tool chest and turning us around so I can lay her on the hood of the car. She's fucking gorgeous, sprawled out with her hair loose and splayed over the red paint.

She pulls me down on top of her, and I groan, grinding into her.

I pop the button on my jeans and draw down my zipper, but then she swallows hard.

"Wait."

My mouth stops moving along with my hand halfway in my pants, and I study her face. "Fuck. Is this not okay?"

I start to straighten up, but she shakes her head, latching on to the back of my neck. "Of course it is."

"Then you'd better have one hell of a reason for stopping me."

Eden rolls her head to the side, checking the empty shop. "We're kind of in the open."

"Baby, I'll fuck you in every dark corner in this place. Take your pick."

I drag her up off the hood of the car, kissing her before she tugs on my hand, pulling me across the building. She bites her smile, eyeing the shitty old limo Jorge has one of the mechanics salvaging for someone.

She leads me toward the back of the car, but I stop and drag her back to me by the passenger door.

"You said anywhere," she reminds me.

"I did. But I'm not really the back-of-a-limo kind of guy."

I swing open the passenger door and lift her up, tying her legs around me before I lower into the car and slam the door shut. Her mouth crashes into mine, the front seat already filled with her scent as I unzip the back of her dress. I'm breathing her, I've tasted her ... only one left.

Pulling down her straps, I lean her back, so I can draw one of her pebbled nipples into my mouth. She moans, and I lift my hips, pushing down my jeans and boxers before I move to her other nipple.

"Fuck. I want all of you on me." I shift her over to the driver's seat.

I peel the dress the rest of the way down and her panties along with it. She leaves both in the seat as I pull her back into my lap. Her bare skin hits mine, and I groan. My hands cover as much ground as they can on her, my hips flexing into her.

It feels like so much of the Bahamas never happened. Every moment with Eden is burned into my brain, but it's somehow rewired into not remembering how, most of the time, I wasn't touching her like this. I wasn't caressing her tongue with mine while rolling on a condom, and she wasn't sinking down on me.

My hands guide her hips while she rides me, bracing her hands on my shoulders. I thrust into her from underneath, and her head falls back.

"God, you feel good, baby."

I kiss the hollow of her throat, moving lower to suck at the skin on her collarbone. She moans, and I grip her ass, slamming her down harder.

"Beck." She sounds needy, pulling at the back of my hair. "Oh my God."

The window beside us catches the heat from our breaths, the condensation building. I wrap my arm all the way around her and pump into her faster. Every time my teeth drag over her skin, she cries out, arching into me for more. It drives me wild—the princess wanting a little pain.

We're pulling at each other, trying to get closer and fuck harder. She's close. So close that I can feel her body starting to tighten around me. I drop the seat back, and she gasps, falling forward.

"Come, Eden," I rasp into her ear.

My hips snap up, driving deep as she falls apart. She moans my name and then breathes it while I speed up my thrusts, dragging her against me.

"Fuck," I groan into her neck as I come. My muscles tense, and I bury myself inside her, holding her tight against me.

I relax back into the seat, running my hands over her flesh until she breaks out in chills. Her lips press to my neck, both of us catching our breaths.

After a minute, I pull the handle and sit us up. I kiss her, my hand around her neck as the other creaks open the limo door. Eden grins at me as I slip out of her and slide out of the car, leaving her gorgeous and naked on the passenger seat.

I pull off the condom, her eyes still all over me.

"You look happy," I say, buttoning my jeans.

She nods. "Very."

When I lean down, I drag my lips from her jaw to her ear. "Get dressed, so I can delete the security video."

Eden's eyes pop wide open when I straighten, and I can't help but smirk as I walk away.

Twenty-Three

Beck

I leave the office door open, providing enough light for me to see the buttons on the console. Eden's slipping back on her shoes when I glance at the camera before switching it to the recorded video. As I rewind, I get a hot, sped-up, reverse version of her coming and her on the hood of the car. I also gain an entirely new perspective of how goddamn sexy she looks with my head between her legs. Her hair falling down her back, her tits heaving.

Pity to delete it.

Then again, if anyone else saw her like this, I'd end up in jail, so for the best.

I hear something out in the shop over the music as I delete everything from after Eden walked in the door. Even if Jorge notices the time missing, he's a smart man. He'll see her in that fucking coat that stops mid-thigh and nothing else below it until her heels and not need to ask any questions.

The screen switches back to the live feed when I finish, and the entire office closes in when my eyes land on the five guys sauntering toward Eden.

Fuck.

Ty and Milo stall out not too far inside the door, but Axel, Lee, and some other fuck keep going until Eden slinks back as far as she can, her shoulders hitting the metal tool chest. Axel licks his lips and slides his hands together as he looks at her, and my vision goes fucking red.

He says something to her then, and she might answer, but I have no idea because I'm already on my way out the door.

As I storm around the corner, pulling my shirt on, every head in the place turns to me. The other three are stopped about five feet in front of Eden, her face flashing with relief when she locks on to me.

"B," Ty says, rushing a step back to further himself even more from the guys who are about a city block too fucking close to my girl.

"You lost?" I grind out, my teeth clenched.

Axel's gaze moves back to Eden, then down to her coat on the floor, and back to her. "Not at all. We were just saying how pretty your little rich girl is."

"Don't," I tell him.

Lee has a wary look to him, which doesn't sit well. He's usually the one with his head the farthest up Axel's ass, so if he's not enjoying their reason for being here, I doubt I will. The third guy I still don't know, and I don't plan to introduce myself.

Eden eases around the tool chest, walking on the balls of her feet to keep her heels from clicking over the concrete floor. She comes to stand between me and the chest, but I bring her to my other side, tucking her against me.

"There a crime against appreciating a beautiful woman now?" Axel asks.

"No, but it can lead to one if you don't fucking watch yourself."

His face goes to stone. "I forgot how disrespectful you can be."

"I'm happy to remind you," I bite back.

"Becker." Ty shakes his head at me, still firmly planted by the door.

Eden's fingers creep up my abs as Axel stares me down. This isn't a one-off between us. Other people might cower and grovel or whatever, but I've never been that guy.

Axel's eyes shift around. "I need your help with a little problem."

"Not happening." I rest my hand on the top of the chest, the other curled around Eden's side. Her rib cage moves under my palm, and I move my hold up to the nape of her neck, brushing my thumb back and forth.

"You need to help me—"

"I don't *need* to do anything," I cut him off, and I see the flare in his eyes.

The cannon just cut loose.

"Maybe you fucking do," he shouts.

He lifts his shirt enough to show the gun tucked in his waistband, but my hand's already dropping behind the tool chest. It catches the safety before wrapping around the stock of the shotgun Jorge keeps in a rack back there—one in the chamber— and when I bring it out, Ty stares up at the ceiling.

"Fucking Christ."

The shop falls silent for several beats, short of the music still playing.

"Axel," Milo calls, "we should go. They patrol this block like motherfuckers with the jewelry store on the corner."

It takes a second, but Axel lets the bottom of his shirt fall. He glances at the two beside him, and they back up a ways before turning and walking back to Ty and Milo.

I keep the shotgun out, arm hanging at my side. I've known Axel long enough to know he's mostly a lot of noise. Mostly. Fuck if this is going to be the one time I expect him to back down. Not with Eden here.

He slowly backs up, his eyes dragging back to Eden again. This time, he looks at her less like a piece of ass he thinks he can claim and more like a problem.

Which I find just as much a problem.

I take a step forward, and his focus snaps back to me.

"You need to get your fucking priorities straight, Donovan."

He reaches the others before he turns around, letting them watch his back as he walks out the door. Lee and the other guy follow him first, and then Milo shoots me a familiar look of understanding. Once it's just Ty, he holds out his hands with his face scrunched.

I shrug at him. We've been there for each other long enough. If it came down to it, he would have my back over Axel's. Until then, I won't blame him for following the money out the door.

It shuts behind him, and I turn, already pulling Eden to me. She's shivering, and she whimpers when her face presses to my chest. I lean the shotgun against the tools and rest my cheek on the top of her head. My insides fucking rip apart while she sniffs, her fingers fisting in my shirt.

"I'm sorry," she mumbles. "I'm so sorry."

I frown, my hands sliding up her face, and I pull back, tipping her head back so I can see her glistening eyes. "The fuck are you apologizing for?" My tone's short, and she shakes her head, trying to look away, but I won't let her.

"If I hadn't been here, maybe…" She trails off because she has nothing.

"That wasn't about you," I tell her. I press my lips to hers hard, needing her to believe me. "That was an insecure fuck who thinks everyone needs to fall in line for him. I would have told him to screw off with or without you here."

She nods, kissing me again, and then buries her face back against my chest. I wrap my arms around her, holding her so tight that she probably can't breathe well, but I need to feel her.

I need to know that even though I'm dragging her through all this shit, she's here.

Because she probably shouldn't be. I shouldn't let her be.

But fuck, I'm in too deep with her for her *not* to be.

Eden

"**D**o you own a gun?" I ask Eli.

It's been over two weeks since the incident at the garage. I *obviously* didn't tell my brother about it, but I've been curious if he's ever been in a similar situation. Not where his boyfriend steals cars sometimes for a guy who showed up with a gun after they'd had amazing sex in a limo, but him having a gun on him in general.

Darla once told me you know you're worth something when someone threatens violence to get what you have, and I think that might be the most fucked up piece of life advice she ever gave me.

Eli's at the opposite end of the couch, reading a book.

Something that might surprise most people about him is how often he reads. His room is lined with books, and he's been cover to cover with every one.

Slowly, his head turns toward me, and then his eyes shift. "Why?"

I tilt my head at him, waiting for him to answer my question.

"Yes." He leans forward and tosses the book onto the coffee table before he relaxes back, bringing his ankle over the opposite knee. "Dad taught me to shoot when I was ten."

My jealousy rises with that one. "He what? Why didn't he teach me?"

Eli shrugs. "Because he's an old-school businessman, and while he loves his daughter, he still thinks you're meant to be a catered-to princess."

I wrinkle my nose at him, but he's right. Daddy's always supported my dreams, but they've leaned toward charity work and helping people in need. If I'd wanted to become a CEO, schmoozing clients at the cigar bar, he might not have been so on board.

"He called earlier," Eli says, scrolling through his phone. "He wanted to know when I was going to be in the office today."

I frown. "It's Saturday."

"That's what I told him. Then he called me back an hour later, asking why I still wasn't there." My brother lolls his head onto the cushions, scanning me over. "Why are you in a dress?"

"I think you mean, *Wow, sis, you look so nice.*" I give him a look, but he shrugs it off, unbothered.

"Beck's picking me up soon," I say.

For once, Eli doesn't even respond to Beck's name. It almost feels like it might be a moment—something to be remembered as the first time my big brother approved of the only guy who has actually mattered outside of him and Daddy.

Except we're just on a delay.

"You haven't gotten over that yet?"

"You are *such* a jackass." I throw a cushion at him as I get up, and he chuckles.

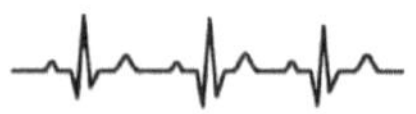

When I step out of the building, Beck's waiting by his car with the door open for me. He still hasn't told me where he's taking me or why I only got an hour's notice, so I plan on crawling right in as an act of protest. I almost make it before he catches my arm and pulls me back out to kiss me.

"You look gorgeous," he says.

And he can take me wherever the hell he wants.

While I mean it, I'm still analyzing every turn he makes for the next twenty minutes. We pass what I think is the back side of the garage at one point, but we keep going several more blocks before he stops in front of a little ranch-style house. White brick with a flower bed started out front.

"Now, are you going to tell me where we are?" I ask.

He raises an eyebrow before he gets out. "A cookout."

"A what?" I whisper as he shuts his door.

I climb out as he rounds the back of the car. He slips his hand into mine on our way up the sidewalk, and once we reach the porch, I see the worn mat in front of the door.

La Familia Donovan.

"Oh my God." I jerk around to face him. "You did *not* bring me to your parents' house without telling me."

He smirks, and I frantically shake my head, looking down at my dress and heels.

"Beck, I'm not dressed for—"

"A cookout," he says, bringing his arms around me. "We're not at the Four Seasons or some ritzy event. It's a barbecue in a backyard, and you look fucking perfect for it."

He frames my face in his hands, lazily pressing his lips to mine like we're not at the front door of his parents' house. Then they leave me, and we are, all the nerves from before springing back to life in my belly.

Beck entwines our fingers as he opens the door and pulls me inside despite my reluctance.

We walk into what looks like the living room with a couch, TV, and armchairs. The entire place smells incredible, spices filling the air. An arch leads to a small dining area with a table and six chairs.

A screen door off to the side of it opens, and a woman walks in with a tray in her hands. She has on a flower print sundress that sets off the bronze in her skin, and her hair is in a tight bun. Within the first few steps, she starts speaking to someone ahead of her, not even glancing in our direction as she marches through.

"Ma," Beck says, but she disappears behind a wall.

Another woman answers her. I took two years of Spanish, but I'm pretty sure my instructor hadn't carried on an actual conversation in the language, so what I learned does me little good in the real world. Most of what I really know comes from people who've worked for us over the years. Eli and I had a nanny who would take us shopping with her, so I can at least piece together that they're talking about clothes.

Beck shakes his head, pulling me with him into the kitchen. His mom has her back to us, a towel in her hand while she talks to a woman sitting on the stool. The stove beside her has most of the burners covered, water boiling and pans sizzling.

"Ma." Beck tries again from inside the doorway, but they keep going, and he blows out an exasperated breath. "For fucks' sake, Ma."

"*What*, Becker?" she says, spinning to him. She almost jumps back when her eyes dart to me, shifting between us before a smile starts to spread.

"I thought you might want to meet Eden before I changed my mind and carried her out of here," he says.

She narrows her eyes at him, saying something that makes his lips curve up on one side before her attention returns to me. "Eden, we're so excited to finally meet you."

I nod and am about to apologize for not bringing anything when she rushes over with an, "Ahh, you're here!"

She throws her arms around me, pulling my shoulders down for a hug and swaying me back and forth. It's so inviting, no awkward pats like I'm used to from my own mother, and my hands go to her back.

I look over to Beck as he drags his mother away from me, folding his arms around her head and whispering something to her in Spanish before he kisses the top of her hair. She swats at him with the dish towel, pulling away, and she squeezes my arm, leaning closer again.

"Now, get out of here before my sister tries to pry those shoes off your feet."

The woman on the stool scowls as she turns around, muttering under her breath. Her gaze drifts down to my shoes then, and she makes a face like maybe she would consider ripping them off me. They resume their conversation with more snippiness to it this time, and Beck ushers me out of the kitchen to the dining room.

"She said that's your aunt?" I ask, my mind going one place.

"Gina's mom," he says.

I slow down beside the table, my jaw setting just at her name, and he comes back to me.

"She won't show up today, if that's what you're glaring at me about. She's still pissed at me for not ruining your vacation."

"You did ruin my vacation." I look around at the wallpaper lining the room, brown and orange with little flowers running up and down in strips. But it only lasts until I have an irritated Beck's face in mine.

"Ruined, huh?" he growls at me, but his lips twitch. "Like I've ruined every day since?"

I nod. "It's been terrible. Awful. Really, I can't stand you—"

His mouth cuts me off, hard and hot, his tongue diving into my mouth and hands dropping to my ass. It's not how he should kiss me with his mother twenty feet away in the kitchen. It's not how he should kiss me with *anyone*'s mother around. But by the time his lips leave mine, I'm incapable of thinking about anyone but him.

"You ruin my days too," he rasps. His blue eyes stare into mine so deep that I can barely breathe, what he says sounding nothing like the actual words. "I can't stand you so fucking much."

He kisses me slowly then, and this time, I feel him everywhere, taking over every piece inside me he hasn't already. And I know I'll never get him out. Beck's there now, and I don't have a say in it.

When he breaks away, he groans, setting his forehead on mine. "This was a mistake."

"Introducing me to your family?" My voice sounds weak. From him and from the sense of doubt that's managed to creep in over the past millisecond.

He shakes his head against mine. "Not accounting for how much I fucking missed feeling you." His hands run up my back, his nose skimming over mine. "I have to make it through God knows how many hours before I can touch you the way I want to."

Never getting him out.

I smile, and he brushes his lips over my cheek, then he breathes out and leads me to the screen door his mom came in earlier. It creaks as he pushes it open, banging shut once we're on the other side.

The backyard has a chain fence around it, and a large oak stands in one corner. My heart warms when I see the tree house nestled in the branches, a swing hanging from the lowest one. I've only ever lived in apartments and penthouses, but the summer I begged for a tree house, Daddy bought a lake house specifically for the tree out back. I slept in it every night until we left to go back to the city.

There's a little girl on the swing, dark hair and a set of eyes that light up when she spots us stepping onto the paved patio. She squeals, sprinting toward us, and Beck's hold loosens on me as he catches her with his other arm.

"Christ, Grace." But he smiles and presses a kiss to the side of her head before setting her down.

His little sister is gorgeous with warm brown curls and amber eyes.

He runs his hand over her hair as she looks up at me, her mouth curving up when she glances back to him.

"She really does look like a princess," she says.

I feel my cheeks heat, and Beck chuckles softly, rubbing up my back.

"Trust me, she acts like one too."

Before I can jab him in the ribs, the door behind us swings open, and Beck moves me out of the way of the man walking through with his arms full of canvas shopping bags. His gaze catches on me, and he stops short.

"Well, I'll be damned," he says.

He unloads everything into Beck's empty arm before he drags me forward for a hug. It's still strange for people I've never met to be pulling me and holding me, but unlike the maternal affection, this embrace feels right immediately, his arms curling around me. He steps back after a second. His eyes are a similar blue to Beck's but his hair is a dirty blond.

"We told him he couldn't eat unless he brought you," his dad says, and given the way Beck's mouth perks up, I completely believe him.

We've barely settled in at one of the picnic tables with the beers Mr. Donovan shoved at us when the screen door bangs open again, and Ty walks out. Milo follows him into the backyard, and the chill from the other night creeps into my muscles. I lean a little closer to Beck. His arm's already snaking around me, pulling me against his side.

But Ty has the same vibe he did the night in my car, and the other one gives me a tight-lipped smile, almost reassuring. We're backward on the bench, and Ty plops down in front of us at another table with Milo sitting closer to the end of their bench.

"Sorry about the other night, man," Milo says.

Beck shrugs it off, and I relax into him.

After a while, more people start throwing open the screen door in regular intervals. New ones carry dishes of food in and out of the house, Mr. Donovan not moving from the white plastic chair he set beside the burning grill.

So much talking and laughing. I don't think Beck introduces me to a single one of them, but my name is yelled from neighbor to family friend over the tops of heads and around me while I'm already in an embrace. Kids are running around, screaming and chasing each other.

And I'm feeling lost in it all.

Family's not something we have a lot of, and when we had a lot of people around the table, growing up, it was mostly for a dinner party to celebrate a deal. We weren't grabbing food buffet-style or blaring whatever was on the radio.

It's warm—and not just from the spring sun splashing down, but in the heart of it.

By the time everyone has eaten and claimed their place in the backyard, it's late afternoon. Ty only sticks around for the food. Milo leaves even sooner, hopping the chain-link fence separating the backyard from what Beck says is his grandma's house.

Grace disappears with most of the other kids into the house. She reappears a little while later to whisper something to Beck's mom, and she sighs, raising her eyebrows and gesturing with her head in my direction.

"Incoming," Beck says.

"What?"

He doesn't have a chance to answer before a barefoot Grace tromps over to us and jerks her head for him to come closer. He leans over, lifting his gaze to hers when she pulls back.

"Ask her yourself."

She gives him a scowl I've seen on his face countless times. Her shoulders heave after a second, and she swings her gaze to me. "Can I borrow your shoes?" she asks so quietly that I almost miss it.

"My shoes?" I say, confused.

I skim over the little girl, noticing her outfit has changed from earlier. Now, she has on a dress similar in color to the one I'm wearing, and she's pulled her hair into a loose bun with pieces framing her face, almost the same as mine.

Beck's teeth tug at his lip ring as he smirks, and I slip off my heels, hanging them off my finger and offering them to Grace. She twists her wrist around, and her fingers hook in the back straps, so she can hold them the same way.

"Oh." I reach behind my neck and unclasp my necklace. "This will go perfect with your dress and those shoes."

She grins, letting the chain circle down into her palm before she shoves it at Beck and turns around. He dutifully drapes it around her neck while she pushes her hair up higher. It's possibly the sweetest thing I've seen him do, and I can't stand him more than ever in this moment.

He drops his hands when he finishes. "Now, run to the pawn shop before she can catch you."

I laugh as she darts off, back into the house after a quick smile at Mrs. Donovan.

She winks at me and mouths, *Thank you*, and I nod.

It sinks into me though. I only notice the hole Darla's left in me when I'm around a real mother. Usually, it expands when I see what I've never gotten, but for once, it seals a little with his mother's approval even if it's only for a second because I gave up my shoes for the day.

When I look away from her, Beck's watching me.

"What?" I say, sure my mommy issues are written all over my face.

He shakes his head, leaning closer to brush his lips over mine. "Just thinking about how miserable you make me. And I mean it this time," he adds. "You're making me hate every person here who's stopping me from sneaking you inside and making you come in the bathroom."

"Maybe you should do it anyway." I tip up my beer bottle, feeling his eyes burning into me.

He traces down my spine, stopping on the curve of my ass under the table, and I think he's about to drag me in the house until the screen door flies open again. A bunch of the kids march out in a line, all in new outfits and carrying cardboard and random items.

"Fuck," Beck says, his hand falling away. "A parade of cockblocks."

His parents both jump up when they see Grace, carefully bringing up the rear as she teeters in my heels. Beck shifts around beside me, turning around the right way, so I do too. His parents settle in across from us, facing toward the kids lining up between the patio and tree across the lawn.

The more people focusing on the children, the farther up Beck's hand slides on my leg under the table.

"This really isn't fair," I tell him.

"You're right."

He grasps my wrist, moving my hand down to his crotch, but I rip it away when his mom turns around with a glimmer in her eye.

"Gracie is always roping the other kids into plays. She's been *in love* with acting since last year. Any chance she gets to be dramatic."

"Or sing," Mr. Donovan interjects. "The girl fucking sings everything."

"Does she do plays in school?" I ask.

All throughout elementary and junior high, we were forced into these terrible renditions of musicals. Layna still has PTSD from the giant animatronic plant they used when we performed *Little Shop of Horrors* in sixth grade.

Beck's dad shakes his head. "They cut the art program from her school a few years ago. They tried to keep some activities going after school for a while, but the funding didn't last."

"That's awful," I say.

He shrugs. "It was that or stop serving free breakfasts. They've already gone to every other day for those, and kids need to eat."

My heart sinks as all of the children loudly shush the adults. Beck's parents turn back around as everyone else quiets down, many still talking but in more hushed tones once they start their play.

"What's going on in that head of yours?" Beck asks, bumping his shoulder into me.

"Nothing," I lie, but he keeps staring.

Eden

The air cools once the sun sinks behind the horizon, but it's almost ten when the last neighbor leaves. Grace fell asleep on a porch swing, and while Beck carries her to bed, his mom gives me one last hug outside their front door. At this point, I've gotten over any aversions to physical affection, the cookout also serving as an intense round of immersion therapy.

Mr. Donovan gives me a wink before they go inside. They pass Beck, and he gives his mom a kiss on the cheek and then pulls the door closed behind him. He backs me off the porch as the light above the door flicks off.

"You ready?" he asks.

I nod, assuming he means to leave in his car, but then he picks me up by the backs of my legs. He ties them around him as he carries me around the side of the house. I squeak a little, glancing over my shoulder and back to him.

"What are you doing?" I whisper since we're still close to the windows.

He pushes open the gate and strides through to the backyard. "Those baby blues have stared at the tree house more today than they have me."

I laugh, more than a little excited to climb the ladder and lie on the wood floor. Although, *I* don't climb anything. Beck lets go of me, leaving me to cling to him while he ascends the planks. He ducks through the door to clear it and lowers us down in the center as I look around. It has a mini table and little red chair in one corner with a tablecloth and vase of silk flowers in the center.

"My dad built it for Grace before his accident, and they decorated it for her. Then my sister announced it was too dirty to play in and hasn't used it other than the swing."

I glance around again, seeing the muted-rainbow rug we're on and the broom standing in the corner. "It looks rather clean to me."

"Yeah, because they guilted me into cleaning it last week. My dad's back and Ma's allergies." He braces himself on his hands behind him. "That means, it's mine now. I can do whatever I want in here."

"Just you?" I ask, fingering the neck of his shirt as I lean forward. "Or can I do what I want?"

He lifts his chin up the closer I get. "It depends on what you want. If you plan on moving in and reorganizing my shit, then no fucking way."

"Oh, we're living here now?"

Beck's mouth tips to one side like he's considering it. "There's no box for a coffee table, but—"

"It's a crate," I tease. "And we're not living in a tree."

"No?" He sits up, so we're face-to-face, and he's grasping my hip with his left hand and running his right through my hair. "Where are we living then?"

His stubble scrapes the tips of my fingers as they run up his jaw and back down to smooth over his lips. He kisses them, and I move them, so he'll kiss me instead.

"Somewhere with a bedroom," I say.

"Mmhmm." He skims up, drawing my earlobe between his teeth. "You'll probably want a bed too."

I nod as he shifts us, laying me on my back on the braided rug. "A bathroom with a sink and lots of counter space. And a huge tub."

"Next, you'll expect a kitchen." His mouth works down my neck, his hand pushing the material of my skirt higher. "So needy."

I smile, closing my eyes when his breath hits my chest. "Fine, then what do you want? A massive sound system and leather sofas?"

Beck peels the straps off my shoulders. "Just you, baby. We'll live wherever you want as long as I can do this every fucking day." He cups my breast, sealing his lips around my nipple as I arch into him.

"Every day," I breathe out.

My hands rake through his hair and down his back until I'm pulling off his shirt. His mouth leaves me long enough for him to take it off, and then he's moving to the other side, one of his hands gripping my ass as he grinds against me. I unbutton his jeans and draw down the zipper. I nudge the waist down until he finishes, pushing his boxers off too. His hand catches mine on the way up, pulling it to him. He's long and hard, and I wrap my fingers around him, stroking up and down his shaft.

"Shit, and a lot of that." He kisses me, pulling my panties down my thighs. "You get the fucking tub, and I get you." Another kiss. "All of you." Kiss. "In every room."

I don't know how he can tangle everything up inside my head this easily—make me not remember if what we're saying and doing is real or pretend, but right now, it feels as real as breathing. Like, tomorrow, we'll go to open houses and find our perfect place. Somewhere it's just us. Like this. All the time.

Beck's grabbing his wallet out of his jeans. He opens a condom with his teeth, and then he's sliding it on while he licks and sucks his way up my breasts to my neck.

"You don't want to live with me," I tell him, my voice airy. "We barely survived a week at the hotel."

He hums against my skin, nestling his hips between my thighs. "We haven't been there for a long time. We've been here, with you pulling the crazy out of me."

"I thought you couldn't stand me."

I mean it as a joke, but Beck hovers over me. He's one thrust from being inside me and looking at me like he'll never stop, never let me go.

"Baby, I don't want to fucking *breathe* without you. What I can't stand is how deep I am with you."

He grips the back of my neck, his eyes staying on me as he pushes inside me. We both moan, and his mouth descends onto mine, his tongue invading as much as his words. I lift my hips to meet his, and he curses, hiking my legs up and locking them around his waist so he can drive even farther in.

Beck buries into me.

Deep.

That's where we are now. It's where I've been with him.

"Beck," I sigh out his name, scraping my nails over the working muscles in his back.

No matter how many times he's inside me, I always feel different after—during. Every smooth thrust and groan from him scores him even further into my chest. When he marks me with his teeth, sucking at my skin, it goes beneath the surface.

Our bodies move together, grinding, Beck's rhythm relentless. It leaves me aching, desperate, and whimpering for release. I'm almost there, ready to fall when he shifts us enough so that the angle changes. His hips slow, and he takes long, deep strokes, letting his hands and lips roam over me.

His gaze stays on mine, our foreheads together, and he has me. Completely. It's not a choice anymore. Beck won't leave scar tissue; he'll rip out my whole fucking heart.

As I come, he picks up his pace again and slams into me, harder and faster. His muscles ripple on his last thrust, and he holds himself inside me, groaning into my skin.

His lips come back to mine for a second, trailing down my jaw before he rolls to his back beside me. He pulls me to him, my head on his bare chest, and I can hear his heart beating rapidly, thrumming away under my cheek. I feel it match my own as I close my eyes.

"My lease is month to month," he says. When I don't answer, Beck grasps my chin, lifting it until we're face-to-face. "What are you thinking, crazy?"

"That I don't really care that much about the tub."

He huffs out a laugh, and I smile, cuddling into him.

Everything rushes by outside the tree house, but inside, it's just him and me.

Beck

If I thought I was in over my head with Eden before, I've sunk so far down that I can't even see the surface anymore. It happened fast, unexpected, and in all honesty, I'm still scrambling to catch up with my fucking heart.

The week after the cookout, she's grinning while I follow her through the door of an apartment about halfway between the garage and where she's living now. I meant what I said about my lease. It went month to month after the first year. I could have moved, but I didn't want to be locked in again. Plus, I would have ended up in another cheap place. At least at mine, the other tenants know to leave me the fuck alone.

I didn't want to start over, retraining a bunch of assholes.

"What do you think?" she asks as we stand in the middle of the living room.

"It has walls and a floor."

Her eyes roll. "They all do," she says.

The bedroom has clean carpet, and the drywall is all intact. It smells of freshly baked cookies from the candle on the kitchen counter, but I can throw that out the window—which isn't nailed shut.

"You could always fill out an application," the apartment manager says. "If you're approved, then we'll let you know, and you can decide then."

Eden plasters on a fake smile and nods, holding out her hand for the app.

"Where to?" I ask her once we're in the car.

She tosses the apartment application into her back seat as I pull away from the curb, and then she chews on her lips for a second. "There's one more we could look at."

The apprehension in her voice has me looking at her out of the corner of my eye, but she programs the address into her GPS anyway.

This building is much closer to the Loop than the garage, and the realtor who helped Eden find the place glides toward us as we walk up the sidewalk.

She talks the entire way in, giving us a full history of the building and throwing open the door with an actual, "*Voilà!*"

Eden spins when we reach the center of the living room. The dark hardwood floor offsets the exposed brick in the corners of the room. A fireplace, barstools at the counter, bay windows that have a seat.

"This is in our price range?" I ask, already knowing the answer.

It's in *her* range, but there's no way in hell it's within the one we agreed to.

"It might be a little higher, but it's perfect, right?" She beams on her way over, and the realtor heads toward the door.

"I'll leave you two to discuss," the woman says. "Don't forget to check out the closet space in the bedroom."

Eden's eyes light up, and she tugs me with her down the hallway. I poke my head in the bathroom on the way by, and her hand slides out of mine. Steps up into a whirlpool tub, two sinks, and enough counter space that I might even have some of my own without her shit invading.

I catch up to her in the bedroom, and even though the lady went out into the hall, I still shut the door behind me. Eden bounces over, but then she sees my face, and hers falls.

"You hate it."

"How much over is the rent?" I ask.

"About nine hundred," she says.

"Fuck, Eden." I blow out a breath, my teeth clamping together. "It's another thousand dollars?"

"Beck, it's not that big of a deal. I can afford the extra." She blinks up at me with her big doe eyes, and she really doesn't get it.

"Yeah, I know," I snap. "You can afford to buy the entire fucking building, Eden."

She winces, and I swipe a hand over my face, trying to calm down, but *fuck*. I need to get out of here and walk away, but as I reach for the door handle, she says, "You said you didn't care where we lived as long as you got me."

I stop, and when I turn around, Eden's still in the center of the room, unmoved.

"Who cares if I pay more, Beck? It shouldn't matter as long as we're together."

Maybe she's right. Maybe the nagging feeling in my gut is just some sense of pride I need to get over if I want her.

"We can fill out an application," I say.

She huffs out a surprised laugh. "What?"

"We'll fill it out, but I'm paying my half of the first, last, and security. The rest…" I leave it off. Because if I think about it now, she'll stay where she is, and she's too fucking far away from me.

Eden lights up and dashes across the room. Our lips collide as I pick her up, her hands cupping my face. It's the candy and flowers and Eden haze in my head as I walk her back into the bedroom wall.

We end up making the realtor wait in the hall a little while longer.

Eden

A car alarm goes off before the one on my phone in the morning. My eyes crack open, only to fall shut again when Beck groans behind me.

"Fuck," he growls, jerking out of the bed.

He mumbles more, and I roll over, watching his gorgeous form until he drags on a pair of gym shorts. His hand catches my face when he leans down.

"Don't move from this bed." He kisses my forehead. "I'm cutting wires and then coming back in here to wake up the way I wanted to this morning, and you're a necessary component."

I smile as he shoves his feet into his boots and clunks out of the room. His apartment door slams a few seconds later. Since he's gone already, I flip onto my side again and grab my phone off the floor, where it got shoved last night.

The first message I see is from the Harris Hotel downtown. I've been waiting to hear from them about using their ballroom for an event. When I emailed about two weeks ago, they said they'd let me know if they had any cancellations for sooner than this fall. I skim through, checking the date that's opened up, but I roll my eyes when I see it's tomorrow night.

So helpful.

The car alarm has stopped outside, and a minute later, Beck walks back in. The door has barely shut when he appears through the doorway, already toeing off his boots and shoving down his shorts. My eyes follow him.

"Did you really cut the wire?" I ask.

"Nah," he says, crawling up the mattress to me. "I just disconnected their battery."

His lips press to mine as he pushes between my legs, pulling the blanket back over us and leaning me back onto the pillows. He slides the phone out of my hand and tosses it to the other side of the bed.

"No distractions, Edes. You're mine until the alarm goes off—the *right* alarm."

I sink into the mattress, draping my arms around his neck, Beck's hand running up my thigh. "Not like it mattered anyway. You know that hotel I've been waiting on?"

He grunts an answer, working his way down my neck.

"They finally have an opening."

"Perfect," he purrs, not listening anymore.

"No, it's not. It's the perfect location, but I would only have thirty-six hours to pull something together."

"Uh-huh. Do I need a tux?" he asks.

I smile, shaking my head and dragging his face up to mine. "Yes, Becker. You need a tux for the fundraiser I'm going to line up in less than two days for Chicago's biggest philanthropists. Like a fucking pop-up store in Malibu—"

His lips seal over mine, and then I'm moaning into his mouth, forgetting everything as his hand teases between my legs.

"Focus, baby," he says, pressing his erection against my thigh. "Then you can tell me all about your little pop-up fundraiser."

My eyes fly open at his words. "Oh my God."

I sit straight up, and Beck rolls onto his back on the mattress, blowing out a breath.

I twist around to him, sitting up on my knees and grinning down at him. "That's *exactly* what I should do."

His eyebrow arches, his hand splayed out over his lower abs. "Isn't that what you were just saying?"

I laugh and jump on him, dropping my mouth onto his. "No, but you're a fucking genius, Becker Donovan."

He grabs the back of my head to keep my lips on his. "A fucking genius who's hard as fuck and wants to feel you come."

I kiss him again but then wiggle away, snatching my phone off the mattress beside him. "Just let me take care of something and send a text *real* quick."

He sighs as I sit back against the headboard, replying to the hotel to hold the ballroom for me. Beck rolls toward me and kisses the inside of my thigh, my arm, and my cheek.

"My little humanitarian." He rolls off the bed then, rubbing the back of his neck as he heads for the door.

"I thought we were having sex?" I say.

"Only if you get to the shower before I finish." He glances over his shoulder and winks. "Time starts now, Monroe."

I squint at him until he disappears, and then I finish my email. As I'm climbing out of bed, I send a text to a caterer who always comes through for me, stalling out at the bedroom door when she answers right back. The shower turns on, and I hurry to fire off a couple more messages.

It's going to take a hell of a lot to line everything up, so we can be set up for a late dinner tomorrow night. Invitations will need to be hand-delivered to the guests, and I'll have to pack weeks of planning into a morning and afternoon.

But this cause is special and will be worth every stressful second. As soon as the caterer agrees and I have the first piece slid into place, my heart's already warm. I smile, sending one more message before the bathroom door jerks open and Beck drags me inside.

My phone clatters into the sink, his mouth on mine as he picks me up and carries me into the shower. And I hear the dings start coming in while he fucks me against the wall.

Not such a shitty morning after all.

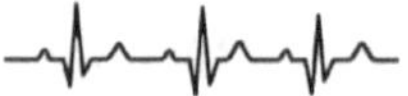

By the afternoon, I have the venue booked, the food ordered, the decorations planned, and the invitations are being printed. I've hired half a dozen actors from a small theater company to dress in formalwear and hand-deliver each one. It only took telling a few select individuals about the exclusive, invite-only gala and begging them not to say anything to *anyone* for the word to spread like wildfire. My phone hasn't stopped vibrating with veiled inquiries and hints from some of the city's most charitable, high-profile names.

Some people lower on stealth have even offered sizable donations simply for an invite.

I have about an hour before I need to be back at the hotel to finalize the table settings. The realtor's office isn't far away, so I stop in and pick up our lease agreement for the apartment. The application we filled out last week was approved, and all that's left is our signatures. They'll hold the apartment for a month, but if we can get the agreement turned in sooner, we can move in a couple weeks.

And as much as I've *loved* sharing space with Elijah and his parade of women the past two years, I'm ready to wake up in Beck's arms every morning. Preferably without horns honking or shouting from the hallway or outside the window. Or the gunshot from the other day.

Since I have a little time left, I swing by the garage. He's been working extra hours between classes lately, writing papers and studying at night after he gets to the apartment. He won't let me be there without him, convinced something will happen to me, so by the time I get there some nights, he's already fallen asleep.

I wave at Jorge on my way through the shop's open bay door. We met once when I dropped lunch off for Beck. I felt bad for not bringing more food and ordered more the next day for them. Beck complained that they like me more than him now because I have tits and also fed them.

He gives me a nod and juts his chin toward the hallway at the back. I pass the open office door because the light's off, but after a row of lockers, the only other door is to a restroom. Backtracking, I glance into the office, and in the back, on a grungy couch, is Beck. He's stretched out, his arm over his face and one of his textbooks on the floor beside him.

I go over and crawl on top of him, lying on his chest. His other arm moves to my back, but he keeps his face covered.

"I'd panic if you didn't smell so fucking good," he rasps.

His arm slowly slides up, and his eyes slit open.

"Hi," I say.

"Hey." His thumb brushes over my cheek, his face scrunching. "What time is it?"

I glance at the clock on the wall. "A little after two."

"Fuck," he says, sitting up and taking me with him. He rubs the heels of his hands against his eyes with me still in his lap. "I have class in twenty minutes. I finished an oil change and thought I could cram in an hour of studying."

"Can't you work your normal shifts until after finals?" I ask. "You only have what, three weeks?"

He nods. "Your pretty little apartment won't pay for itself."

I sigh, biting back the urge to tell him for the hundredth time that he doesn't need to worry about the rent. He won't listen, and last time I mentioned it, he scowled at me for a solid hour. But it seems ridiculous that he's trying to fit so much in that he's falling asleep in a garage in the middle of the day.

"Speaking of the apartment…" I trace my fingers over his jawline. "I picked up the lease to sign."

His forehead creases, his face pulling away so he can look at me. "I thought we had a month to sign it."

"We do," I tell him. "But the sooner we sign, the sooner we can move in."

He studies me for a second. "You in that big of a hurry to lock me down?"

I smile, draping my arms over his shoulders. "Once we hand over first and last month, and the security deposit, there's no getting rid of me for a year."

Something flashes over him, a heaviness behind his eyes, but then he kisses me. His hands frame my face, and even though we're in a dim office in the middle of the afternoon, all I feel is him. His lips are slow against mine, the kiss deep in every way possible. It's like he's using our mouths and tongues to extinguish whatever was passing through him a moment ago.

I don't know how long we stay like that, kissing and feeling and avoiding, but when my phone dings, all the things we should be doing come crashing back in around us.

"You've got to get to class," I tell him. "And I have about a million things to do."

I slide off his lap, and he scoops up his book, dragging his shirt off as he stands. He stops at one of the lockers for the one he left in this morning and his book bag. On our way out, he tells Jorge he'll be back later.

He follows me to my car and kisses me again before heading to the gravel lot beside the building, where the employees park. I climb in, noticing he's still waiting for me. When I wave him off, he gives me a look that says he'll leave when my ass is gone, so I throw my car in reverse.

The shop is off a rather busy street, so why he thinks anything will happen to me here—and in the middle of the day, might I add—I have no idea.

I'm stopping at the intersection when he tears out of the lot behind me, heading in the opposite direction. It's only then that I check the time, realizing his class starts in two minutes.

Shit.

I sigh and grab my phone, so I can send him a text, swearing I'll make it up to him. But when I unlock it, I see the message I missed.

> *In town for the weekend, baby cakes. Lunch tomorrow?*

As always, the timing couldn't be worse. I toss my phone back on the seat and let out a frustrated groan, connecting it to my car so I can call Elijah.

He answers after only one ring, his voice filling the car. "I got breakfast."

"Trade me," I beg him. "I have thirty hours to finish pulling off this pop-up fundraiser, and the last thing I can afford is to end up stuck at a two-hour-long lunch."

"Not a chance," my brother says fast. "I did lunch last time, and it ended with me *carrying* her back to her hotel."

I whimper, whining and trying everything I can to find the heart I know is buried in my brother. "Eli…"

"Nope. You can send me a list of things you need done for the fundraiser. I'll track down waiters, pick up your dress—whatever you need. But you, little sister, are going to lunch with our mother."

Fuck.

Beck

The last week has been rough. Between all the extra hours at the shop—trying to scrimp every fucking penny I can to help my parents for the month *and* put together as much as I can for the apartment Eden wants—*and then* hitting all my classes, I'm over it.

I drop onto the couch with my computer to start on my econ final. The professor handed out the requirements early, but I haven't had time to breathe long enough to even look them over. Usually, once I start, I can hammer out the basics before getting distracted, but tonight, I'm so fucking tired that I only last ten minutes before I'm spacing.

I grab my phone, looking to see if Eden's on her way yet.

She texted about an hour ago that she was finishing up a few things for tomorrow before she leaves her dad's building. From the way it sounds, she's taken over a conference room, turning it into a war room for the charity event tomorrow night.

She hasn't told me what it's for, but whatever it is, I'll be expected to show up and smile like I'm not stressed the fuck out by everything in my life right now.

I've been trying to figure out how to tell Eden we need to hold off on the lease until after finals. We'll still have a week to sign, and even if I won't be able to pay my entire half, I'll at least be able to contribute more than my dick and pretty face to the equation.

I almost told her at the shop after she sprang it on me, but she was so damn excited. Her face is what gets me into this shit. Her smile and the way her eyes light up. It doesn't hit me in the chest; it pile-drives. I'm not ready to be the reason it fades.

I've even considered asking Ty if Axel has anything coming up, so I can make some cash. One more job to maybe push me ahead or at least cover the cost of moving into the apartment. But then I'd have to start over with walking away from him.

My head falls to the back of the couch, and I take a deep breath, refocusing. After another second of drowning in the bullshit, I sit up and pull up the info for my paper again, wanting to get as much done for it as I can before Eden walks through the door. Because the second I see her, none of this shit seems to matter anymore. Except it always matters—and lately, anytime I finally get back to it, the water level has risen.

⎯╲╱╲╱╲╱╲⎯

I wake up on the couch. The apartment's dark, except the lamp, and my computer is on the floor with the screen off. Fuck. I never plugged it in. I sit up and swipe my phone off the table, checking the time.

My chest constricts, my eyes flying to the door when I see the time. *Six in the fucking morning.*

I'm on my feet, and when I throw open the door to the bedroom, Eden's not in the bed. She's not in the bathroom, and all the crap she leaves on my counter looks untouched.

Fuck.

I run back out and grab my phone off the table, checking through the blinds behind the couch as I call her. I'm not sure what I'm looking for—her body on the sidewalk maybe. Her last message said she'd be here in an hour, and that was around eleven.

The sky's a soft gray, the sun not quite up yet, but there's no blonde.

I walk back into the bedroom about to hang up and try again when the ringing stops.

"Shit," she says. "Shit, shit, shit. I fell asleep."

The air returns to my lungs, to the entire fucking room.

"Christ, baby. You scared the shit out of me." I fall onto the bed, the adrenaline of needing to find her still pumping.

"I'm so sorry, Becker. I'm packing up now. I have to drop the invites off with the people to deliver them, but then I'll stop by before you go to work."

"Bring coffee," I tell her.

The line goes dead, and I let the phone slip to the mattress. Even knowing she's at a building with a team of security patrolling, I feel like I should check the hallway and the stairwell, making sure no one touched her on her way to me.

It's that thought that has me taking a quick shower and changing, so I'm watching out the window for her long before she pulls up to the curb. I shake my head, watching her get out and rush to the back to grab stuff out of her trunk.

I meet her on the stairs, glaring at Phil more than usual to send a message in case he forgot not to fuck with her. Eden gives me a cautious smile when she hands off a stack of cardboard to me.

She follows me back to the apartment. I hear her shut the door as I set down the pile in the kitchen.

"I swear I didn't mean to worry you," she says as I turn around. "I was finishing the invitations—"

My mouth crashes into hers, and she sighs, kissing me back. I back her up to the fridge, pressing against her. With everything piling on and thinking something might have happened to her because I keep dragging her here to me, I need to feel her.

I set the tray of coffees on the counter without looking, but when I push up her skirt, Eden breaks her mouth away from me. My lips move down to her throat.

"I have a meeting in less than half an hour."

"I only need five," I growl against her. "Less if I try."

She laughs, gripping the sides of my face and pulling me up to hers. "I expect you to prove that tonight."

I push my forehead to hers, my dick still very much interested in proving it now.

"My meeting's across town, and I still need to stop at my apartment to change."

"You have clothes here," I remind her.

She started leaving them when we kept failing to get out of bed on time in the mornings, claiming two-day chic is for hair, not clothes. Whatever the fuck that means.

Her eyes go soft, her teeth digging into her lip. "I'll make it up to you. I promise."

She nudges me in the chest, and I take a step back, scratching the back of my head. She goes over and picks up the cardboard, leans it against a cupboard.

"Cardboard is an interesting choice for decorations," I say. "It might not bring in the donors you want though."

Eden wrinkles her nose at me. "They're moving boxes. I picked them up yesterday, so you can start packing."

My fingers flex at the mention of the apartment. She hands me one of the coffees and the papers that were balanced between the two cups in the carrier. I sip the coffee, scanning over the lease agreement. And when I flip to the last page, she's already signed it. Dated yesterday.

"If you sign it today, I can leave it in their drop box in the morning when I take your tux back." She's already grabbing her coffee and keys. "Which is being delivered here at two, and the dinner starts at seven."

I set the lease agreement on the counter. "You're not coming back before the event?"

She shakes her head, backing toward the door. "I still have all the minor details to finish this morning and then the last-second ones for this afternoon. Oh." She smiles the one she always does when she's up to something I'm probably not going to like. "And I have some very special invitations to hand-deliver myself."

"Very special," I repeat, following her. "Maybe I'll get one of those since you refuse to tell me what you're raising money for tonight."

"It's a surprise." She presses her lips to mine but ducks away before I can stop her. Eden beams at me, reaching for the knob. "Be there at six, all pretty."

Then she's gone, and I sigh, looking over at the unassembled boxes and the lease with her name written in on the line. The *E* and the *D* and the *EN*.

In black ink.

Beck

It's a quarter to three when I climb the steps outside the apartment. Late for the tux to be dropped off, but I managed eight hours' worth of work at the shop in under six, so I'm giving myself a pass. Even if it means I'll have to go track the suit down.

On my way up the steps, I glance down the street at a sexy little black Porsche just begging for someone to steal it. We'll blame me being tired as fuck for it not occurring to me that the only time a car that hot is parked on the block, it's here for me.

I hit the top of the stairs to my hallway and stop short when I see the profile of Elijah Monroe.

Fucking Christ.

He has a garment bag slouched against my door and his phone in his hand.

"Delivery boys usually stay downstairs," I say, reluctantly engaging. "We prefer the lobby attendant to bring the deliveries up."

Elijah pockets his phone, not missing a beat. "Would that be the strung-out guy at the bottom of the stairs or the dealer outside?"

I shrug. "Phil would have gotten it to me."

Grabbing the bag, I unlock the dead bolt and walk in. Despite the lack of an invitation, Elijah follows me inside. I've dealt with him enough over the last three and a half months that I don't need to check to be sure he's judging every single inch of the place.

"You expecting a tip, or…" I toss the tux on the recliner and turn around at the latch of the door.

He's walking into my kitchen, and I'm about to not-so-politely tell him to leave when he reappears. "Moving boxes and a lease," he says dryly. "How exciting for you, huh? You land a princess ready to take care of your pauper ass."

My teeth grind together. Even if I wasn't already in a mood, his comment would grate, but as it is, it fucking scrapes to the bone. "She's not taking care of me. I'm paying. And if you have a problem with your sister moving out and moving in with me, then just fucking say it, Monroe."

He stops in front of me, an easy expression on his face, like he doesn't care what way this goes. "I have no problems with Eden moving out. If she wanted to load a truck and drive everything to her new place herself, I would be there, carrying boxes. The problem I have is with the second part. The one where my sister moves in with her current project."

"Fuck you, Elijah," I spit at him.

His jaw tenses. We're both ready to tear each other to shreds, but one thing is keeping the distance between us. The blonde we're talking about right now. But with her not here, I have no idea how long it will hold out.

"You think you're not a project?" he asks. "Why haven't you met our parents?"

I shake my head, not fucking answering him.

"I haven't heard anything about you being at the penthouse downtown. Where our father lives. It's actually closer to you than *our* apartment. And what about Darla?" he asks.

"Get the fuck out, Monroe." I'm a comment away from not caring if he's Eden's brother, and I take a step before catching myself.

"I've got to run anyway. I have a list of things she gave me to do for tonight, but I'm sure she asked for your help plenty to pull this off."

Elijah slides his hand into his pocket and checks his phone, heading for the door. Then, like the smug asshole he is, he opens it and pauses, turning around. "One more thing to think about, Donovan," he says. "And this isn't me being an asshole because I don't think you're good enough for my sister, but a serious question. If you're permanent, then why aren't you at lunch with Eden right now, meeting our mother? Does Darla even know you exist?"

I lose it, stalking toward him until he's backed into the hallway, and I slam the door. My fists clench as I will myself to stay the fuck inside the apartment and not go throw him down the stairs to help him leave.

What pisses me off the most is, Elijah's not fucking wrong. He's an arrogant fuck who needs to mind his own business, but he's not wrong.

At no point has Eden indicated that she wants me to meet her dad or even told me much about him.

Anytime she mentions him, she goes cagey and quiet. I assumed it was because of how well Elijah and I get along, expecting her old man to have similar feelings about me. I'm not a meet-the-parents type of guy in general, so I haven't pressed it, but I would meet him in a heartbeat if she asked me.

And her mom … lives in California. And is apparently in Chicago right now.

I pull out my phone.

> *Where are you?* I send. *I don't want to wait until tonight to see you.*

I get another minute to cool down before Eden answers.

I'm just finishing lunch.

Halfway through another text, I tap out of it and call her. I stop in the doorway to the kitchen. The boxes and the lease have a sound—a buzz I can't tune out.

"Hey," Eden says, and my muscles relax. "You miss me that much already, huh?"

"So fucking much." I walk back to the living room to drown out the cardboard and paper. "Let me come to you. I'll be your errand boy or whatever you need."

"We'll be revisiting the *errand boy* thing in the future, but I've actually got it all under control right now. I'd much rather you catch up on studying or sleep. After I finish here, I'm dropping off something, and then I'll be back at the hotel to tell people where to put bouquets and how to space place settings."

"After you finish lunch?" I say. "You go with anyone?"

Eden answers with silence. I hear shuffling and people around her but not a damn thing from her.

"You there?" I ask.

"Yeah," she says quietly. "I'm actually with Darla—uh, my mother. She flew in last minute and demanded a lunch date."

I nod, grimacing when I realize she's not going to say a word about me meeting her. Maybe I could push, tell her I'm on my way and meeting her mom. But I don't get the chance.

"Oh, did Eli bring your tux? He texted me a bit ago that you weren't there."

"Yeah, he found me."

"Perfect," she says, a smile in her voice. "Sexy, black-tie Beck is one of my favorite Becks. I'll see you at six."

I toss the phone on the couch, staring at the garment bag with the tux someone else paid for inside and feeling like the dancing monkey all over again. Only this time, I wasn't aware of it.

Eden

Beck doesn't show up at the hotel. He doesn't answer his phone when I call. His place next to mine at dinner stays empty, and it's hard to hold the fake smile as I make up excuses for where he's at instead of being here.

With me.

"Miss Monroe?" One of the security guards taps me on the shoulder.

I'm behind the stage at one end of the ballroom, making sure there aren't any last-minute details that I missed in my rush to pull everything together. The theme is fairy tale, and the space is decorated like the inside of a castle. Before dinner, we had various performers set up around the room for the guests to watch—dancers, musicians, painters. But no singers. That I saved for the main stage.

When I turn around, the guard gives me a meek smile.

"I'm so sorry to bother you, but—"

I hear it then, and I don't need him to finish.

"Baby cakes," Darla calls, and I close my eyes, cringing. "They don't have my name on the list."

I take a deep breath. "Let her in."

The guard walks away, and I glance over just as my mother sashays through the door. I look out at the tables, filled with guests, and my eyes connect with Eli's. He's at the table with our friends, but once he sees her, he rolls his eyes and stands up, heading our way.

She beats him to me, pulling me in for a hug.

Pat, pat, pat.

"What are you doing here?" I ask, my voice tight.

We talked about the gala at lunch, but she was hardly paying attention, too busy flirting with our waiter. Darla has her blonde hair styled too closely to mine for comfort, her dress a dark wine color and her cleavage the main event.

"You didn't think I was going to miss a chance to see all of my old friends, did you?" She laughs like it's the most ridiculous thing she's ever heard even though I didn't say it.

I also don't say how most of those old friends are currently tensing in their chairs at the sight of her. She and Daddy might have had one of the cleanest divorces imaginable after gaining what they wanted from one another, but none of his associates were sad to see her go. Darla always has an agenda, and it typically has to do with money. Even Eli and I are fair game when it comes to her.

"Well," I say, trying like hell to get her to leave the backstage area, "I have to go up onstage in a second to—"

"Is Ashton here?" she asks.

My eyes dart to the side as the *very special* guests start walking toward us. I swallow, the heat creeping up my neck. "I don't know. Like I said at lunch, he was invited. Hey, Eli!"

I try to redirect her as my brother reaches us, but Darla barely glances at him before she's focusing on me again.

Please, God, no.

"I know you said you're with this new guy," she says, trying to sound motherly, "but I *really* think you need to give Ashton another chance. He's a Hayes, baby cakes. No one will be able to take care of you better than him. Certainly not some mechanic you found—"

"Mom," I say fast, my eyes pleading with her to shut the fuck up.

About then, Grace comes twirling over to me in her blue princess gown, everything about her brilliant. "Eden, it's perfect." She touches the tiara I gave Mrs. Donovan to put into her hair.

She and Mr. Donovan are right behind Grace, him in his dark blue blazer and her in a peach floor-length gown. They smile at me, and I force the same one back at them I've given them all night. Because the hurt in my chest right now is from their son.

"Mom," Eli says, hooking his arm around Darla, "let me buy you a drink." He gives me a look, softer than earlier as he ushers her away. "Or seven…"

The rush of panic seeps out of me once they round the corner of the stage, and I spin back to Grace and Beck's parents.

"How's my star performer?" I ask. "You ready to go show them why they need to fund your after-school program?"

I really throw the enthusiasm on thick even though I don't feel it, and when she nods, I grab her hand. She gives one more tentative look at her parents before she follows me up the steps onto the stage, and we stop in the center, in front of the banner.

Then Beck's baby sister sings her heart out, and he's not there for either one of us.

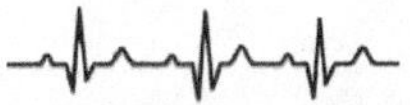

When the town car stops in front of the gray brick building, I gather up the skirt of my red dress and throw the back door open. The two dealers who are always by the steps whistle at me as I pass them.

"Fuck off," I tell them, storming inside.

I stop at Beck's apartment, shooting a glare at the guy from the stairway, who's watching me from the end of the hall, and then

I start pounding on the door. It only takes a second before Beck jerks it open, and our scowls collide.

He's in a T-shirt and jeans, his hair still damp from a shower. I shove past him, my eyes landing on Ty and Milo in the living room.

"Out."

Neither of them moves, their gazes darting to Beck as he walks in. He hooks his head for them to go, and they can't get out fast enough. I turn my head as they're passing me, and once Ty's out of the way, I see the unfolded boxes where I left them this morning, leaning against the cupboard. My chest tightens when I walk into the kitchen to see the apartment lease still on the counter.

I lift the pages to the last one, and when I hear the door shut, I spin around.

"You didn't sign it," I say.

Beck relaxes back against the counter, tipping back his beer, his face expressionless, like he doesn't give a shit about standing me up or that I had to track him down—*again*.

"Where the fuck were you tonight?"

He shrugs. "Here."

I shake my head, crossing my arms over my chest. "Yeah, I got that part. Why the fuck weren't you at the hotel?"

"Because I'm not some puppy you can parade around whenever the hell you want." He tosses his empty bottle in the trash. "I put in some hours at the garage, and then I studied—like you told me to when you didn't want me to meet your mom today."

I stare at him. "Is that what this is about? That I didn't introduce you to *Darla*?"

The muscles in his jaw work under the skin, and he grabs another beer out of the fridge before walking to the living room. I'm right behind him.

"Becker, *I* don't even want to know my mother. She's terrible and shallow and money hungry."

"Does she even know about me?" he asks.

"Of course she does."

"And your dad?" He pauses for a second, and suddenly, my belly twists. "He lives in the same fucking city, Eden. You've never once asked me to meet him."

I lick my lips, looking away. "This has nothing to do with tonight." I open my clutch and pull out my phone, bringing up the video of Grace performing. "*This* is what tonight was supposed to be about."

He takes the phone when I shove it at him, and his Adam's apple bobs in a hard swallow.

"She was amazing, Becker. We made more tonight than I have at any other event. And it's all going to after-school programs at underfunded schools. The charity involved sets them up to—"

"You had my baby sister there tonight to help you raise money?" he says. His eyes lift, and I nod. But instead of being surprised, like I thought he would be, his face hardens, his nostrils flaring. "What the *fuck*, Eden?"

"Beck," I start, but he pushes the phone back at me and wipes a hand over his face.

"If you want to use me as a dancing monkey, that's one thing, but my fucking family?"

"What?"

"They aren't props you can use to get donors."

I shake my head. "I wasn't using them for anything. I would never do that. I was trying to help."

"How?" he asks. "By dragging my sister out in front of a bunch of rich pricks and acting like she's some charity case? You made her the poster child for your cause."

"That is *not* what happened tonight," I snap. "But you weren't even there, so why would I expect you to know that?"

"Would it have mattered if I were? You don't fucking listen. I would have said I don't want Gracie up there, and you would have done it anyway."

"No, I wouldn't have."

"So, she wouldn't have performed?" he asks.

"No," I say, but it's too fast. More a reaction to him than the truth.

"And what about the lease and us not signing it until after finals? Or the whole fucking apartment?"

I groan in frustration. "Who cares about the apartment?"

"I fucking do," he shouts back.

We stand there for a second, my breaths coming faster the longer he looks at me. He runs his tongue over his bottom lip, stacking his hands behind his head so his shirt lifts.

"I'm not signing the lease," he says.

And my eyes shift up to his. "What? Becker…" But I stop, feeling everything slip.

He lowers his arms to his sides. "I told you I couldn't afford it, but you guilted me into it anyway. I *said* I needed the extra time to come up with my half of everything, and you showed up with moving boxes. Then you pull this shit."

"I'm only trying to help, Becker! The program for your family and the apartment."

"We don't *need* your help, Eden," he says, almost desperate in his words. "No one asked you to do anything or get involved."

"I thought I was being a supportive girlfriend," I say, my voice short.

"No. You're a trust-fund princess who needs to mind her own business."

His words sting, and my lower lip trembles, but I lift my chin and refuse to let him see it.

"Well, if that's what you think, then maybe I should get back to the perfect life you hijacked at the beginning of the year."

"Yeah, Eden," he says, his face hard, "you should." And then Beck grabs a hoodie off the chair and pulls it on over his T-shirt, passing me for the door. "Call a ride. I'll wait downstairs until it gets here."

He leaves me in the living room, slamming the door as my tears start to fall. He doesn't even give me time to tell him that I can just call back my town car.

But I don't think I would have told him that anyway.

Eli's crawling out of the town car in front of our building when mine stops at the curb. I get out, and he glances back when he hears the door shut. He turns around and sighs, holding his hands out.

"Well, Darla is passed out in her hotel room, and the buzz around the charity was that you fucking killed it tonight."

I nod, managing a small smile as I pass him, but he rushes around in front of me. His hands touch my arms, his eyes studying every inch of me. Rather than let him jump to conclusions about why my eyes are red, I sigh.

"I think Beck and I broke up."

He frowns. "Fuck, E." He pulls me to him, wrapping his arms tight around me. "Maybe it's just a fight. Give it some time, let him cool down."

I nod, my arms slung around his middle. "I don't know how things got so twisted, so fast. This morning, we were…" I stop because I don't know how we were this morning.

I've known since we looked at the apartment that something was off with him, but I truly thought it would fade once we were moved in. Once we were in our own space and we didn't have to either be on his turf or mine all the time. We'd have mutual ground—a tree house where we were us without all the noise from outside.

When Eli lets go of me, he gives me a sad smile and gestures toward the door. I make it halfway there before I stop and turn to him.

"Why did you say *Beck* needed time to cool down?"

My brother's brow furrows. "You said Beck broke up with you."

"No." I shake my head. "I said I think we broke up, but I didn't say…" I stare at him, sorting through the cool expression.

We're in the sixty percent. Somewhere in the range of completely full of shit.

"Elijah…"

He shrugs off my warning, but I stop him when he tries to walk around me.

"What did you do, Elijah?"

"Nothing," he says. He weighs his response and adds, "Much."

I set my jaw, folding my arms and waiting for him to tell me.

He sighs. "I might have implied you weren't serious about him because you haven't introduced him to Dad. Or Darla, who you were conveniently at lunch with at the time."

I slap at him with my clutch. "Damn it, Eli. You know why he hasn't met Daddy, and Darla is fucking Darla. Why? Why can't you just stay the hell out of it?"

But I don't let him answer because everything feels like it hits at once. My chest hurts. My heart. And I just can't be here right now.

Eli dodges out of the way when I shove past him, and I march down the sidewalk toward the exterior entrance of the parking garage.

"Edes," he shouts after me, "it's after midnight. Where could you possibly be going?"

"I'm going to Daddy's," I yell back at him.

And I know how it sounds, coming from the woman stomping down the street in a red ballgown and Louboutin stilettos, but I don't care.

Everyone needs a place to fall apart. Someone to hold them every now and then and just let them be and process. I thought that was Beck, but since he doesn't want to be that, I'll go to the one person I have left.

When I step off the elevator into the penthouse ten minutes later, I drop my clutch on the table and walk straight out of my heels. But when I round the corner into the sitting area, I stop. My heart sinks at the sight of the empty recliner. The TV and lights are off, except for a lamp on an end table.

"E?"

I don't even look away from the chair. "He's in bed already."

It's a statement, but Coleman answers anyway, "Half an hour or so."

I sigh, my eyes drifting over to him, where he's leaning on the counter in the large, open kitchen.

"Shit, doll." He shakes his head, as disappointed as I am. "If I'd known you were coming…"

I wave him off, smiling through the fresh tears stinging my eyes. "No worries, Coleman." I head toward the staircase across the room, giving a forced smile over my shoulder. "I'm going to stay, if that's all right?"

He holds out his arms. "Your home, E."

"Right," I say. "Night."

My room's at the top of the stairs. Daddy insisted on keeping one for me. Eli too. They're fully decorated, the bedding changed weekly whether we've slept here or not. I can't remember the last time either of us did. At one time, I tried to stay a few nights a month. I don't even know why I stopped. Eli's used his once or twice as a crash pad after a rough night of partying but not recently.

I pass my closed door, padding down to Daddy's at the end. It sits ajar with the glow of the TV creeping out into the dark hallway, and I push it the rest of the way open, smiling when I see the split screen with multiple channels playing at once.

"Never enough time, Edes," I mumble to myself, lower, like he would grumble it.

Leaving the door open, I cross the room to the bed. Normally, I'd just go to my room, but right now, I need the one man who's never let me down. So, I crawl in on top of the comforter, still in my gown. God, I probably look like a nutcase right now.

Daddy doesn't budge when I curl up on the pillow beside him. Unsurprising. He'll be out for most of the night, if not all of it, from his sleeping pill. I feel better, though, having him here, and I watch whatever newscast plays in the center, just breathing. And crying. There's a little more crying.

Beck

My phone died sometime in the night. I wake up in the morning, notice it, and don't plug it into the charger. It's Sunday anyway. No school. No work.

And after last night, no Eden.

I feel that one. I felt it when the tears spilled over her eyes and when I walked down the stairs, leaving her in my apartment. And then when I watched her walk out of it.

I fucking hate how last night went down with her. I wanted to make a point by not going to the dinner—to stop the cycle I'd fallen into of ignoring my gut, my instincts, because of her. But then she blew in and showed me the video of Grace, and I lost it.

My family lives in a shitty neighborhood in a poor school district with a lot of parts of society working against them in one way or another, but they're strong and proud, and they don't need to be saved by her. And I'm not the guy to sit idly by, letting someone else tell me where to be and how to act because they pay my bills.

I finally charge my phone Monday night, and when I turn it on, I text Ty. He keeps asking me to help him get some piece he bought cheap running. I've been putting him off, but right now, I need a distraction.

Two hours after he texts back, we're at the garage with the car's engine hooked up and ready to lift out, so we can swap it for another one. That's the first time my phone vibrates since Ty. I feel it before I check.

Eden.

She starts easy, which I appreciate.

Hey.

I can hear her say it every way she's ever uttered the single syllable to me.

"So then, I stripped off my pants in the middle of the bar and told them all to suck my dick. And you know what? They did."

My mind processes what Ty just said, and I look up from the screen.

"The fuck did you just say?"

He grins, shaking his head. "I'm just fucking with you, man. You checked out on me, and I wanted to see how much it took to bring you back."

I roll my eyes and set my phone on the bumper of the car. He starts bringing the engine up with the hoist, and I watch it, making sure it's going to clear the front of the car. I see the screen light up on my phone again, but I wait until Ty starts pulling the hoist back away from the car before I grab it.

Can I come by?

Fuck. Her text has me stuck in a loop of reasons why I want to say yes and why I need to say no.

"Did I tell you about the shit with Axel?" Ty asks.

I grunt a response, still staring at the most complicated four words I've read.

"He has a big job coming up—ten cars—and he wants to deliver them all in one night. I told Milo there's no fucking way it happens with the guys he has tearing cars apart now. We did, what, five that one time?"

"Six," I say, reading Eden's next message.

Please?

"Right. Six, and that was with you, where we could dismantle an entire car in an hour. These guys are taking three—"

The snap of the chain has my eyes flying up just as the engine swings loose. I lunge forward, trying to steady the hoist before the weight sends it over, but with the momentum of the engine, I'm too late. The entire rig tips, and I push from one side while Ty pulls from the other to keep it from falling all the way over.

"*Fuck!*" Ty yells as the wheel of the hoist comes down on his foot.

I shove it back and steady the engine. By the time it stops swaying, Ty's backed up to the car, sitting on the open hood with his eyes wrenched shut.

"Broke?" I ask.

He's made it a habit over the years of calling bones when one of us decides to fall out of a tree or lay over a motorcycle on the highway. I wouldn't say the guy is the bone whisperer, but he hasn't been wrong yet.

He sucks air through his teeth, wincing. "Broke," he chokes out. *Fuck.*

I feel my phone vibrate in my pocket again as I run back to the office for the wheely chair. He shifts from the car to the seat, and I drag him through the garage, locking the service door on our way out.

Eden

I wait half an hour for Beck to answer my texts before I drive over to his apartment.

As much as I want to see him, I also need to get the tux Elijah dropped off on Saturday. It's on loan from a designer, and given our last conversation, Beck would most likely have an issue with me buying a two-thousand-dollar suit for him.

"You gonna tell us to fuck off tonight, honey?" one of the guys outside his building says as I climb the stairs.

I keep my chin tipped up and stride into the building, not reacting to them. When I get to Beck's door, the guy from the stairs comes farther down than normal.

"He's not here," he says.

I knock anyway, more than I usually would as the guy creeps another door closer. My pulse picks up when there's no sound on the other side. No movement.

When I turn to come back down the hall, the guy's scratching his forearm only one apartment away from me. Other than the first night I was here, he's never strayed too far from the stairs, not wanting to deal with Beck.

But like he said, Beck's not here.

I reach in my bag as I walk toward him, and I pull out my phone. My thumb taps the nine and the one, hovering over the one as I pass him. Once I reach the stairs, I hit the last button just in case, but I make it to the bottom and out the door without any issues other than my heart ready to thrash out of my chest.

"Last chance, baby girl," the same dealer says when I walk out the door. "Tell me to fuck off again and see what happens."

I keep my phone out until I'm in my car and a block away.

It was fucking stupid of me to go inside without checking to see if Beck's car was in the parking lot. I start to turn to go back home—home being the penthouse because I'm still mad at Elijah. He showed up yesterday morning at Daddy's for breakfast, and I glared at him across the table while he put jam on his toast.

At the last second, I turn the opposite way and drive toward the garage. It's about the time Beck leaves when he's working late, so I might catch him if he hasn't locked up yet. But really, I just need to see him.

I check the employee lot, my belly fluttering when I see his car parked on the gravel. The light's shining from under the shop door as I crawl out of my car, and I breathe a sigh of relief as I grab the handle.

Except it doesn't turn.

"*Shit*," I say, jiggling it around, just in case.

I take a deep breath, reaching for my phone to try and call him when I hear voices and turn around. Three guys are walking by on the street, and they slow down, eyeing my car. Then they're eyeing me.

The next block up is a larger intersection. Stoplights. Cars. People. And I walk in that direction instead of my car. Instead of toward the guys. They were heading the opposite way before, so when I hear the crunch of gravel behind me, my chest rises faster.

This is not happening. It's all I can think. All the times I've been here and Beck's apartment, I've been fine. Now isn't any different. I'll get to the corner and under the brighter lights.

But the sounds are louder, and it's more than one pair of feet trailing me up the block.

"Hey," one of them says, and my muscles cool.

They keep talking, telling me to turn around and asking what I'm doing tonight. There's a chuckled comment about my skirt, and *the pretty little ride having a pretty little ride.*

The chill has worked its way through me now, my entire body on high alert and wanting to break out in shivers. I reach the side of the jewelry store, and I'm almost at the corner when I glance back. Just as I do, one of the guys grabs my arm. His fingers dig into my flesh immediately, and he's pulling it at a weird angle, but I try to jerk it away anyway.

"Let me go," I cry out, shoving at him with my other hand.

Another rushes up, and I've managed to get another step closer to the corner, so the streetlight above glints off the metal blade in the second guy's hand. The blood pounds in my ears, my pulse throbbing in my face. When the guy who has my arm reaches for the strap of my bag, I slip my arm out of it and push at him again. His grip gives enough so that I can twist away, and I run the last couple of feet to the corner, but as I'm rounding the jewelry store, I slam straight into someone.

My chest's heaving when I look up, and Milo's gripping my arms, his face about as shocked as I imagine mine would be if I could feel anything other than absolute terror.

Milo's eyes snap up as one of the guys darts around the corner with a grin on his face while another tells him to get me. He sees Milo, and I see the blade in his hand as Milo jerks me to the side, reaching in his waistband. The guy realizes he's going for a gun and bolts back around the corner.

"You okay?" Milo asks, searching me over. "Did they touch you?"

I shake my head. "They just took my purse."

"Fuck," he hisses.

He takes off at a dead sprint after them. I want to tell him not to leave me, but I don't have time. I sniff, trying not to burst into tears, and I force myself to move over enough so that I can see around the corner. Their figures are almost all the way back at the garage, dim yellow in the streetlight when one crashes down on another, and the other two keep going until I can't see them.

It only takes a few seconds and swings before one gets up, leaving the other on the ground. Milo starts back toward me with my purse, but he stops when he sees me, watching from the safety of the busy intersection.

"Come on," he calls to me. "I'll drive you home."

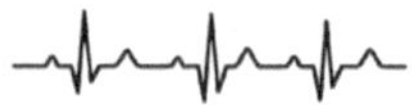

It's the middle of April, but I turn on the heated seat, shivering as Milo drives my car to the penthouse.

"You're sure they didn't touch you?" he grinds out.

I look over, and I don't think I've ever really looked at him before. He has almost black hair, a harsh jawline, and when he glances over and I see him straight on, I notice the slight offset to his nose, as if it had been broken once or twice.

"They didn't touch me," I say softly. "Just my arm, I guess."

Milo's fingers tighten on the steering wheel as he speeds through a light as it turns red. "I checked the one's wallet after I knocked the piece of shit out. I'll make sure Beck gets the name."

"No." I swallow, turning in my seat to face him. "Please don't tell Beck about any of this."

His eyes dart to the side and then return to the road. "You two didn't work shit out the other night?"

I let out an audible breath, and he nods.

"Shit. So, he'll really kill me if he finds out I'm driving you home." He accelerates more, suddenly in a hurry to get away from me.

"I doubt he'll do anything. But I still don't want him to know I was at the garage, looking for him."

Milo sighs, not saying more.

When we reach the building, I direct him around to the parking garage and up to the penthouse level. He parks beside Daddy's car, his eyes skimming over the other vehicles.

"Please don't steal any of these," I say, immediately hearing how terrible it sounds.

But Milo chuckles, looking over and nodding. "I'll do my best."

I grab my keys from him when I crawl out, and he follows me to the elevator. I thank him. Again maybe. I can't remember if I said it before or not, but I don't think too much gratitude for what he did tonight is possible.

"Give me your phone," he says.

I hand it to him without a fight. He saved me from three dudes with a knife who called me a *pretty ride*, so if he wants my phone, he can keep it, and I'll pay for the service plan.

"Call me if you ever need anything." He gives it back, and I nod. "I *mean it*, Eden."

I look up, and his face is dead serious, so I nod again.

His eyes fall to my arm, and he shakes his head before he walks away. After he disappears around the corner, following the decline to the lower level, I hit the button for the elevator. The doors open, and I walk in, leaning back as the metal doors close. In the reflection, I see my upper arm where the guy grabbed me, the skin a deep red from his fingers.

And I can't even cry about it. Because this isn't something that happened.

Broken. Just like Ty said.

We spend hours in the emergency room with him bitching the entire time about the cost, but I don't know why since he gave them a fake name. I drove his car, so it wouldn't be stuck at the garage, and after I drop him off at home, I walk back to the shop.

It takes me a while to clean up and get the engine put out of the way, so I can finish it up later in the week. I'm walking out, across the lot to my car when I stop dead in my tracks. *Fuck.* I forgot about Eden's texts. I climb in my car and read the one I missed while getting Ty's ass loaded in his car.

> *It's fine if you don't want to see me, but you could at least answer.*

Then I look at the one she sent over an hour later after still not getting a response from me.

Just get me the tux back.

I toss my phone on the passenger seat. Earlier, I was so damn torn over whether I should see her or not, and if not for the intervention of Ty and a rusty chain, I don't think there's any question which one would have won out

The next day after classes, I drive over and check on him, sure the painkillers his uncle always keeps on hand have made it into his system. They have. He's like a dopey golden retriever with a smooth grin, and his eyes are slit open the entire time I'm there.

It's when I'm leaving that he props himself up on his elbows. "Axel's going to need a guy for that job in two weeks. He's paying big, B. It could solve a lot of problems."

I don't even turn around in the door, pushing it open and letting it slam behind me.

But if I thought it would be that easy to walk away from, I haven't been paying attention to my life lately.

It's only a couple of nights later, when I'm locking up the garage after working late, that I get the reminder. Everyone else left hours ago, but I wanted to finish a car I had half-torn apart and scattered around the shop.

I reach for my keys in my pocket as I walk around to the gravel lot, but I stop when I see Axel's lumbery fucking frame reclined against the side of my car. No one else is around, not even a car parked on the street with someone waiting for him, so I know what he's here for, and it settles in my gut.

I blow out a breath, slinging the strap of my bag over my shoulder.

"You decide to catch me outside to avoid the shotgun?" I ask, walking up.

He ignores my comment, not even looking at me but out at the street. "I'll assume Ty ran his mouth about the cars?"

I shrug. "No idea what you're talking about."

His eyes lazily shift over to me. "That kid would tell you if he got a hangnail. I know how it works. If I tell him something, it goes to you."

But I still won't admit to anything, so he sighs.

"Ten cars, three nights."

"You offering me a job or bragging?"

He shakes his head. "Job. You do all three nights, and I'll give you fifty."

I stare at him like he's fucking lost his mind. "Fifty grand for ten cars?"

"No, B." Axel straightens up, pulling out his phone. "Fifty grand for thirty cars. We're doing ten cars a night for three nights in a row. We rented a bunch of storage units around town, and we'll alternate between them. We have a few of Monte's guys helping us out."

The number bounces around in my head like a fucking pinball, making a *ching* sound every time it taps one of the things I could do with fifty thousand dollars. It would take care of everything— catching my parents up on bills, moving them out of here, getting Grace into a decent school where she's not sharing textbooks, and then I cut myself off because my next thought is that I could afford not only my half of moving into the apartment with Eden, but also the payments.

Axel swipes at something on his screen. "Ticktock, Donovan. I don't have all night to stand here while you try to pretend like you're not jumping on this."

I clench my fists at my sides. I hate what I'm about to do, but Ty was right; it solves so many problems.

"I walk away after," I tell him. "You and me, we're fucking done."

"You walk away. But I won't be surprised when you walk right the fuck back when you need more cash. Does that mean you're in?"

Axel's stuffing his phone back in his pocket when he looks up at me, and I nod.

He taps my shoulder with the side of his fist and walks away.

When I get in my car, I don't head to my apartment. Instead, I drive to Eden's and fish the garment bag out of my back seat. A nicer guy would have brought the rest of her stuff, but I haven't moved any of it from my sink, my counter, my closet.

And maybe that says a lot fucking more than I want to admit.

I look up when the door swings open, and Eli's shoulders lower when he sees me.

"Becker Donovan," he says, walking away from the open door. "The mechanic that will not go away."

I roll my eyes and shut the door behind me.

Eden's not here. If she were, he wouldn't have let me cross the threshold without a fight. He clinks glasses around in the kitchen, and I drape the tux bag over the back of the couch.

"Let Eden know it's here," I say, already on my way out.

"She's mad at me," he calls.

I should keep going, but I pause in the entryway, waiting to see if there's more.

"As much as I dislike the idea of you dragging my sister down into the shit with you, I hate her being mad at me more. So, if you manage to slither your way back into her life, put in a good word for me."

Like I said, I should have kept going.

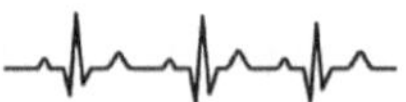

After I leave the tux at Eden's apartment, I don't hear from her for almost a week. But when I do, she makes her opinion known very eloquently.

You're an ass.

Simple, to the point, and not something I necessarily disagree with her on. The next message is more flattering than I think she means for it to be.

Perfect face and dick but SUCH an ass.

You're drunk, I reply.

Doesn't change the fact that you're an ass.

I close my laptop, moving it to the cushion beside me when I see the bubbles pop up again. More than once, I've thought about texting her, but I always shut it down.

Tell me you miss me.

I tap out the reply right away but hesitate to hit send. Because I do miss her. God, do I miss her. It's tearing me up inside, leaving me in shreds. But Eden needs someone she can take care of, and that's not me. It will never be me.

I miss you.

She doesn't send anything after that, and I probably wait a lot longer than I should before I stop checking my screen. I promised to swing by my parents' house tonight to help my dad move boxes to a shelf in the garage, so I abandon studying and drive over.

I'm only a block away when Eden's name flashes on my screen. All the reasons not to answer her call knot in my chest cavity. This is how I fall back in headfirst. I answer. I break. I convince myself I can deal with her making decisions based on what she thinks I need.

By the time I swipe the phone off the seat, the screen goes dark. I park in front of the house and am deciding if I should call her back or not when she once again makes the decision for me.

This time, I answer.

"Becker?" she says—but not the *she* I wanted. "It's Layna."

"Where the fuck's Eden?" I ask.

Of all the people I don't want to talk to, the best friend is up there on the list.

Layna sighs. "She's trashed in a bathroom stall at the moment. We might have gone a few shots too far while trying to forget you exist. Since you're the reason we've taken up residence in here and given the text messages I just looked through, I think it's only fitting that you come assist."

"Where are you?" I glance up the sidewalk to the house. The porch light hasn't turned on yet, so they haven't noticed me, and I shift back into drive, pulling away from the curb.

She tells me they're at Club Bleach and gives me a tipsy-woman's explanation of how to get there. I happen to know the guy working security, so I get in without the cover, and I weave my way through bodies and pounding music to the back.

I don't even stop, walking straight into the club's ladies' room.

A chick at the sinks jumps when she sees me, and I hold the door open, staring at her until she wobbles out on her heels. Flipping the lock, I catch sight of Layna in the long mirror. I round the corner to the stalls, and her shoulders sag.

"Thank God," she says. "I love Eden more than my actual family, but there was no chance in hell I was going to lumberjack carry her out of here. And since she's not talking to Elijah—"

"You could have cut her off sooner."

Layna tips her head to the side, giving me an Eden-worthy glare. "And you could have not called her a trust-fund princess who needs to mind her own business. But here we are, *Becker.*"

She hands me a black clutch and then carefully swings open a stall. As she steps in, I lean on the counter, crossing my arms. I can only see Layna's shoes after she closes the door, and I hate how much I want to move further down to see Eden's.

"Okay, babe." Layna crouches down on the other side of the panel. "I'm sending you home with a bodyguard. Do not sleep with him. Do you understand me? I don't care if he starts spitting out an apology for acting like an asshole or makes you come with his stare alone. You're better than Becker Donovan will ever deserve."

I rub my jaw, letting out a slow breath.

"Where are you staying tonight?" she asks, softer now that she's made her point. "Okay. Text me in the morning."

She stands up and mumbles something else before the door opens, and she walks out.

"Quite the endorsement, Layna." I push off the counter, and she stops in front of me.

"I'll apologize in my maid of honor speech—*oh, wait.*"

Christ.

She holds out Eden's phone for me. "I texted you the address to where she's staying and the code to the elevator. Go up the stairs, first bedroom on the left." She pulls the phone back when I reach for it. "If you so much as blink in a way that hurts her, I swear to God, Becker, I will pay someone to burn your fucking apartment building down."

"Might break a nail by striking the match yourself?"

Plucking the phone out of her hand, I walk around her. I didn't show up for a standoff with her. I came for the drunk chick hiding in a bathroom stall.

When I swing the door open, Eden's in the corner on the floor, which might shock me if this wasn't one of the cleanest bar restrooms I've seen in my life. She has her head resting on the wall beside her, and I scoop her into my arms, shifting her as I stand so her head rests on my shoulder.

Layna opens the door for me and follows us out, but she stops once we're on the sidewalk outside.

"You need a ride?" I ask.

She shakes her head, already on her phone. "I'll order one. And until then, he'll keep me company."

Her chin points to the guy working security, and he gives me a nod.

"And, Becker?" Layna says, looking up. "This is your only pass with me. I won't call you again."

She wanders over and hops up onto his stool then, and I carry Eden to my car.

She's asleep when I set her in the passenger seat. Once I get her settled, I check the text Layna sent from her phone. The directions send me into a parking garage downtown, attached to a towering building. I pull into a space on the top level near the elevator, and on the way around the vehicle, I check out all the security cameras. At least a dozen just with one sweep, but with a cool two million in cars in six spots alone, I can't say I blame them.

The elevator takes us up after I enter the code, and I walk out the other side and into a huge apartment. I have a marble floor under my feet, vaulted ceiling above me, a wall of windows ahead of me, overlooking the city.

Well, Eli, I've been to the fucking penthouse.

As I climb the stairs, Eden stirs. She brings her hand up around my neck, and I fucking hang my head down closer to her, so I can breathe her in. I creak open the bedroom door and leave the light off, using what filters in from the hall to find my way to the bed. Four-poster canopy with pink fabric draped around. Like you'd expect a princess to sleep in.

I toss back the covers and lay her down. I'm setting her heels on the floor when her heavy eyes flutter open. They're sad right off the bat, and knowing it's because I'm here is a crowbar to the ribs.

"Hey," she says quietly.

"Hi." I lower beside the bed, looking at every inch of her I can before bringing the blankets up over her. "What were you doin' tonight, crazy?"

Eden gives me a shrug. "Trying to forget you."

"How'd that work out for you?"

She shakes her head, and I can't help myself, reaching out and pushing her hair back. Her eyes fall shut for a second, but she peeks them open again. My thumb strokes over the rise of her cheek.

"Do you think I love you?" she says after a minute.

I nod, sinking deep. "Probably."

"Do you love me?" She blinks at me, and I know this will all be a haze for her in the morning—not quite real, but on the cusp.

"Definitely."

"And if my probably is a definitely too?"

"Then call me when you wake up and tell me." I lean in and kiss the corner of her mouth, tangling my fingers in her hair for a second before I stand up.

I leave her phone and clutch on the table and ease the door not quite all the way shut on my way out. Farther down the hall, I see another door partially open, the blue glow of a TV escaping. I'm sure a place like this has security cameras on the assets inside, like it does on the ones in the garage, but I don't feel like announcing myself to her dad. Especially if he has no fucking clue who I am. Or maybe that would be the worst scenario.

As I hit the bottom of the stairway, I glance up and see someone standing in the living room, and I stop. They have their arms crossed over their chest, looking me over.

"I brought Eden home," I say. Then curious if it makes a difference, "I'm Becker."

The man gives a slow nod. He's middle-aged and shorter than I expected given Eli's height. Only then I find out his height has nothing to do with Eli's.

"I'm Coleman." He moves through the living room toward me and thrusts his hand into mine. "I'm Mr. Monroe's nurse."

I raise a brow, questioning if I heard him right. "Nurse?"

He lifts a shoulder. "Assistant, housekeeper, security. Whatever needs done really."

Those three make sense to me, but the first one still sticks in my head. I glance back up the stairway, wondering if this is why she'd go all quiet and tense whenever he was mentioned. But why the fuck wouldn't she tell me?

"You didn't know he's sick," Coleman says, and I look back at him as he lets out a breath. "Shit. I'm sorry. As much as Eden talked about you before the breakup, I thought she would have told you."

I shake my head. "No, I had no idea anything was wrong with him."

He grimaces, dragging a hand back through his hair.

"Cancer?" I ask, thinking it's the most likely. Something he is taking treatment for and will recover from, so Eden doesn't consider it an issue.

Coleman sighs. "That's something you'll have to ask Eden. I've overstepped as it is, and the Monroes have been nothing but amazing, so…"

"Yeah," I say, my eyes making one last pass up the stairs and around the apartment I never thought I'd set foot in. "I'll let myself out."

I walk back to the elevator, and on the ride down to the parking garage, the air still smells like her. So does my car, and the candy and flowers swim around me the entire drive to my apartment. But when I walk into my living room, it fades, only lingering on my shirt and skin.

I already miss it, and for a second, I let myself admit how much I fucking wish she'd call me tomorrow.

Eden

My head is heavy, the heartbreak whiskey more menacing than security vodka or rainy-day tequila.

It takes a second to realize the pull at my wrist isn't part of a dream. Then the rest starts to fade in, Daddy yelling and the overhead light bright in my dry eyes when they open. I blink a few times and then jolt up, seeing him at my bedside in his pajamas and robe.

"What the hell are you doing here?" he shouts down at me.

I shake my head, my pulse hammering under his grip. "Daddy—"

"How did you get in here?" His hand tightens on my wrist when he twists, and I cry out. "Why are you in Eden's bed?"

I glance at my phone on the end table, but he grabs it, throwing it across the room and into the wall.

My eyes well as I try to get my arm free, prying with my fingers. "Daddy, it's me. It's Eden." I try to keep the tears out of my voice, try to sound calm, but the last part chokes out, "I'm Eden."

His brow furrows for a second, and I wait for any sign he recognizes me, but he shakes his head, the confusion flashing over his face. "No. No. You have to leave before Eden gets here."

My gaze darts to the doorway when Coleman flies through, and Daddy turns to him.

"Call down for security, Coleman. And tell them to hurry the fuck up. I don't want them all here when Elijah and Eden get home."

I force slow breaths, not wanting to upset him more, and Coleman gives me a subtle, reassuring nod on his way over.

"Already called them, Mr. Monroe," he says coolly. He slides his hand over my arm, keeping his tone even. "I'll get it all taken care of for you."

Daddy hesitates but then releases me, and Coleman steps in front of him. Neither of us moves, waiting for Daddy to leave the room. The second he steps down the hall, Coleman drops onto the bed beside me, pulling me to him as the first sob breaks out of my chest.

"Shh, doll." Coleman smooths his hand over my hair, his other arm tight around me. "I got you."

I crumple into him and bury the sounds in his shirt. I'm shaking with a mix of adrenaline and devastation over my own father not recognizing me. And once the hurt starts, I can't stop it, one heartbreak morphing into another, the new hurt belonging to Beck. It floods out of me. Every second I've missed him and knowing he was here earlier, so close, and now he's gone again. Slowly it all shifts again, to what happened at the garage with Milo and then to Eli, and eventually it's all together, just a mess of emotions forcing their way out.

There's a creak in the doorway then.

"Edes?"

I sit up quickly, wiping my eyes with the heel of my hand. My breaths are uneven, my lip trembling, as I look at Daddy in the doorway, his face washed in concern. Suddenly, he's crossing the room to me, taking the place of Coleman and rubbing my back.

"What happened, princess?" he asks, his voice soothing me more than anyone else's could. "You can tell me."

My tears stay quiet then, and I relax against his side while he tells me it's going to be all right. While he's the man who's always been there for me. Except when he had no idea who I even was to him.

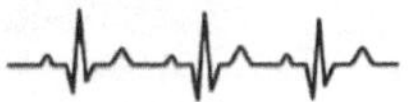

It started with little things a few years ago. He'd call, asking his assistant to draft up a contract twice or leave for a meeting but drive home instead. The first time I even thought it might be something more than him overworking himself was when he invited me to dinner for my birthday—three months after we celebrated my birthday.

The doctors said it's extremely difficult to diagnose the exact type of dementia affecting him, and with him being older, it could be more than one. But they mostly contribute it to the vessels in his brain restricting blood flow.

The symptoms started mild with forgetfulness and have slowly progressed. More than once he's confused Eli with someone else, but this is the first time he hasn't recognized *me*. And no matter how many books or pamphlets I've read, nothing could have prepared me for it.

Daddy wants to keep in control of the company for as long as he can, give Eli more time to fall into his role before he fully takes over. Since the diagnosis, though, Daddy's relied more on a hands-off approach, so when he has bad days, he can stay home. Both here and at the office, he has Coleman—an absolute saint who interned for him years ago before switching his major to medicine.

They hadn't talked since those two summers, but one call from Daddy, offering him a job as a nurse/assistant/driver/everything, and Coleman was moving from NYC to Chicago.

He finds me at the island in the kitchen about an hour after Daddy goes back to bed. He slips the lukewarm mug out of my hand and reheats the teakettle for me. I stay, staring at the shattered screen of my phone. It was already cracked from last week when Milo tackled the guy for my purse, but now, it has splinters and spiderwebs.

Coleman slides pain relievers and a glass of water in front of me, and I almost forgot part of the reason I feel so terrible is the night I had *before* Beck picked me up out of a toilet stall.

Classy.

"I look that bad?" I ask, forcing a smile.

"Don't pull that shit with me, E." He opens the cupboard for another mug. "You don't have to smile here. You can be sad or mad or—"

"Scared?" I offer, and then I shrug. "Because I'm scared."

He lets out a slow breath. "You should be feeling guilty instead of scared." He pauses, serving a judgmental look. "Because the picture you showed me of your little bad boy did *not* do him justice."

I appreciate his attempt to change the topic, but he could have picked one that wasn't equally sore. My mind goes rather fuzzy after texting Beck about whether he misses me. It was splotchy by the time Layna opened the stall door and I caught a glimpse of his boots. I've never had a physical reaction to boots unless they had a heel and were part of a fall collection until then.

The last clear thing I have of Beck is his lips grazing my cheek when he put me in his car.

"He still a good guy?" Coleman asks, bringing the kettle over and pouring. "Or do we *hate him* today?"

He mimics Layna, from the speech she gave earlier before dragging me out tonight.

"We've never hated him." I wrap my hands around the mug, wanting the heat more than the tea itself. "We just don't know what to do about him."

Coleman nods and leans over the counter, bracing on an elbow while he takes a sip. "You don't need to figure it out right now."

"Oh, yeah?" I say dryly. "What do I need then?"

I ask the question and then realize I really do want the answer. It's what I'm supposed to be sorting out during my semester off. Elijah might hate having his life mapped out for him, but I would kill to have someone point me in a direction and tell me to go.

After the last few months, I know that's what I was getting with Ashton. And there lay the doomed attraction to Hayden Prescott. They came with the GPS already programmed.

"Tell me what I need, Coleman."

He settles his other elbow on the counter, holding his cup with both hands. "Nothing but yourself, doll. You find out how to be there for you, and after you've shown up for the person who matters most"—he lifts a finger and mouths, *You*—"then you show up for everyone else."

"And what if they don't want me showing up?" I drag my nail over the screen, tracing one of the cracks until it's lost in the others. "They is Beck," I admit after a second, glancing up. "Every time I thought I was helping, he didn't want it."

"Then you show up anyway. Just because he doesn't want your help doesn't mean he doesn't want you there."

Thirty-Five

Beck

Eden doesn't call. She texts me in the morning instead.

> *Thank you for your help last night.*

I reply, *Call me the next time you try to drink me out of existence.*

And I think I read her next message a thousand times over the next week.

> *Definitely.*

The day after my last final, I finally make it to my parents' house to move boxes. I flip on the overhead in the garage, but they're already on the top shelf in the far corner.

Fuck.

It's late, but I go toward the house. After classes and work, I've been fixing Ty's car by myself while he rolls around in the desk chair, spouting nonsense. I figure finishing his car is the least I can do since the guy's out fifty grand because of his foot.

I'd never say I'm avoiding my parents, but I'll admit to screwing around more at the shop as a way to put off being here. But it's the end of the month, so my excuses won't hold up anymore.

When I pull open the back door, my dad glances up from the dining table, his reading glasses halfway down his nose and a stack of papers in front of him.

"Do we know you?" he says.

I shake my head. "Nah, I'm here to steal the TV."

He points toward the living room. "Have at it, but take your shoes off. Your mom just vacuumed."

Bending down, I untie my laces and toe off my boots by the door. I pull the envelope out of my back pocket and slap it on the table on top of the bills as I sit down at the chair on the end. My dad shuffles it off to the side, and I reach over and drag it back.

"Use it," I tell him. "And it's cash, so you can't pull that shit where you try not to deposit the check."

"All right, *mijo*," he says, and I crack a smile.

"Don't fucking do that. Your accent's terrible."

He chuckles and sits back in his chair, setting his glasses on top of the envelope of cash. "You and Eden?"

I shake my head, picking at the pattern on the white tablecloth. "Not since she paraded Gracie around at the fundraiser."

My dad considers this. "Your sister enjoyed it. Your mother's still bragging to your aunt about the dress she wore."

"What about you?" I ask, genuinely curious if he sees it as his daughter being used as the poster child of poverty for the night.

He sighs. "Would I have signed Grace up for it? No. But I wasn't going to take the opportunity away from her either. She got to sing and dance in costume on a big stage in front of all those people. Eden even had a spotlight set up. The only time it was used was for that little girl, and her smile when it hit her was brighter than the damn bulb."

She was happy in the video, but I could also see him just off to the side of the stage, the look on his face matching the one in my gut when I was staring at the screen.

"Is that the only reason you're about to rip a hole in your mother's tablecloth?" he asks. "Or was there more going on with the two of you?"

I quit fucking with the fabric and relax back. "We were going to move in together. But she decided she wanted something way out of my price range. I thought I could deal with her paying for it, but…" I lift one side of my mouth with my shrug. "I couldn't stop feeling like I'd be an object there. Eden would have her expensive couch and a pointless bowl on the coffee table and then me, filling the space wherever she needed it."

"Something else she bought?" he suggests.

It hits right, and I nod. "I don't want to be a kept man, relying on her for shit."

"So, you wouldn't be." He grabs the envelope, and I think he'll try to give it back again, but instead, he sets it on top of the checkbook. "You can accept someone's love and support without compromising yourself. If I didn't believe that, then I'd kick your ass out of my house every time you showed up with money."

I give him a look, and he holds out his hands.

"It's true. You don't need to take care of us any more than she needs to take care of you. If you ask me, the real problem is, you're both used to being the one solving people's problems. She raises money for charities and causes, and you work eighty-hour weeks on top of school to pay *my* bills."

"You talked to Jorge," I say.

"We're not your responsibility, Becker. And we've been making the rent long before you picked up a wrench. Growing up, you never went hungry, your mom taught you what the school failed to, and given what's sitting in front of me right now, we raised you to be strong and proud. Too proud, in some cases."

I don't say anything. I don't have anything to say.

"You finished finals?" he asks after a breather.

"This afternoon."

My dad picks up his glasses. "Graduation is the day after tomorrow."

I lift my eyes to his. "Like I told Ma, no chance in hell I'm walking across some stage in a cap and gown."

She, of course, nodded to my face and then ran down to the campus store and signed me up for both, which are now hanging in the hall closet.

"We'll still be there." He skims a pen down and circles the total due on their electric bill. "Your mom plans to sneak in and put you on the registration sheet."

I half-smile, having no doubt she will. "I'm still not going."

I don't mention what I'll be doing instead. By the time they're settling into metal folding chairs in a humid auditorium, I'll be in a storage shed with a stolen car in pieces.

My dad doesn't even look up or try to change my mind. "We'll just be proud to hear them call your name."

His words stay with me through the next day at the garage and all day before I leave my apartment and head to Axel's house, where we're all meeting up for the details. He never shares much until the day of the job—the less people in on them, the less chance of someone running their mouth. I won't even know who the hell else will be inside for sure until I get there.

I park at my parents', knowing they'll already be gone, and I start down the street. With all the noise in my head, I need the space. The air. But as soon as it all starts to clear, I'm thinking about Eden, so I walk faster. The last thing I need is to be daydreaming about the princess tonight.

"Beck."

I'm crossing the street to Axel's when Milo strides down the driveway. He stops me in the middle of the street, catching my hand and slapping me on the back. It's a little more buddy-buddy than we've ever been. I have nothing against the guy, but we weren't exactly in the same circle in high school, and he started in with Axel after I walked away.

He taps me in the chest with the back of his hand. "You and Eden work things out?"

I shake my head. "No, but thanks for reminding me."

His mouth hitches up on one side. "Sorry. She seemed cool. Like, she'd be the kind of chick to tell you when what you're doing is a *bad* fucking idea."

I nod, not following him in the least. "Yeah, she'd probably have an opinion."

Definitely.

Milo nods, glancing over his shoulder, and I notice the fifth guy from when they were at the shop by the corner of Axel's garage. I still don't recognize him, and I wonder if he's one of Monte's guys that Axel mentioned would be helping out. He has his eyes set on us. Milo pushes his hair back, turning around again, and then he slaps at my chest *again*—which irritated the shit out of me the first time, and I gotta say, I'm no more a fan the second.

"Hey," he says, grinning even bigger, "you're graduating this semester, right? I have a buddy who just finished up too. You going to the ceremony tonight?"

I lift an eyebrow at him, trying to decide if he's high as fuck or if he's always been so out there. "Uh, nope. I kind of have somewhere else to be tonight."

I look behind him to Axel's house, where we're *both* supposed to be instead of standing in the middle of the fucking road.

"Nah," Milo says. "Your graduation sounds like the *only* place you should be tonight."

His eyebrows rise at the end, his face dead serious despite the light tone. My eyes drift over his shoulder again. The guy I don't know is talking to Lee, but then he glances at us again, shifting right back. And Milo is still in front of me, his jaw tight. His look isn't saying that graduation is the only place I should be but that this is the one place where I *shouldn't* be tonight.

Fuck.

The vibe changes. He knows something. What I have no fucking clue, but I'd be an idiot to stick around to find out.

I lick my lips, glancing around. "Yeah." I clear my throat and nod, forcing a quick smile. "You're right. I just saw you here and wanted to see if you'd tell your grandma hi from me. If she ever needs anything, my family's just over the fence."

Milo claps his hand onto my shoulder. "Thanks, man. I'll let her know."

I swallow and nod at him, and then I turn around and walk the opposite direction. I walk without looking back—without even thinking about the fifty grand or how pissed Axel will be when I'm not there. I walk back to my car, climb in, and drive away. Far fucking away and where I should have been all along.

The entrance is abandoned when I rush in, and I slow down once I hear the voice over the speakers. I quietly open the door to the auditorium and scan until I see my parents and Grace, not far from the back row of chairs set up on the floor.

I'm not the least surprised to see the empty chair by my dad, and I slide past the couple on the end and move the program to sit beside him. He looks at me out of the corner of his eye, his mouth turning up, and he moves his arm back to slap me on the back, leaving it on my shoulder.

And they not only get to hear my name called once, but three times when no one shows up to walk across the stage.

They move on, reading through the rest of the names, and once the other graduates have filed out, the auditorium erupts in chatter and bodies, everyone fighting to get out the door at the same time.

We're in the middle of it. Ma's hanging on me and pinching my face because she knows I fucking hate it, and Dad pulls an envelope out of his jacket. My jaw sets before I even open it, and then it almost cracks when I read the amount on the check.

"I never said I was using your money, Becker. I just said I'd deposit the checks."

He aims a glare at me, reminding me where the pride and the stubbornness originate from—and it's not entirely from the woman who's demanding I put on the cap and gown for *just one* picture.

As I put all the money I've given them over the years in my wallet, my phone vibrates. I pull it out and check the text from Ty.

Tell me you weren't with Axel tonight.

The chill scrapes down to the bone, and I nod to my parents as I shove my way through the crowd to the front before I call Ty. I get some space, my heart racing as the people flow by, and then he answers.

"Thank fucking God," he says.

"What happened?" I ask, but I already know.

"They hit all the storage units with the first batch of cars, dude. Fucking *Milo* and that Arthur dude from Monte's group set the whole thing up. Did you know Milo's a fucking cop?"

I'm shaking my head in response, but the timeline fits. He showed up right after Monte went down for everything and the other guy I didn't recognize too. I knew it was too convenient. Everything just worked out with a neatly wrapped-up bow.

I tell Ty I'll be by later, so he can fill me in on the rest.

It's when I'm lowering the phone that I glance up and see the legs. Ahead of me, just a flash of them between all the other legs. But I've been able to pick them out of a crowd since three days after I first laid eyes on them.

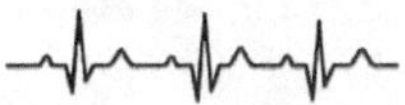

When Grace dives into my car a week later, I let out an annoyed sigh. "You think I want to sit outside an elementary school, looking like a creep, for half an hour?"

She rolls her eyes, reaching for the seat belt. "I hurried, okay?"

"Next time, I'm leaving you." I smirk when she wrinkles her nose at me. "How was play practice?"

"Great," she says, smiling.

They started the after-school program during my finals, wanting the kids to be able to have a performance before summer break starts at the end of the month. Ma said they were having trouble with volunteers at first and thought they'd have to wait, but it all worked out.

"We get to see our costumes next week." Grace clicks her seat belt. "But I got to see mine early."

"You like it?" I ask.

She nods and hands me her book bag like I'm her chauffeur or something. "Your princess says it's going to look *amazing* with my eyes."

I stop with the backpack half over the seat, my attention fully focused on Grace. "Eden?"

She gives me the side-eye, like the question is ridiculous, but I stare at her until she says, "Yes. She showed me on her phone. She also makes us help clean everything up. So, it's her fault you were a creep."

About then, the side door to the school's gym opens, and out walks Eden Monroe in a sexy little blue-and-white flower print dress and heels. It's like a pulse when I see her. Even after all this time, the space on my arm feels her. That was the first part of me she owned. And she didn't even have to buy it. I gave it to her, free and clear. Whether I was ready to admit it or not, the rest probably belonged to her then too.

She disappears around the corner of the building to the parking lot on the other side, but I still feel her, and it goes far beneath my skin. No matter how much I remind myself we don't fit, she's more out of place by not being in my life. Even now, I'm just as deep as I've ever been with her.

After I drop off Grace, I go back to my apartment and find the other thing with Eden's name on it. I run down to the store on the corner and buy the biggest black marker they sell. Then I scribble out my name beside hers—because it only took her five days to be the mark I never want to lose.

Eden

I went on vacation after my chat with Coleman. *Alone*, alone this time. Just three days in the Bahamas and at a different resort.

When I came back, I got a new tattoo. This one is on my other foot, the black outline of a palm tree with a heartbeat line that connects to the outline of a city skyline. I told myself it had nothing to do with Beck, and I think it's mostly true.

But having something that reminds me of him isn't the worst thing I could have permanently ingrained into my skin.

He also has nothing to do with me volunteering to help with Grace's play. I happened to be at the foundation when they were discussing the lack of volunteers. With all the time I've spent organizing galas and enticing donors, I've never been a part of the other side. I'd see photos and read thank-you letters from people that were helped, but I never *experienced* it.

Every day of rehearsals was a mess, and even the night of the play is a disaster. The kids forget their lines and break props. They also beam when they go out to bow and squeal as they rush backstage when it's all over.

It's incredible.

I look for Beck after the play. Not running out into the gymnasium and frantically searching the crowd for him before he floods out with the rest of the faces, but I peek around the curtain. And it might have happened during the play several times as well.

He's out there. I can feel the pull even if I can't see him.

But my eyes do land on Daddy and Coleman in the back row. Behind them, propped against a wall, is Eli. He moseys backstage not long after with a look of utter amusement on his face.

"That was shit," he says.

I laugh and nod. "Yeah, but it was pretty great."

He gives me a hug and kiss on the head from Daddy. "He said he's proud of you," my brother tells me. "But he also thought it was shit."

Eli stays to sort costumes and tear down a set, looking completely out of place in his button-down and slacks from work. My brother might be a lot of things, and sometimes, I might want to strangle him for not keeping out of my business, but one thing is for sure about Elijah Monroe: he'll always show up for me.

People are still milling around when I leave through the side door of the gym. I step around the kids racing each other from one end of the building to the other, and I'm almost to the corner when I hear my name.

It stops me. All of me.

When I turn around, Beck's striding toward me to catch up. He has on a plain T-shirt and faded jeans with his hair unruly. The not-my-type Beck who ended up being the all-my-heart Beck.

He stops in the same concrete square on the sidewalk as me. They always seem so small when you're walking, like you have to line your feet up just right to get two steps in without hitting the crack. Somehow, it feels larger with him on one side and me on the other.

"You helped with my sister's play," he says.

I nod. "But it had nothing—"

"And you came to my graduation."

My heart beats faster, harder. I knew he wouldn't walk, but it didn't matter. I was going to be there in case, through some act of God, he did.

When I nod to answer his question, he's not across the square anymore. He's on my side, close enough that I feel him.

"But you didn't call," he says. "Is that because you haven't been trying to forget me or because you already have? Because I'm happy to remind you."

His fingers reach out and skim my arm on one side. The tips graze my skin enough that I remember how much it's ached without him touching me.

I still haven't answered, and he steps even closer, his entire palm moving over me now.

"Tell me what you're thinking," he says. "Because I can't deal with fucking missing you anymore."

"You hurt me," I whisper.

"I can't fix that." He runs his hand up my neck, his other curling around my side. "But I sure as hell plan on spending a lot of time making up for it."

"I don't need you," I breathe out. It seems important he knows it, or maybe I need to remind myself in this moment because it feels like I might need a lot of him.

And Beck doesn't miss a beat. "I don't need you either."

"Oh," I say, his words cutting deep even if I just said the same to him.

"I don't *need* you, Eden. But I fucking *want* you."

His eyes lower to my mouth, and then our lips crash together. Beck pulls me closer, kissing me hard enough to leave a mark. It shatters me and heals me, all at once, because the way he's kissing me, I know he means it.

"I love you," he says, his lips still on mine. "So fucking much, I can't stand it."

I nod against him, throwing my arms around his neck. "I love you too. Definitely."

The memory is cloudy of him in my bedroom, stroking my cheek while I asked if he loved me, but I've heard his answer in my head every day since he left me in my bed.

I gasp when he picks me up, right there on the sidewalk in front of the elementary school.

"Beck," I mumble, but he pushes his tongue into my mouth, and I don't even care where we are anymore. I want his lips on me, his hands, his breath—everything I've learned to live without because, now, I know I can, but I don't want to.

We pass people in the parking lot as Beck carries me past my car and to his only three spots away. He opens the passenger side of his car and sets me right onto the seat, kissing me again before he runs around to the other side. Once his door shuts, he drags me toward him by the back of the neck, his lips punishing and perfect.

My eyes slit open, and I see the boxes in the back seat.

I break my mouth away, his moving down my jaw to my neck. "Are you going somewhere?"

"I'm moving," he says, working his way back up until we're face-to-face. "I got the apartment."

My breath stops along with the rest of the world, like he always manages to do to me.

"You..."

"I might have adjusted the date you signed the lease, so it would be closer to mine and not look suspicious." His lips twitch, and he looks amused as I stare at him, not sure what to say or if I dare even move. "I picked up the keys today," he says, "assembled a bunch of moving boxes, and started packing our stuff."

"*Our* stuff?" I ask.

He nods. "You left all that shit on my sink."

I swallow, my mind playing catch up. Minutes ago, I was aching for him to cross a cement square, and now we're moving in together. "But what about the rent? I thought you didn't want me to pay more."

"I don't. And you won't." His mouth hitches up on one side when I stare at him. "Let's just say I had a savings account I wasn't aware of. It should make up the difference until the lease is up.

After that, I thought we could find something else. Maybe closer to your dad?"

My heart sinks at his words. Coleman told me he'd talked to Beck the night he brought me home. "I'm sorry I didn't tell you." I shrug a shoulder, wanting to look away but not willing to stop looking at him. "I think it was one of those things if no one knew, I could pretend it wasn't real."

That all changed when he didn't recognize me. It became more real than I imagined it could.

Beck sweeps his thumb over my bottom lip. "I met him tonight."

I smile a little. "Yeah?"

He nods. "Coleman stopped me on their way out. He introduced me as the guy you don't know what to do with, and I think your old man might have wanted to murder me right there in the gym."

I smile even wider, and he leans in, gently kissing me.

"Maybe I'll have to con him out of a job," he says. "Tell him I'll stay away from you if he makes me a department head or something."

As I shake my head, laughing, I look down and see the new tattoo on the inside of his forearm. Where I wrote my name and number before he left the hotel in the Bahamas. My eyes dart back up, and Beck's lower, a slow grin spreading over his face.

"If I was going to be miserable, I at least wanted to have a pretty reminder until I got you back."

"And now that you have?"

He casts his gaze up to mine. "Now it's there like the rest of you. A part of me."

I press a kiss to his skin in the same place as the first time I marked him, and then I trace the fresh ink with my finger.

Ever Deeper Even Now.

Beck

Six Months Later…

While Eden leans against the closed bay door, I finish up with the car I'm helping Ty fix up. My best friend sold the first one we salvaged within a week of it being drivable and was pushing this one into Jorge's garage days later, reminding me of all the things he's ever done for me. Never mind half the shit he brought up I had done for him.

This car isn't nearly as bad off, but the progress is slow since I only have time on the weekends to work on it with him. Even though I started at E&E Holdings months ago, I still cover jobs for Jorge some nights when I can. It lets me slam shit around and burn off some steam after spending too much time in meetings with Eli—which some days is *any* amount of time.

Eden's brother might have laid off his crusade against me after he realized I'm not going anywhere, but he wasn't exactly thrilled when Anthony brought me on at the company. I was reluctant to take the job at first, worried how it would look to accept a high paying position in an empire I have no claim to. Only then I went to the garage where I started working because of a connection my dad had made, and I couldn't figure out how it was any fucking different.

By now, I've earned my place, proven I deserve my swanky office with a view. And I won't lie, I'm looking forward to the day Elijah hears one of the comments his old man makes about having *two* princes to leave his crown to.

"So," Ty says as I flip off the work light and unhook it from under the hood. "You two taking me out to dinner or what?"

I give him a look. "The fuck would make you think I want to eat with you?"

His mouth falls open. "I am your *best friend*, and you treat me like I'm—"

The hood drops, cutting him off, and he rolls his eyes. "Fine. I'll swing by your mom's. She always feeds me."

She feeds him because she's obsessed with cooking in her new kitchen. They might not have let me buy them a house, but they agreed to a little rental not far from me and Eden. Grace has choir and art classes at her new school, and Ma even joined a gardening club with her neighbors.

Ty flips me off and backs away, spinning about halfway through the shop and nudging Eden on his way out the door. She gives him a quick smile, and I shake my head as I put the last of my tools away.

After I clean up, I hook an arm around her, pulling her out the service door with me. She's scrolling through her phone, so she squeaks and laughs. I let her go to lock up, but I have no intentions of keeping my hands off her for long. Ty was already here when she showed up after her last class of the day, and while I couldn't give a shit, Eden prefers I not feel her up in front of people.

"Hey," I say, gripping her hips and backing her toward the parking lot. "My turn."

She smiles and starts to drop her phone into her bag until it goes off in her hand. Her eyes return to the screen, and her eyebrows shoot up. "Oh my God."

Her wrist turns to show me the screen, and I can't finish reading one text before the next rolls in, so I have to tap on one of the screenshots her friends are sending her. Ashton Weare-Hayes pops up, his arm around a blonde with her hand jutted toward the camera.

"Fuck. Is that the same ring he gave the other chick?"

Eden nods, putting her phone away, and I wince.

"Does this mean you're leaving for the Bahamas again?" I smirk when she pushes at me and spin us, tugging her against me as I back toward my car. "Because we might as well move there if you plan on going anytime this guy gets engaged."

She wrinkles her nose at me, and I kiss her, more than ready to take her home. But when I pull back, she's blinking up at me, and I don't need to ask what's going through her head right now.

I sigh and glance over my shoulder before I tip my head in that direction. "Come on, crazy. Let's walk while you tell me how I'm supposed to propose to you."

Eden beams at me and pulls me away from the car.

"White gold band," she says, and I wrap my arm around her, walking up the dark street while she rattles off her requirements. "Emerald cut diamond. I have pictures on my phone if you want to see them."

I nod, holding her tighter against me. "I'm sure you do."

"As for where, restaurants are a classic, but I think the location needs to be more special, so maybe…"

She keeps going, not even paying attention when we turn the corner, and I open the door to the jewelry store, dragging her in behind me. It's when I nod to the guy behind the counter and loosen my grip on her that she trails off, looking around.

"Beck, what—"

My lips press to hers to stop her. "I've been in over my head since I met you, Eden Monroe. You're challenging, sexy, gorgeous, and no one has a better heart." I lead her over to the case and point to a ring that fits about half her requests. "We can get you something nicer later. Fuck, I'll even drop to my knees in a fountain with birds flying around."

"Doves," she whispers, her mouth turning up.

"We can do all of that," I tell her, pushing her hair back. "But for now, the only thing I fucking care about is you saying yes."

Eden's eyes bounce between mine, her fingers twisting in the greasy T-shirt I changed into at the garage. I kiss her deep and slow, only stopping after I hear the *tink* as the guy sets the ring on the glass beside us. I already have one for her, hidden away at the apartment. The one she has pictures of on her phone.

"You're really going to ask me to marry you in a jewelry store that also sells ammunition?" she asks.

"Yeah, baby, right here." I pick up the ring and kneel down on the grungy carpet. "Marry me, princess?"

Eden

A Year Later...

"How the hell did you talk me into this?"

Beck wraps his arms around me from behind, his lips skimming the shell of my ear. I sigh, relaxing into him.

He asked me the same thing this morning when he rolled out of bed because Layna was pounding on the hallway door, threatening him if he'd snuck back into the suite last night after she kicked him out. And when he snuck in *again* to kiss me after everyone had already gone down to the beach for the ceremony.

I spin in his arms, looping mine around his neck. "The same way I always do."

"Well, I plan on collecting as soon as I get you the fuck away from all of these people." Beck kisses the tip of my nose, pulling me so we're chest-to-chest, no space between us. "But I'm thinking the promise I can do whatever the hell I want to you isn't going to cut it in the future. Unless you get really good at acrobatics."

He's abandoned his navy suit coat, his matching tie hanging loose around his neck. We've danced and cut cake and smiled for hundreds of pictures. All the things we didn't do when we got married a year ago.

After Beck proposed in the jewelry store, he did drop to his knee again. The next day, he slid the perfect ring onto my finger in front of our families.

Five days later, Daddy was smiling at me from the bottom of the stairs in the penthouse. He walked me down our makeshift aisle, kissing me on the cheek before he handed me over to Beck with a wink. The moments there made up for him not being here, not that I haven't wished he were every second. He watched Mr. Donovan walk with me, though. Jones streamed the ceremony for him and Coleman in Chicago, and Ryker and Puck were on reception duty.

The one person not to receive an invite to either ceremony was Darla. It was for the best since she's busy, landing her next prenup. Which happened to be the only thing she asked about when I told her I was getting married.

"We should do this every anniversary," I say, running my fingers through the back of Beck's hair.

"Go to the Bahamas or get married?" he asks.

"She Lives means come here." Winston walks up, resting his forearm on Beck's shoulder. "She has quite the crush on me, in case you haven't noticed."

As soon as the words leave his mouth, he's checking over his shoulder for Sasha. She's right there with a glare ready for him and their beautiful little girl in her arms. Winston gives us a grin before he goes to give her a kiss on the cheek and take Amalia from her.

He was the first call Beck made when I told him I wanted to have a ceremony here, and Winston was at the airport when we walked out. Grace is in love with Amalia, and from the looks Mrs.

Donovan has been giving me the past four days, she has every intention of becoming a grandma in the immediate future.

She'll have to wait though. Not that Beck hasn't offered to put a baby in me anytime I want, but I'm working to set up a foundation, and he's about to become a lot more involved with E&E.

I've abandoned my heels, Layna being a lifesaver with a pair of flats in her purse. She hands my shoes to Beck, and he takes them. I have yet to get either of them to tell me *why* she apologized to him in her maid of honor speech, but the hostility level between them remains minimal, so I don't press my luck.

Ty kidnaps Beck then, dragging him over to the bar for a drink with him and Milo, and soon enough, Brad Sinclair waltzes over to join them. He and Julia were in Chicago not long ago, and we met them for dinner. He has every intention of being Beck's financial advisor whether Beck wants him to be or not.

They only get through half of their drink before Beck abandons them, stalking toward me. He swipes up his jacket from the back of a chair and catches me around the waist, coaxing me away from the guests and DJ and leftover wedding cake.

"I think they've seen enough of you," he says.

"Is that so?" I ask, and he nods.

With our official photo-ops over, I'm surprised he's held out this long.

We pass Eli, leaning against a beam at the edge of the outdoor reception area. He hands me his whiskey as soon as I reach him, but Beck pulls it away.

"I want you sober," he growls, giving the glass back to Eli.

My brother chuckles, finishing off the last of the liquor. "Fucking had to say that in front of me?"

But regardless of the irritated smile on his face, he and Beck are getting along for the most part. My brother and my husband might not be best friends, but Beck has secured his place at the murky bottom with the rest of us as far as Eli is concerned. Eli didn't have much of a choice once he realized Beck was just as willing as he was to burn the world for me. And when Daddy retires next month and leaves the company to both of them, I have a feeling they'll be unstoppable.

Beck scoops me up off the path on our way to the suite—the same one we stayed in the first time around. He kisses me while opening the door, hot and demanding. He bites my lip, sucking it in to his mouth, and I'm already lost in him when he lowers me down onto the bed. It's only when my arm brushes against something not bed related that I open my eyes. My eyes drift around, taking in the dozens of baskets on the bed and spread everywhere else around the room.

"Why are we surrounded by sex baskets?"

Beck hovers over me with a smirk. "I might have made a special request with the front desk."

I laugh as he drops his mouth onto mine, mumbling that we're not leaving until we've worked through every single one.

Everyone has their breaking point. Mine brought me to where I needed to be. Where I was supposed to be.

It led me to my heart.

To Beck.

This book, you guys. It's been a ride.

First and foremost, I want to thank my readers. You are all kick-ass. Thank you for sticking with me and loving the words that fight their way out of me. To the bloggers who shout, share, and review, the support you give indie authors is amazing. I can't tell you how much I appreciate the time and heart you put into what you do.

Joe—you are a goddamn rock. I'm sorry for how much I screw with your sleep schedule as I trudge into bed at four in the morning, and for how often I stare straight at you, nodding along, even though I'm listening more to the characters in my head than you. I love you. I appreciate you. Fuck 2020, though, am I right?

My nine. Where've you been all my life? You just sent me a GIF of Cardi B waving money and called me a big money baller, so that pretty much sums it up. I'm going to mail your box. Expect one yearly.

Murphy Rae, you are gold. This cover is everything.

My editor, Jovana. I can't even express how grateful I am for you. This story was not going down without a fight. Thank you for your patience and willingness to work around my ever-changing schedule.

A special thanks to Callie and Emmily and all my early readers. Also, all the incredibly supportive authors I've met or stalked along the way. The Cool Kids, LitChicks, and those who stay floating at the top of my DMs.

To my family—the ones who are in it. You are strong, brave, and capable of so much good. I love you.

And here's a general shoutout to the ones I've no doubt neglected. If you flipped back here only to be disappointed, then maybe it's time we talk about expectations because I'm a GD mess, and you should get used to it.

Party on, fam.

CG

C.G. Blaine writes Contemporary Romance and New Adult novels. At one time, she was cool. Now she lives in the middle of nowhere with her husband and plays pillow to a forever-hangry, blind cat. She's terrible at texting back, and if she's overly nice to you, chances are she's not a fan.

Instagram: @cgblaine
Facebook: @cgblaineauthor
Website: cgblaine.com

Snag a **FREE** story when you join C.G.'s newsletter and be the first to receive updates on future releases, bonus content, and giveaways.

Sign up at https://www.cgblaine.com

www.ingramcontent.com/pod-product-compliance
Lightning Source LLC
Chambersburg PA
CBHW050822190726
48286CB00007B/1958